WHERE LOVE LIES

M.N. FORGY

Where Love Lies

By M.N. Forgy

Edited by Nerdword & Fairest Reviews
Cover by Tall Story

Created with Vellum

INTRODUCTION

This book contains elements that may trigger some readers. Discretion is advised.

WHERE LOVE LIES

M.N. FORGY

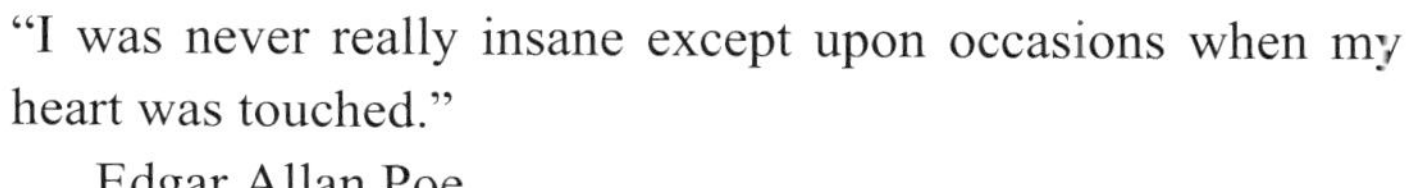

"I was never really insane except upon occasions when my heart was touched."

Edgar Allan Poe

1

The sun's rays brush yellow hues across the naked sky as I drive away from the city of Charlotte, South Carolina. My entire childhood in the rearview mirror. Windows down, a warm, earthy breeze fills the car, causing an open cardboard box in the back to flap with the wind. With both hands on the wheel, my seat way too far up because I'm short and can't reach the pedals, I adjust my round sunglasses, focusing on the road.

My thirteen-year-old daughter, Paige, shuffles in the passenger seat, huffs then places her scuffed Converse on the dash, a smiley face on the tip, from a permanent marker, beaming at us. Her brown eyes stare out the window, her jaw pulled tight in irritation.

"Babe, you can stay in touch with your friends."

"It's not the same," she says with an exhale, rolling her eyes. I can't help but notice how much she looks like her dad right now.

"You excited for a bigger room?" I try to make conversation, hoping if we focus on something exciting, it will distract her from all the things that aren't. Sighing, she drops her phone in her lap.

"I don't know. Everything seems wrong without Grandma." She squints up at me, her usually bright eyes bathed in grief. Moving to the suburbs placed forty miles out of town without my mom feels unnatural. She should be here. It was her dream for all of us to move to the suburbs because she couldn't give me that life when I was a child. We wouldn't even be moving now if it weren't for the inheritance she left behind. I have a feeling I would appreciate it a lot more as an adult anyways. Licking my lips, I try to ignore the pressing loneliness that freezes time now that she's gone. It's been two weeks since she died but it feels like it's been three months.

Squealing tires peal behind me, snapping me out of my thoughts. The sound of metal crunching and glass shattering echoes around me. My body stiffens seconds before I'm thrust forward then snapped back against my seat from the seat belt catching. The quick tug makes my chest tighten and my body instantly ache. A loud whoosh of dust fills the car as the airbag deploys, punching me in the left side of the face. Our SUV careens to the side of the road before coming to an abrupt stop on the edge of the shoulder of the highway. Smoke plumes around the car, and I can't help but cough. I bat at the airbag, adrenaline flowing through my body as I reach into the passenger seat for my daughter.

"Paige! Paige! Are you okay?" My hand swipes nothing but air.

Debris starts to settle, and I finally see her through the fog. She has one hand on the roof, one on the console between us, her body resting against the door. Thank god she had her seat belt on. She could have slammed into the dashboard or thrown from the car cracking her skull open. Her chest heaves as she looks around, her face pale from shock.

"Oh my God, Paige! Are you okay?" I grasp her by the cheeks, looking into her wide, scared eyes. Turning her head to look for injuries, I find a small cut on her cheek.

"Shit," I whisper, inspecting it closely. It's pretty deep for how small it is. I slide my hands down her arms to her hands, searching for other cuts. She seems to be fine other than her trembling state and labored breathing.

"What the hell!" she finally screams, spittle spewing from her bottom lip. There's that mouth. She's fine. Pulling her to me, I slowly release a breath, thanking God that she's okay. I start feeling the pain from the wreck. Suddenly, I feel the tight pull in the nape of my neck and the strain in my chest. My head throbs. I think I might puke from the anxiety racing through me like a drug. If I'm this bad I can't imagine what pain Paige is in.

"We should call an ambulance to get you checked out for internal injuries, babe."

"No! How embarrassing! I'm fine." She smacks my hands away, forcing me to back away. Her eyes fill with tears and body shaking she looks around the car. The first thing I notice is that damn cut; it looks bad. Blood spills from the wound, the magenta and plum hues from inflammation making her cheek look like a starfruit. She needs to be seen, regardless of what she wants.

Pressing her hand to her face, she applies pressure to the wound and kicks the airbag away from her. "I'm fine, Mom, really."

Looking over my shoulder, I see traffic has stopped from the wreck.

"I should go check on the people that hit us."

"Yeah, go. I'll stay here," she says on an exhale, resting her head on the headrest.

I nod. "Yeah, okay, I'll be right back."

My hand slides along the driver door, reaching for the handle and opening it. I instantly fall out of the car, my legs not working properly. My eyes scan for who hit us, and I spot a blue SUV with a dented front end, sitting about fifteen feet away, with smoke billowing around the hood and filling the air. It looks like their airbags didn't deploy; I should make sure they're okay. Forcing myself to walk I head toward the vehicle, the driver door swings open and a man steps out groaning. He seems calm compared to myself. His head snaps up, looking for who he hit, and our eyes lock. Bright as sky blue eyes infiltrate my own. He has sharp cheek bones with full lips and short ash brunette curls. His broad shoulders stretch, working out the knots. Despite the dirt and grime from the accident, he's nothing short of the actor Ryan Phillippe.

"Sorry about that, I didn't see you." Sincerity wraps around his apology, his soothing voice like still water on a summer evening. Knowing he's fine, I look back to my car; it's definitely in worse shape than his. How are we supposed to move without a working vehicle?

Placing my hand on my forehead, I try to push through the anguish and despair and remain strong. I'm okay and Paige is going to be fine, that's all that matters.

Forcing myself to think positive thoughts, I bite my bottom lip and take another glance at my car, the same one I've had since I was eighteen. "It's definitely totaled," I mutter, my words quivering with emotion. Stepping closer to it, I look through the back window. One side is broken and the other has spidering-like veins cracking throughout it. Some cardboard boxes are smashed against each other, but thankfully, all the breakables are with the movers.

"I can pay for the damages. I'm so sorry," the guy says from behind me, his tone a bit too upbeat, considering the situation. Looking over my shoulder at him with a deadpan expression, he tilts his head into his shrug. I hate how calm he is. Why isn't he even a little bit startled? Affected?

"Are you serious? Your insurance will cover it because it wasn't my fault!" I spat, my tone as sharp as a blade. "And what do you mean, you didn't see me? You had to be speeding around that corner to slam into me!" I'm talking with my hands at this point, waving them around for effect, which is what I do when I'm really upset.

Crossing one arm over his chest, with his elbow resting on his other arm, he holds his chin with his hand.

"Or, maybe you were driving too slow?" Dropping his arms, he grins as if his poking fun is cute. Now gone with the apologetic attitude his true colors coming to the shitshow.

My mouth drops, anger fuming inside me. Is he messing with me?

"You hurt my daughter, how can you stand there and act like this is my fault." Lines crease among my forehead as I scream at the asshole.

"Mom!" Paige hollers from the car; she must hear me yelling.

"Stay there, Paige!" I shout with annoyance, knowing if she comes out and sees me upset, she'll follow suit, and this will be an even bigger scene.

"Who's that?" the guy asks. His body shifts to the right, trying to get a look at who I have in the passenger seat.

"My daughter…" I murmur, but then remember she's hurt because of him. "Who is injured because of you!" I point at him with my index finger, wishing it would slice through him right now. His negligence resulted in hurting my child and ruining my car. It should be him bleeding, not her.

Stepping past me, he heads to my car.

"What do you think you're doing?" I ask, but he ignores

me and goes to the passenger side. I'm right behind him and ready to attack. He better not touch her!

"Let me see," he speaks to Paige. She turns her face for him to see. "Yeah, that is a nasty cut. Let me grab something from the car to help with that." Scooting past me, he jogs to his SUV.

"Is that who hit us?" Paige asks, looking out the window at him.

"Yeah…" I'm a bit lost at what to say to her about this man. Watching him rush back to us, he hands Paige a blue rag. It looks brand new.

"There ya go, just hold it on there. Apply pressure." He's bent over, hanging into the broken window to help her. He's so attentive and calm but that rag isn't going to cut it.

"Thank you, really, but I need to get her to the hospital to be checked out."

"The ambulance must be held up somewhere," he throws his hand out towards the backup traffic.

"Just my luck," I mutter, the urge stinging my eyes.

"Well, your car definitely isn't going anywhere. Let me take ya'll to the hospital and I'll get a tow truck out here—"

"That's not necessary. I'll take care of it." I've been caring for Paige and me on my own, since I left Cam and I've become stronger and wiser for it. Some would even say stubborn. Cam is Paige's father, and my ex-husband.

His chest rises with a hard inhale; he's not pleased with my independence.

Silence falls between us, cars starting to honk impatiently, wanting us to move the wrecked cars off the highway, so they can pass.

He smiles, his chest silently shaking as if he's laughing at me.

"What's so funny, because this," I point to my car and then Paige, "isn't anything to laugh about!"

"Are you always like this?"

"Like what?"

"Refusing to let others help you when you clearly need it?"

"I don't need your help!" I can feel my cheeks becoming hotter by the second, anger mounting inside me.

"Clearly," he remarks with amusement. I'm so over this guys. I need to get him out of my face and take Paige to the hospital. Then get to the house and meet the movers. I go to my car and search for my phone to put in his information.

"Mom, can I get out?" Paige asks, sitting up in her seat. Her cheek still bleeding.

"No, there's traffic everywhere, just sit tight for now."

She groans and slumps back in her seat, in silent protest. I'll deal with her later. I find my phone under my seat then walk back over to Mr. Ryan Phillippe, who can't seem to take anything seriously.

"So, my name is Rain Adler," I start, hoping to get him off the idea of taking us to the hospital.

"Rain, that's a pretty name." I still, our eyes locking again, and he's being genuine. Shaking myself from staring too long , I clear my throat.

"My name is Heston Thayer. Let me take you to the hospital." My hands drop to my sides. He just won't give this up. First, he's overly calm and then poking fun at me, and now, he's being kind. I can't make up my mind how to feel about him.

"Your car isn't in the best shape either," I gesture toward the smoking SUV, wondering if he forgot he was part of this wreck.

"Nah, she'll get us there."

"Mom, I don't feel good," she sobs. Shit, I really need to get her looked at. Maybe he's right, maybe I do need his help. But he needs to understand that I'm not making this easy on him, not the least bit. He hurt my kid, and my car.

"Fine, you can take us to the hospital. I'll call a tow truck on the way," I finally give in.

I open Paige's door and see that she's still holding the rag on her cheek. From the color of the cloth and all the blood soaking in, it looks more like a purple rag.

"Come on, he's going to give us a ride to the hospital." I help her out, noticing the powder from the airbag sticking to her hairline and arms it makes her look in worse shape.

Paige doesn't say anything as we slowly walk toward the SUV, keeping my arm around her shoulders to make sure she doesn't fall. Opening the back passenger door for Paige, she boosts herself up and climbs into the back seat, resting her head on the headrest. A somber pull at her natural beauty, she places the rag back on her cheek and glances at me with a forced smile. Pulling my gaze from hers, I get into the passenger seat and shut the door. It's very clean in here, the dash shiny, and floorboards without a speck of dirt. The leather seats polished and without wear. I'd think he just drove it off the lot, if it weren't for the steering wheel. The sides are worn and ragged from driving, pieces of it tattered. The smoke dancing around his hood and into the cab catches my attention, and my brow rises. Is he sure he can even drive this the way it is?

He slides into his seat and shuts his door, his hands resting on the steering wheel.

"You sure you don't need a tow truck?" I ask him, gesturing to all the smoke.

"Nah, I can fix it," he insists, a bit of arrogance in his tone. He has to crank it twice before it finally starts then he glances over his shoulder before he pulls into traffic. Slipping my phone out of my pocket, I hold it tight. Being in a strange man's car is scarier than I imagined. Not wanting him to sense I'm uneasy, I Google a local tow truck company to come and get my car. They pick up on the first ring and I quickly give them the location and condition of my car. They assure me they'll handle it and they're on their way. It took a whopping five minutes to get that settled, and now I'm left sitting next to a man I don't know anything about. Awkward silence fills the cab as the three of us sit confined in one small space, which causes my heart to race for a different reasons than just being in an accident.

"You wanna exchange information?" he casually asks, his words breaking through my panic. My eyes snap to him, without moving my head to look at the attractive man who hit my car, tended to my daughter and is now taking us to the hospital, despite what it's doing to his car in its condition.

"Sure…" I finally respond.

He gives me his cell number and insurance information, and when I begin to tell him mine, he holds the wheel with one hand and swipes along his screen to enter it. Panicked, my hands rise, as if they'll protect me from the dash if he wrecks or the car gives out.

"Whoa." My heart begins to race as cars pass us with not much room to spare. "Umm, maybe you should wait until we get there?"

"Nah, I got it." He clearly doesn't sense my discomfort. We just got into a horrible wreck and with the condition his car is currently in, you would think he would be a little more attentive.

Closing my eyes, I focus on breathing and hope he'll hurry the hell up and get off the phone.

He laughs, and I open my eyes to see what's so funny.

"Why you got your eyes closed?" A boyish grin on his face shows off two dimples.

"I guess I'm a little gun shy about wrecking again."

"I'm actually a good driver…well, except for earlier." He rests one hand on the wheel, looking at me with endless blue eyes. An electric charge fills the air causing me to stir uncomfortably. Glancing over my shoulder at Paige, I say, "Are you okay back there?"

"Sure," she groans, holding the rag on her face.

"We'll be there soon." I give a reassuring smile before hastily looking out the window wanting to avoid Heston's cobalt blue eyes. The magnetic pull between us is confusing, and I don't know how to dissect it right now. He's so nice and calm compared to my ex-husband. If it where Cam he'd be yelling and kicking the bumper in a fit-of-rage. Sighing, I focus on what's outside my window. The sun sits high in the sky, touching everything in its sight with warmth, and whispers the promise of a beautiful summer. Something Paige and me really need after the last two weeks.

We finally make it to the hospital. It's huge, and on the far-left side, a construction company is adding on to increase its massiveness. The accident happened closer to our new place so I haven't been to this particular hospital.

"Well, thanks for taking us." I paste on an appreciative smile, nervously tucking a brown strand of my hair behind my ear. Getting out, I open Paige's door and take her hand to help her down.

"Sure you don't want me to wait? I don't mind."

"No, thanks, I have someone who can take us home. But thanks," I lie, I don't have anyone now that my mother is dead and that realization hits me in the gut a little too hard. I guess I can have Cam come get us, even though I'd rather walk in the desert without water or shade.

Closing the car door, I give one last friendly wave and take Paige inside. The emergency room smells like latex and citrus cleaner that's almost as strong at the florescent lighting that's beaming down on us as we walk over to the desk to get checked in. A robust woman, with breasts bigger than I've ever seen rest on the desk, smacks her gum as she types in Paige's information. Raising her left hand, she scratches at her over-volumized black hair, still looking at her computer screen.

"Alright, if you can take a seat the doctor will be with you shortly." Sighing, we turn away from the receptionist desk, only to find there's no place to sit. Every dark blue chair is taken. It's packed, but there doesn't seem to be anything visibly wrong with the people sitting in them. Paige, who just got into a wreck, has a blood-soaked rag on her face, and they're making us wait. I hate fucking places like this, instead of seeing patients by their level of injury, it's first come, first serve. Meaning the woman across from us, who is on her phone laughing, will be seen for something as silly as elbow pain before Paige.

After two hours, we're finally called back to be seen and Paige has to get twelve stitches.

Twenty minutes later, she's all stitched up, we head back out to the waiting room and pray that, Cam, Paige's dad, comes quickly. We're standing outside, Paige leaning against a rock wall, when my phone dings.

How is Paige? Is she okay? Would it be alright if I come by and see her, bring a stuffed bear. I feel real bad about what happened.. – Heston

What the hell? I can't decide if he's charming or unsettling. He doesn't even know us to care this much.

Me: She's fine. I text back.

What about you? Are you fine? - Heston

My fingers hesitate over the screen, a man asking me how I feel is a new to me. Cam never asked or cared. It's also peculiar that this guy, Heston, is so okay with everything that happened today. Shaking my head, I reply back.

Me: Better, not so shaken up. Thanks for asking. Are you okay? I don't want to be rude; he's checking on me and my daughter, and he did give us a ride to the hospital.

Heston: I just wanted to check on you guys. I feel terrible. My brows furrow with apprehension. Why is he so concerned? I would think he would be frustrated, and pray to the gods that his insurance doesn't rise through the roof.

Me: Why?

Heston: I want to get to know you.

Biting my bottom lip, I stare at his last text. It seems a little forward… kind of weird too. Do Paige and I seem that interesting? I don't know how I feel about this.

"Dad's here," Paige murmurs. I lock the screen to my phone and look up. There he is, my ex-husband, with his big and boisterous self. He glares at me with the same beady eyes he did not so long ago.

Whispering under my breath, "here we go," I prepare myself for another round of fighting. It's what we're good at.

2

TWO WEEKS LATER

After the wreck, and having to listen to my ex-husband yell at me over the accident and the cut on Paige's face that wasn't my fault, we missed the movers. They couldn't redeliver for two weeks because they were down a driver, putting me and Paige in a hotel to the new house. Cam didn't even offer for us to stay with him, I'm not surprised. We're finally moving into the house today, but she's currently with her dad, so I'm left unpacking most of our things by myself. Our new place is bigger than our apartment and has more space than I know what to do with. It's two stories: gray siding with white panels. It's hard to stay inside and unpack when all I want to do is smell the fresh cut grass, and flowers. Walking outside, a cup of coffee in hand, I can't help but scout the porch and yard. It's bare of anything but a concrete walkway. Even then, the grass creeps over the edges like skeleton hands wanting to take it into the deep dark soil. Patches of the yard are discolored from the sun, weeds popping up like acne everywhere. The yard has been long abandoned of any care.

I look at the house beside me, its lapis-colored door

matching the pots filled with beautiful blue flowers. The next house has a red front door, an abundance of crimson roses lining the property. Then yellow, green…every door is a different color. I look back at my house.

Black.

My nose scrunches up.

Despair. Darkness. Rebellion.

All things I don't want for our fresh start. This is the other side, where the grass is greener and everything is supposed to be brighter.

First thing I'm doing is painting the damn door. But what color? I'll have to see if Paige has any ideas. Drinking the last of my coffee, I step into the house. The fresh smell of paint and balmy coolness from the air-conditioner settles on my skin. Our old place above the Chinese restaurant barely kept us cool with an added window unit. I remember Mom covering the windows with vibrant-colored throws to mask the heat from making the place hotter. Reds, oranges, yellows. You couldn't miss our apartment when you walked around the corner.

My phone dings from beside the boxes on the floor. Sitting back down in the circle of chaos, I grab it and unlock the screen.

Heston: So, *are you settled in?*

He's been texting me here and there, just small talk. The crash has turned us into little pen pals, and the interaction is nice. At least I have someone to talk to. He has a sense of humor, and even though he's kind of an ass, there's a touch of softness to him. Or maybe the cracks of loneliness from my mother being gone has me longing for anyone to fill the void.

He asked me to go to lunch with him yesterday, but I don't date. I wouldn't know how to act or what to say. I just want us to stay like we are, blindly talking from our sides of the world.

Me: *Almost.*

Heston: *I wish I could see you.*

My heart stutters, the feeling reminding me of missing a step and almost falling on my face. The only difference is, I can't help but smile. His charm makes my heart warm. *What should I say back? Something just as sweet?* I shake my head No. I don't want him to think I'm the girl who falls heads over heels for a man because he's persistent and nice.

How about naughty? Hmm...his response will tell me the kind of man he really is...

Me: *Nudes will cost you.*

Heston: *I'd settle for lunch.*

I wasn't expecting that response. Maybe he is a nice guy, after all—not just playing a part.

I sigh. A lunch date might not be a bad idea. After my divorce a few years back, I moved in with my mother and haven't been in a relationship since. I've sheltered myself and my heart from being broken, protecting it from ever having to feel like I'm replaceable again. Moving here is supposed to be the start of something new, right? Something better? This is what Mom wanted for us. If I don't take a chance, her wishes will be in vain. If anything, my mother showed me you never know when your day is up, so what am I waiting for?

Me: *Maybe.*

"Hello?"

I glance over my shoulder at the unfamiliar voice. A tall woman with blonde hair flowing over her chest stares back at me inside my home. "Hi. I'm Tenly Brights. I live across the street. The house with the green door." She gives a small wave, her smile overly big, and one foot tucked behind the other. I can't help but notice how gorgeous she is—and the epitome of a suburban housewife. Standing up, I brush my hands off on my shorts and walk over.

"Hi!" I shake her hand. "I'm Rain." She tilts her head to the side, looking at me intently. I can't help but notice the softness of her palm and her perfectly manicured nails. She's wearing a loose-fitting purple top, black yoga pants, and stark white sneakers without a spot of dirt on them.

"That's a beautiful name. Where are you from?" she asks, with curious eyes.

"Thanks. We just moved from Charlotte."

"Ah, city girl. Well, I was just coming back from my morning jog, saw your door open, and thought I'd introduce myself. Do you need any help?" She gestures toward the temple of boxes in the living room.

"I think I've got it. I'm almost done," I say, stunned she even offered. People in the city don't do that. They keep their head down and walk on by like they see nothing.

She looks around, her foot untucking as she becomes more comfortable. "Is it just you?"

"Me and my daughter. She should be here soon."

"Bless your heart being a single mom in today's world." She shakes her head, sympathy pouring from her deep green eyes. I can't tell if she's giving me a compliment or being critical. "I mean, some people around here wouldn't understand choosing to split up a family and raise a child in separate households, but I totally respect it." She presses her hand to her chest, and I can't help but wonder if people really are that quick to judge around here, or if Tenly is just a gossip. There's always one woman on the block, isn't there—acts like your best friend and talks behind your back?

"Well, her dad and I didn't work out, and we didn't want to stay together just for the sake of Paige, you know? We weren't happy and didn't want to project that onto our daughter."

Wait—why am I explaining myself to a stranger?

It's this place. I want to make a good impression. Come off as a good mother, who only wants the best for her daughter.

"I get it." She nods, her silky blonde layers framing her face. "My husband and I have been trying for kids." She holds both hands up with her fingers crossed. "Hopefully, this month will be the lucky one!"

"How exciting! Good luck to you guys," I encourage. I don't know anything about trying to get pregnant. I wasn't expecting to when I had Paige. Ever since, I've been scared to even look at a penis, fearing it might happen again…well, and the whole not dating thing.

Her bright smile fades. Her eyes dart from side to side, scoping out the place again. "Yeah…well, it's been three years. I don't have my hopes too high." The joyfulness in her voice from moments ago has been cut with something dark and broody. Loss and loneliness stir the depths of her eyes into that of a fine mist hanging over the everglades after a morning rain.

"Well, I'll get out of your way." Tenly takes a step back, slipping her hands into the pockets of her pants. "Nice to meet you!"

"You too," I reply. As she leaves, I cross my arms and rest my hip on the doorway, watching Tenly as she walks across the street to a big house with foliage spidering up the side, matching her forest-colored door.

3

Sitting on the floor going through boxes, it's taking me longer than I expected because I keep running into mom's things. Turning behind me, I grab the top of a cardboard box, dust feathering my palm and tug it toward me. Opening up the top, I reach inside and pull out something soft. It's my mom's horribly colored crochet blanket. It was such an eyesore in the living room of our old place, I remember sneaking it back into her room all the time. I have no idea why she loved it so much, but she did. Running my fingers across the twisted silk knots, the orange and black bleed into green. Bringing it to my face, I inhale the sweet notes of the strawberry lotion she always used. It makes me miss her more. My eyes gloss over, thinking about how her smell will soon fade.

Car doors slam outside. I jerk my head up, peeking out the front window, catching the corner of a sun-stained red truck.

Placing the blanket on top of a box, I navigate the circle of my mother's knickknacks and photos. If you didn't know any better, you'd think I was performing a ritual of some kind. Paige rushes in and comes to a complete stop, her eyes widening as she looks around the place. I can't help but grin at her astonishment.

"Holy crap! This place is huge," she mutters, her warm mocha eyes smiling with excitement. She spins in a circle, her hands gripping the bottom of her Dutch braids. She always wears her hair like that, along with some hoodie, no matter what the temperature is outside.

Wrapping my arms around her, I pull her close. Being alone in this big empty house today has made me miss her more than ever. Being by myself feels different now, knowing I'm on my own creates the loudest echo of solitude. She tenses beneath me. Snuggling her like a little kid is probably crossing some teenager line, but I needed to feel her, to smell her pineapple and peony perfume.

"You good?" I whisper into the top of her head, wanting to make sure her father didn't do anything stupid.

"Yeah."

Holding her by the shoulders, I move back to get a good look at the stitches in her face.

"I'm nervous it'll scar." She raises her fingers, barely touching the black string snaking through her porcelain skin.

"Nah, you're young. It'll bounce back in no time." Cam's cold shadow envelopes my body before he fills the doorway. Tension thickens. My arms drop from Paige's shoulders. I'm sure he'll have something horrible to say about the house. I murmur to Paige, "There are two rooms upstairs. Pick the one you want. I'll use the other for my studio."

"Sweet," she says, taking the stairs two at a time.

"Studio?" Cam scoffs, before stepping completely into the house. His square shoulders and lanky six-foot height take over the foyer, causing an unsettling energy to raise the hairs on my arms. I feel like a deer watching a hunter enter its territory. Even though the intruder is on your land, a place you call home, you're the one who has to tread lightly. "It must be nice living off dead mommy's money, huh? Now you don't have to get a real job." His beady dark eyes stab into me. Sourness swirls in the pit of my stomach. He always considered my pottery trash, demanding I get a real job with a steady paycheck. I never did. Moving in with my mother was a different pace, she encouraged my creative side and didn't care about a steady income. Being a starving artist is part of the career. Like actors not having enough sleep, or family time. It's a sacrifice to do what you love.

"Thanks for dropping her off." Grabbing the door, I wave my hand, gesturing for him leave. We're not married anymore. I don't have to put up with his condescending shit.

"Living in a place like this, don't think you're going to get another dime out of me." He starts to leave, and I still my nostrils flaring with rage . He's such a dick. I don't know how I was with him for so long and never saw how ugly he truly is until we divorced.

"You'd have to pay fucking child support for me to raise it, Cam," I snap.

Now on the other side of the doorway he glares back at me, his jaw clenched. I slam the door in his face before he can say another shitty thing to me.

Asshole.

Sliding the lock into place, I drop my head to the door, taking a deep breath. Cam unravels me. One look at his face, and I'm back to the many times he was mad, violent, or abusively drunk. No matter how hard I try to forget that part of my life, it's always lingering, hiding in the shadows of my mind.

I take my time going up the stairs to see which room Paige chose. Cam's truck revs, rumbling through the neighborhood, sounding like a pissed-off drunk teenager on a joy ride. I close my eyes, my teeth clenched, trying to calm my anxiety. I remind myself he's not my problem anymore, but it does no good. The impression he's imprinted on Paige and me in our new safe heaven is not the first impression I was hoping to make.

One box has been moved from the landing, but I still have to maneuver around the rest she left behind. Something clatters against the floor, and I follow the noise, finding Paige inside the room on the left side of the house, above my room downstairs.

"Nice choice," I say, entering the room.

"Yeah, I like the view." She points to the window. Soft sunlight streams into the room, lighting the space in a beautiful glow. The floor creaks beneath my weight as I move to take a peek outside. The neighborhood comes into view beneath a few swaying branches. It is nice. This house is nice. Everything about the place is nice. I can't wait to make it ours.

Walking out of her room, I stop at the doorway and glance over my shoulder at Paige as she jerks her blankets free from a plastic bag. "What do you think of the place?" I ask as I turn to face her. She plops the comforter on her lap and looks around the room with curious eyes.

"I mean, it's a lot bigger than our last place." She's right about that: the kitchen and living room alone are bigger than the spread we had before. The kitchen was so close you could cook while watch TV on the couch. Ok, not really, but it was small.

"Even with all our stuff, it feels empty." Looking up at me her brows raise with awed energy from the fact she's never been in a place this nice or big. This house is big enough to actually to do something with, and I have zero experience with decorating. Even when I had a home with Cam, my skills were a perfect example of Pinterest epic fails from one room to the next.

"You still mad at me for making us move out here?" I chew on the inside of my cheek, waiting for her to reply.

Huffing, she opens the bag wider and finds it empty. Shoving it to the side, she stares at it in thought.

"I don't know, just so much is happening. Grandma, the wreck, moving. The thought of being the new kid at school is just too much to think about right now." There's a lot of weight hanging in her words. She's been through a lot lately, but Paige is stronger than she thinks. She underestimates how much she can handle. She'll fit in here just as well as she did at her old school.

"Give it some time. You'll make new friends."

Her eyes rise, narrowing at me in irritation. I get it; she doesn't want to make new friends. But if I'm trying, she can too.

"I'm hoping to finish unpacking at least one room tonight. Holler if you need me." I tap my nails on the doorframe and turn to walk away when she says, "Um…can we order pizza?" She doesn't look up from digging in a box, a stray hair that escaped her braid falling into her face.

"I swear, you're going to turn into pizza as much as you eat it, child." When I ate pizza at her age, my face would break out so bad, but her skin is always clear, and I don't think she'd care if it did cause acne.

Not used to stairs, I hold onto the banister. Bickering male voices make me stop at the second to last step. Shadows move about on the other side of the blurred glass.

Grabbing the knob, I open the door to two men. They both jerk forward, plastering smiles on their faces.

"Hi!" they say in unison.

My eyes fall to the plant in the guy on the left's arms, then to the bottle of red wine in the other man's hand.

"We're your neighbors." The man holding the wine points to a house behind him. The one with the blue door.

"I'm Flynn, and this is my partner, Owen," he introduces them both. Owen is shorter and a bit leaner than Flynn. His blond hair is really thin like candy floss , and freckles dust his nose. His white shirt is tucked into navy-blue Chinos, both without a wrinkle.

"This is for you. I can't imagine the hell moving brings these days." Flynn sighs, as if the thought pains him. Pursing his lips, he presents me with a dark bottle of wine. His toned arms flex as I take it, showing just how fit he is compared to Owen.

"And I said not everyone's an alcoholic, so I brought a plant to—" he peeks into my living room, my mother's eccentric blanket standing out from the box, "—liven up the place." He waves his hand around, then pushes the dark green leafy plant toward me.

"Thank you so much! Both of you. This is so kind," I say around the leaves, trying not to drop their housewarming gifts. I'm more of a Moscato drinker, and a serial killer of plants, but this is supposed to be a new start, and I'm going to really try and keep this plant alive, while swigging red wine and waiting for my green thumb to blossom.

"Mom, who are you talking to?" I glance over my shoulder. Paige is standing at the top of the stairs, one hand on the banister, confusion drawing her brows down.

"Some of our neighbors came over to introduce themselves." My eyes snap back to Owen and Flynn, who are eyeing my daughter like she's a newborn baby. Flynn's mouth hangs open in pure joy.

"Oh my god, she is too much!" Owen says, his hands

clasped together. They're both in awe, starstruck, as if they've never seen a teenage girl before. It reminds me of women whose biological clocks are ticking and anything baby has them gushing all over the place.

"Um…" I hesitate, taken aback, "this is my daughter, Paige, and I'm Rain."

"Oh, honey! The pleasure is all ours!" Flynn waves me off.

"Yes, new neighbors are exactly what we needed." Owen nods in agreement.

"How much do you wanna bet Tenly was here first?" Flynn mutters under his breath. Owen rolls his eyes before looking right at me.

"She was here first, wasn't she?" Owen questions, his right brow raised.

I open my mouth to reply, then stop, unsure what to say. Do I tell them yes?

"She always has to one-up everyone," Owen grunts.

"That woman is a toxic bitch," Flynn hisses, his cheeks turning red. Maybe she *is* the neighbor who doesn't approve.

"Easy now. Tenly and Rain could have hit it off and here you are blabbing—"

"Oh, screw Tenly," he interrupts, and I have to bite my cheek to keep from laughing.

"Who is Tenly?" Paige asks, coming down the stairs. Oh lord, don't get her started on the drama. The girl lives for it. She's never involved, but she craves it like a drug. Watches every reality TV show and knows everyone's business at school.

"A shitty woman who thinks she's above everyone else." Flynn doesn't hold back, and Owen slaps him on the arm.

"What?" He holds his bicep, where Owen just hit him.

"It's true! You can't tell me what she said about us adopting didn't piss you off." He stares at his partner, waiting.

"Of course it did, but we have to live with her across the street, so I just ignore her oppressive beliefs—you should, too."

Flynn scoffs, looking the other way, as if he has better things to do than listen to this crap.

Paige laughs, gaining their attention.

"So, she's like the gossiping bitch of the suburbs?"

"Paige!" I scorn, my heart beating in my chest like a drum. I cannot believe she said that! I've never heard her use that word before.

"Yes," Flynn and Owen say at the same time.

I turn away from the door, taking the plant and wine to the kitchen, unsure what to say to our new neighbors after all that was just said. Do I thank them for the gifts? Continue on about Tenly? Owen and Flynn come farther into the house, their eyes scanning the place like they're in a haunted house rather than one of their neighbor's. I find it odd.

"Wait until you meet the Gradys. Their kids will drive you up the wall!" Owen throws a hand out, shaking his head, gaining a slap on the arm from Flynn.

"Okay, I think that's enough gossiping for one evening." Flynn fakes a smile, clearly nervous about Owen's opinions. "I'm so glad you and your daughter are here. This house could use some light." His head swivels, pointedly looking around the place, and my curiosity piques as to what the heck that means. "Wait—was there something up with the people who lived here before us?" Paige asks what I'm thinking.

"They just…weren't happy," Flynn stammers, and my suspicions rise. The room grows quiet, tension whispering that there's more to this than they're letting on. Owen turns around to leave. "Come on Flynn," he calls. Flynn smiles.

"Don't be strangers!" he says so friendly and over the top, as if he didn't just go gossip queen before tucking tail and running.

Paige takes a slow step toward me; her eyes still on the door.

"That was weird," she says, her voice low.

"Yeah, I can't argue that," I admit, grabbing the bottle of wine from the kitchen counter.

"What do you think they meant about bringing light into the house?"

I bite my bottom lip, staring at the front door. The black paint covers every crack and crevice. The color and what happened here projecting onto Paige and me.

"I don't know, but first thing tomorrow, I'm painting that damn door a different color."

"What, why?" Paige's head snaps up so fast, another strand of her hair comes loose.

"Because it's black. It's sad and—"

"Powerful and strong. Keep it," she interrupts. My brows furrow at the way she sees and feels about the color.

Maybe I've been looking at it all wrong. I've always seen the color as something evil, but maybe it represents something more—like strength and authority. If it weren't for the dark door casting its dominance, every neighbor that has stepped into this house today would have seen how fragile Paige and me are. Instead, they've seen something ruthless and compelling.

"All right, we'll keep it black."

4

Heston: *Thinking about me yet?*

Phone in hand, I stand in my room in my champagne-colored bra and matching panties. I was hoping he'd forget about lunch since I don't know how to feel about it. Should I be excited or dreading it?

The fact that Heston is handsome, especially his sexy smirk and his short, ash blond curls, has a smile spreading across my face. He makes me feel like a high schooler again, I swear. The butterflies and constant urge to giggle at everything he says is mortifying. I hope I never witness myself mid-flirt.

Biting my bottom lip, my fingers move across the keyboard on my screen.

Me: *Thinking about how I don't have a car because of you.*

Three dots pop up as he replies, and I chew on the end of my nail, nervous he took my horrible attempt at flirting as rude.

Heston: *I'm the kind of man who does a lot of things he's* *not supposed to, but I've never regretted one thing I've done. Yet.*

I crack a smile at his massive ego.

Me: *The day isn't over yet.*

I laugh, feeling both sexy and confident after my risqué behavior. I'm not typically the kind of girl that flirts, so I don't know why I even said the things I did, but it feels good. It's this place; it makes me feel comfortable and free. I don't feel hidden away in an apartment where people walking by could care less about who lives there. I matter here and I can feel it.

Heston: *I'm looking froward to your kind of trouble.*

Oh man, he knows what he's doing. He can more than talk the talk and walk the walk.

We chat a little more and I find out his car is in the shop, so he's taking an Uber to where we're eating. I decide to take one too incase the date goes sour and I want to leave.

Now…to find something to wear.

Well, the good news is I've hung all my clothes up. The bad news…I can't find anything I want to wear for my lunch date. Purple light casts a calming shade across the room as I stare at my closet. Baggy shirts and pants are all I wear. I've been hiding my body, seeking comfort in one over-washed hoodie at a time. It's clear I haven't recovered from my divorce with Cam. He made me feel ugly and ashamed of my curves.

Leaning back on my heel, I glance at the rack of clothes once more, trying to remember what I would've worn before I met Cam. How I would have worn my hair. Truthfully, it's difficult to remember who I was before him.

I pull my phone out again, checking to see where the closest Target is. They have same-day delivery, so if I find something more…alluring to wear, it will be here before I need to go.

On the third page of dresses, my eyes snag on a model in a bell-sleeved, lace-hemline Mya dress. It's long-sleeved and brown with a white design. The boat neckline is gorgeous, exposing my shoulders. It's mid-thigh and looks cute with the white wedges she's wearing.

Wait—what am I talking about? I haven't worn heels in so long, I'd probably fall into a bush just trying to get to the sidewalk.

I bite my lip, glancing at the shoes in the bottom of my closet. I wonder if my high-top Converses will look okay with it. Dropping to my knees, I reach for the box in the back. I've never worn them. My mom got them for me for my birthday last year, and I was too nervous I'd get something on them. I felt as if their lively outlook didn't match the way I felt inside. I definitely didn't want to be seen, and my dark colors not only matched my soul but hid me from wondering eyes. I open the lid. Brand-new butterscotch shoes stare up at me. Running my finger over the fabric, my eyes start to water, thinking about my mom. She tried so hard to brighten my life, and all I did was hide within the four walls of our apartment. Shaking myself out of my grief, I take the box with me and head over to the bed.

I'm wearing them.

I order the mini dress, along with a push-up bra and matching cheeky panties. I don't plan on anyone seeing them, but they looked nice and wearing something besides my sports bra and mismatching bikini-style panties might feel nice. Maybe. Is it too much?

Palm to my face, I let out a squeal. I'm going to combust from the uncertainty. Butterflies swarm inside my stomach. I haven't been on a date in years, and the first impression is the most important. I don't want to come off as a lonely, divorced, single mother, but I also don't want to look like a hooker. The outfit I ordered doesn't seem to say either. It's flattering and looks like something a woman who's sure of herself would wear—which is what I want.

Setting my phone down, I sigh. Dating feels a lot harder than it did when I was a teenager. Why is that? I'm older and wiser now, you'd think it would be easier. I feel like I'm cooking blindfolded.

5

After locating the perfect place for my plant—a snake plant, I learned—I find myself staring back at my reflection, closely eyeing the brown dress and the way it hugs my waist. I bite back my smile. I cannot believe I'm going to wear this, but, man, it's so cute paired with my Converse. Grabbing my Sakura Blossom perfume, I mist my body with sweet almonds and tree blossoms.

My phone buzzes on the dresser, the vibration causing it to dance toward the edge. I swipe it before it falls and look to see who it is. The insurance company. A voicemail notification pops up, and I read the dictation. Looks like they're going to lend me a car until I receive my pay out. Good. One less thing I have to worry about.

I'm pretty sure they have my address, but I did just move, so just in case, I email them the new one and set my phone back down to finish getting ready.

"Hey, Mom—" Paige stops at my door, her mouth parted as if she just walked upon a princess. She scans me from head-to-toe, then tucks her chocolate-colored hair behind her ear, her beautiful face clear of makeup. She's wearing her favorite black sweats with a matching sports bra. She's relaxed and comfortable.

"What do you think? Too much?" I glance down at what I'm wearing, not sure if it's just cute to me or if it actually looks good. Maybe I should change, this feels too weird.

"Wow, I mean, when you said you were going out to lunch with a friend, I didn't realize it was a date." She crosses her arms and sits on my bed, staring at me as if I escaped from the zoo. "I mean, I don't know if it's a date. Maybe." My head starts spinning. "Do you think it's too much for a lunch date?" I'm starting to second-guess this whole thing. I should cancel. I can't do this.

"What? No! You look amazing. I don't think I've ever seen you in a dress," she says, her tone filled with astonishment. My body temperature begins to rise as my insecurities strangle me. The more people compliment me or take notice of something new like a haircut or shoes, the more uncomfortable I become. I don't know why I'm like this. You would think any situation that gives you attention would make you want to do more of whatever it is, but it makes me even more self-aware and self-conscious.

"You know what? I know what you need! Wait here!" She holds her index finger up and runs out of the room. Her bare feet slap against the hardwood floor and stomp up the stairs.

"What are you looking for?" She doesn't reply as she continues to rummage, then her feet hit the stairs once more, before she appears in my doorway, out of breath, a smile full of contentment on her pretty face. She holds her fist between us and slowly unclasps her fingers, revealing a pair of drop earrings. They're small with a silver chain holding a radiant diamond in the shape of a teardrop. The tear catches in the light and a spectrum of luster dances across the wall and ceiling. I take them in my hand and look up at her. She's nearly bouncing on her tiptoes with excitement.

"Where did you get these?" I ask, my voice thick with awe.

"Grandma got them from an art fair last year. She said she didn't know if they were real, but they reminded her of me." She shrugs, interlocking her fingers in front of her. "She said she traded a painting for them."

"Wow," is all I can say. My mother was a free-spirit, through and through. She always made bold decisions and didn't care what the world thought of her. I wish I had her bravery. "They look real," I mutter, rubbing the pad of my finger over them.

"You should wear them. I mean, who knows if you'll get an opportunity to dress up again. The guy may turn out to be a loser, so you should go all out."

I've wanted to switch back to my sweats and a hoodie five times now, and I've only had this dress on for twenty-minutes.

I go into my bathroom and slip the earrings into each earlobe piercing. They actually do add something to complete the outfit. I feel pretty and better about myself.

"See? They look good!" Paige whispers, looking at my reflection from behind me. Turning around, I rest my hand on her shoulder, elated she came in when she did. I needed her reassurance. She's turning into an amazing young lady so fast, I can hardly see the little girl she used to be. It's unfair how quickly time passes.

"You sure you're going to be okay here by yourself?" Usually, my mother would be home with her. Now, she'll be alone.

"It's not like it's the first time I've been home by myself,

Mom." That teenage tone snaps back into place, and I'm pretty sure she rolls her eyes.

"When?"

"Grandma left a couple times. I think to see her boyfriend or something. I don't know."

I do remember coming back once or twice and my mother not being there. It had infuriated me at the time because she was supposed to be watching Paige, not sneaking off like a teenager.

"I know, but this is a new place with different neighbors. I want to make sure you're comfortable being here by yourself."

She shakes her head with an annoyed expression. With her right brow lifted, she turns her head to the side. "It's safer here than the city, don't you think?"

I want to throw my brush at her and hold her at the same time. She's grown so much in the last couple years; it won't be long before she wants to move out or go to college, leaving me behind and on my own.

I look at the time. I better get going. Grabbing my purse from my dresser, I head to the front door.

"Is your phone is charged?" I ask. It seems any time her and I are apart and I call her, she never picks up. It drives me crazy.

"Yes."

"If I call, you better pick up!" When she doesn't respond, I toss a stern look over my shoulder.

"What? I said yes," she huffs, holding her hands up.

"No going anywhere…for now." Not until we get a little more settled and know who we're neighbors with.

"Okaaay," she says, boredom thick in her voice. Plopping down on the couch, she snatches the remote from the coffee table. I grasp her head and kiss her forehead, before opening the front door to my Uber waiting outside.

"Be back soon!" I holler, shutting and locking the door behind me.

My phone vibrates as I make my way to the car. A quick glance down, and I see Heston texted.

Heston: *Lighthouse Restaurant. I'll wait for you in the cabana.*

I've never been there before, then again, I haven't been to too many places. Leaving the apartment gave me anxiety, I felt safe and comfortable inside. That's why this is such a big deal for me. I'm stepping outside my comfort zone, pushing for new friends and new experiences to help me strangle my loneliness. It surprises me every day how much I hid behind my mother, even as an adult. If there was a problem with Cam, I would seek her help. If I was depressed, she was there. It was like I couldn't take care of myself after my divorce, and although her help was a Godsend, I'm starting to see how much it hindered my independence. I open the back passenger door and slide into the small car, cherry air freshener invading my nostrils. I glance at the guy behind the wheel. Mid-forties. A rainbow bandana wrapped around his bald head. A long beard braided down his chin.

"Where to, my lady?" he asks over his shoulder, his tone dopey and lacking any energy. I give him the name of the place, and he nods, backing out of my driveway.

The closer I get to the restaurant, the more nervous I become.

I shift in my seat, my hands tugging at the hem of my dress to cover more of my pale thighs. Are my legs usually this washed out or is it the lighting? That little bit of confidence I had is diminishing by the second. I should have worn something more casual, comfortable.

My insecurities begin to spiral.

Did I put deodorant on?

I should have brushed my teeth.

Is my hair frizzy?

We finally pull into a parking lot, taking a sharp right next to a blue and white building, an array of cars right in front of what must be the cabana. The wooden piers hold up a straw roof, and just underneath are a dozen high tables with chairs, and, of course, a bar that can only be described as paradise. There's twinkle lights, and flowers everywhere.

"Thanks!" I give a small smile to my driver before climbing out. I pay and tip him from my phone and walk toward the cabana. My heart jackhammers inside my chest, causing me to breathe harder.

I place my hand on my chest in attempt to calm myself, noticing I'm a little shaky. Why am I acting like this? This is ridiculous. If he likes me, he likes me. If he doesn't, screw him. I don't want to hide in the shadows anymore. I don't want to be shut up in a house watching TV, while constantly glancing out the window, wondering what some couple is thinking as they walk along the crosswalk. I want to be the kind of person who takes risks, goes on adventures, doing something interesting, something worthwhile. I want to believe I'm capable of more.

As music plays through two speakers by the bar, I stop at the entrance and look under and around the cabana. I spot Heston at a table in the far back.

6

When our eyes meet, he does that sexy smirk of his, and a flirtatious smile takes over my lips. My head lowers before I peek back up at him. Damn, if he isn't more handsome today. My fingers ache, longing to tangle in his blond, curly hair. His white shirt hugs his shoulders and clings across his broad chest. His dark-washed jeans compliment his lower half just as well. He makes casual strikingly good-looking. I clench my thighs, forcing myself to look away. I weave my way through the tables and chairs, my ears catching, "Start of Something Good," by Daughtry. I haven't heard this one in a long time. It's perfect for the occasion. Nearing the table, he stands up like a gentleman, his blue ocean eyes sizing me up. My body heats under his attention.

"Wow, you look incredible." He shakes his head, running a hand through his hair while staring at me as if he can't take his eyes off me.

"Thank you." I look down again, that nervous feeling in the pit of my stomach returning. Damn, I need a drink.

I slide onto the stool, sitting directly across from him.

"Have you been here before?" he asks, resting a tanned arm on the table.

"Actually, no."

"Oh, man. You have to try their orange crush cocktail," he insists, and I smile with a nod. Yes. That's what I need right now. Anything with alcohol will do.

"Hey, ya'll!" My attention instantly snaps to my right, where a waitress gawks at Heston with a Pan-Am smile. The kind where the flight attendant is always with bright white teeth forcing her cheeks to touch her eyes. Her colossal boobs press against her navy-blue polo shirt, and she bats her fake eyelashes at him like I'm not sitting here. She probably hopes I'm his sister.

"Two orange crushes," he orders, then winks at me. Small victory!

"Do we need menus or do you already know what you'd like?" She finally glances my way.

"I have no idea what you serve." I look to Heston, hoping I'm not holding him up from giving his order. He smirks then glances up at the waitress. "We need a couple menus, please."

"Alrighty, I'll grab those for you and your beverages." She turns, and I wait for Heston to watch her ass as she walks away. That's what Cam used to do. But he doesn't. He keeps his eyes on me. I bite back a smile, looking down at the table. He's nothing like Cam.

"So, Heston, do you have any kids?" I start in with the questions, really wanting to know who this handsome man is.

"Nah, not yet." He shakes his head, his tone almost somber. He's sexy as hell. How does he not have kids with at least one woman out there? "Do you have more kids or is it just you and your daughter?" he asks as the waitress slips menus onto the table, taking a second longer than necessary to stare at Heston. I want to get jealous, but how can I blame her? Look at this fucking man.

My eyes meet his blue orbs, and I nod.

"Just me and Paige, and she's a handful."

A charming smile pulls at his face. He sits back in his chair, crossing his arms.

"She looks like she could be trouble." He lightly laughs, and I do too.

Taking a menu for myself, I raise my brows. "You have no idea."

My eyes scan the menu, finding crab, fish, shrimp, chicken strips, and more. It all sounds so good; I don't know what to get. Since I moved, my food choices have been slim from exhaustion.

"Oh, I'm sure she has a good role model," he says, insinuating I'm the one influencing my daughter's rebellion. I'm not usually trouble. I'm quiet and let things sit on my shoulders, but he doesn't have to know I'm wallflower. So, I shrug, not letting on if I am or not.

The waitress comes back, her eyes on Heston again.

"Ya'll ready to order?" She carefully places our orange drinks on the table. It looks like a slushy in a fancy glass with a citrus orange soda smell that reminds me of when I was kid. We'd go to a little gas station down the street and get those glass bottles you had to pop the top off. It's a sweet memory in a line of dark challenges in my life.

Heston's sapphire eyes fall on mine, and the waitress glances at me. They're waiting for me to order. Shit.

"Oh…um, I'll have the shrimp and hush puppies."

"And I'll have the snow crab legs with fries," Heston orders. The waitress takes both of our menus and walks away, her hips swaying. She's really putting herself out there despite Heston being here with a woman. It pisses me off.

We sit silently for a few moments. Before the awkwardness sets in, I rest my arms on the table, leaning in to get a little more personal.

"So, what do you do for a living?" Please have a job.

"I'm in real estate," he informs before taking a sip of his drink. "You?"

"I'm an artist. Pottery mostly." I shrug, not really sure where I sit on the spectrum of professionalism. Realistically I'm not even on the cart.

"Really?" His tone takes on one of heightened curiosity. A little spark flickers in my chest. He's impressed? Usually, I get looks of sympathy or "Ahh, the starving artist."

"Yeah, I mean, I make pottery and sell it online or go to art shows." I inwardly cringe at how timid I am. I'm scared he'll judge me for not having a career that matches his eight to nine day job. I don't really flaunt my work because I never love what I make. It's nothing like my mom's.

"That's incredible. You'll have to show me your work sometime."

I smile. "Yeah, I'd like that." The idea of him in my studio, in my new house, gives me goosebumps.

We talk through lunch, until it's near evening. He's so easy to open up to that I lose track of time, but it's been worth it. The date has actually turned out better than I could have imagined. I've learned so much about him. He lives in the city, is twenty-nine years old, hates rap music, despises corn, unless it's popped. I had to give him a hard time about his dislike for rap music, though. I love it. Growing up, you weren't cool unless you knew every Dr. Dre song there was. Leaning down, I rummage through my purse. My fingers graze my phone, and I pull it out.

"I need to check on Paige."

"Yes, of course."

Texting Paige, I ask if she's okay, and she gives me a thumbs up. I swear, she only knows how to reply back with emojis.

The waitress comes in the meantime, setting down the check. I guess she thinks it's time for our date to be over. It is getting pretty late.

Heston pays for our meals and stands, holding his hand out for me to take. My heart flutters. He says and does all the right things. It makes me wonder what his flaw could be. God, I hope he's not married and I'm the side chick.

Walking out of the restaurant, he grasps my hand, his warm palm a little bigger than mine, pulling me toward a dock next to the cabana, so boats can pull up and grab a bite to eat before heading back out. Lights are wrapped around the railing, giving off a nice glow as the sun goes down. Reaching the safety rail, I place both hands on it and look across the crisp water. It's beautiful. The sound of it crashing against the dock is hypnotizing. Heston comes up behind me, resting his head on my shoulder, the smell of bergamot, pepper, and Amberwood making me inhale before letting it go with a sigh.

"Tell me you'll see me again." His lips brush my ear, command lacing his tone, surprising me with his assertiveness. A little red flag waves, and I want to tell him not to command me around. It takes me aback for a second, but I do like him and want to see him again. He's has a charming side, good looking, a romantic. A little dominance is something I can handle.

Turning my head toward him, I whisper, "Yes."

He kisses my cheek, and I close my eyes, relishing in the feel of his lips against my skin. It's so foreign but feels so goddamn good. I'd take him home right now if I could, but sleeping with a man on the first date would definitely have the neighbors talking, and it wouldn't be a good example for Paige.

My phone buzzes in my back pocket and I pull it out.

Paige: Where are you? Are you staying the night with him or something? You've been gone all day and I'm bored.

Bored is not a good state to leave a teenager in. Sighing, I text her back, telling her I'm on my way.

"I gotta go," I tell Heston. I shouldn't have left her alone. She may be a teenager, but she has the heart of a kid.

I pull up the Uber app and request a ride. Five minutes.

"Me too, unfortunately. I have a few spaces in a shopping mall I need to go over for clients, so I better get started on that." He takes a step back, and coldness wraps around my body, reminding me I'm not with him, this is just a date.

Holding my purse with both hands, I glance up at Heston, trying not to come off as shy, but I'm not sure what to really say or do to end the date.

"So, I had a really good time. Thank you. It's nice to get out and go somewhere other than grab-and-go places…" I stop myself. I sound like a hermit, and that *cannot* be attractive.

A sexy smirk pulls at the right side of his face, making my toes curl.

"I did too. Maybe next time I can come to your place, see your pottery, cook for you…" His voice dips, giving off a low, husky tone that's warm and passionate.

"Maybe…" I tease, and his eyes gloss over with something mischievous. I like it.

"I think you like to taunt me." His hand on my hip, he blinks his smoldering blue eyes. As If the ocean was doused in gasoline and set on fire. "It's okay. It just makes me want you more." My mouth parts, my body warming.

A Jetta pulls up, the headlights shining right on us.

"That's my ride," I whisper. Heston grabs my hand, breaking our circle of burning need, and walks me to the car. Such a gentleman. He opens the door, and I slip inside, telling the man my address again. I look up at Heston, hoping he says something I can hang onto until we see each other again.

"Call me later." He winks, that dominant tone dipping in before we part. I nod, unsure which cue to follow, as he shuts the door.

Sitting in the back seat I replay the whole evening. I wish he would've come home with me and told me more about himself. I enjoyed his company, but the feeling of isolation beings to slip up my chest and snake itself around my neck, strangling my confidence.

7

"Mom!" Banging on my bedroom door wakes me from a hard sleep. Stretching my arms, I arch my back and flip over onto my side.

"What?" I mumble, not wanting to get up yet.

"I think Grandma's here." My eyes widen, and I lift my head. The bedroom door opens, and Paige stands in her checkered pajama pants, her hair a mess. Her brows furrow, followed by a quivering lip, anguish brushing across her face. I throw the blankets off me, and Paige points toward the kitchen.

Turning into the open space, I instantly notice a brown package sitting on the counter. The idea that my mother is in a box, horribly taped and covered in dust, makes my chest ache. Is this really what life comes to—dead in a vase, inside a box packed among socks? A woman, who was five and a half feet, weighing over a hundred pounds, reduced to ash in a baggy.

Carefully, I take it into my hands and peel the tape off the sides until I can pull the rest of the cardboard apart. The gold and black urn greets me, and my eyes water. I bite back a sob and slip my fingers into the sides of the box to grip the cool vase and gently pull it out. It's heavy. I set it beside the box before I drop it. Holding back tears, I can't help but notice the house doesn't feel so empty anymore, like she's actually here with us.

"Well, Ma, this is the new place." My voice cracks as I speak to the seven-by-nine-inch urn.

"Where are we going to put her?" Paige asks. It's a question I've asked myself a million times.

We both look around the house for the perfect place.

"What about there?" Paige points to the dining room. I follow her hand. There's a built-in cabinet for fine China on the wall behind the table. We don't have fancy plates. Half the time, we use paper plates. I had no idea what I was going to put there. Until now.

"That's a good idea." Taking the urn, I place her high on the top shelf and center her. She can look over us, and we can see and feel her presence anytime we're in here.

I take a step back, placing both my hands together, and just stare at it. I can't believe she's actually gone, but it's nice having her here. It a confusing feeling.

"I really miss her," she mutters, and the tears I've been fighting finally cascade down my cheeks. Sniffling, I grab Paige by the shoulder and pull her close. We have each other. Since the day I found out she was in my belly, we've treaded through everything that has brought together. And as Paige's mom, I can't let this consume her. She has her whole life ahead of her.

"Why don't you go watch some TV?" I suggest. Walking away, she says, "I'm going to go to my bedroom." I sigh at her response and go to the kitchen to make some coffee, my eyes slipping over to the urn. I want to tell my mother about the neighborhood and Heston, but maybe it's weird talking to a bag of ashes—to carry on a conversation as if she can really hear me…

I glance at it again, then over my shoulder, making sure Paige is gone, so she doesn't judge me.

"Well, Mom, the new place is really nice. Well…aside from a couple weird neighbors." I pause, thinking what my mother's response to that would be. Probably something along the lines of *weird means character—which this world lacks.* Smiling to myself, I continue, "I also met a guy. You'd like him. He's a gentleman, nothing like Cam." I turn around, my hands on the counter. The Keurig brews behind me, brushing the air with the scent of light coffee beans. "I wish you could meet him." I wonder what she would say about Heston. She encouraged me to move on after Cam, but I never did. I don't know what words of wisdom she'd have to offer now.

She was the type of person who either liked or hated you. She despised Cam from the moment she met him, and I'd been heedless to her opinion. She'd say he looked like an asshole and talked like one—and all I saw was that damn smile and the way his ass looked in a pair of jeans. I'd like to think Mom would approve of Heston being so different from Cam. I've always looked to my mom for approval. Not having her to run to has made me make so many bold decisions on my own. Getting a house, going on a date, dressing up—it's all been amazing but also stressful. It's hard not having someone standing behind me, telling me if it's a good idea or not.

If she didn't like Heston, would I listen this time?

8

It's near noon, and I still stand here against the counter, quietly drinking my coffee. I can't help but stare at the urn on the cabinet right in front of me. My mind's a complete blank as quietness wraps around me like a gentle blanket.

Knock, knock, knock.

I jump, nearly spilling my coffee down my shirt.

The doorbell rings, replacing the hard knocking. Someone is obviously trying to get my attention. I hurry to the door and swing it open to a medium-sized man in a striped button-up and black pants glaring at me. Standing next to him is a young girl, maybe Paige's age. Her black hair is pencil straight with pink tips. She's in a tight, ripped-up black shirt with lace trim, and her small waist nearly swims in jeans that are way too big for her.

"Your daughter got mine drunk last night," the father informs angrily. My mouth drops at his tone and what the hell he just insinuated. My Paige?

"Are you sure?" Scratching my head, I look at the girl

next to him, then back to him. This doesn't make sense. Paige doesn't even know this girl!

"Yes, I'm sure." I have no idea what to say. Paige must have done this while I was gone all day. But why? This is so unlike her.

"No, I don't think so, sir. We just moved here," I inform him. Besides, Paige has never touched my wine.

"That's great to know trouble just moved next door! Layla doesn't need any more bad influences in her life. Maybe get ahold of your kid before she taints the whole neighborhood!" He's nearly shouting now, his cheeks flushed, sweat dripping from his forehead. Even if Paige did what he's accusing her of, does he understand it was his kid *and* mine? How dare he come over here and talk down to me! My shoulders rise, anger spreading inside, ready to burst. I have to remind myself this is a new place and I really want to make friends with everyone—including this jerk. I want the good and the bad this suburb has to offer. I want to live the American dream. Inhaling a calming breath, I look away, finding Owen and Flynn walking around their yard. Owen kneels down, looking at his plants. Flynn stares up at the sky as if an airplane is coming, but there's no plane. Owen glances up, and we lock eyes before he jerks his attention to the plant.

"I'm sorry, what was your name again?" I ask the man, propping our door open with my hip. I haven't met this man yet, making this encounter beyond awkward.

"I'm Earl, Earl Grady. My family and I live right next door." He points to the left, the one with the white front door. His yard vacant of flowers or bushes. It's plain, boring.

I take a sip of my coffee and watch him carefully, thinking about what to say. Tossing my coffee in his face is out of the question for now, but I don't want to be a pushover either. I remember the time I was playing music too loud, while making a special piece for a show my mother was going to, the neighbors across the landing came over yelling and cussing that I woke him up and now he's going to be late for work. The situation ended with me paying him fifty dollars, just so I didn't have to fight.

"Look, I hear you. The whole block can. I'll have a word with my daughter."

"A *word*?" His head tilts to the side, as if I've lost my mind, his tone insinuating my "talk" is too easy of a punishment. He's really starting to piss me off. It's too early in the day for this crap.

"Look, my daughter has never done this before, so yes, I'm going to talk to her and figure out why she decided to sneak out with a stranger and drink, if you don't mind," I reply with a sharp tongue, flicking my scowl to Layla.

He stands up straighter, glances at his daughter, then back to me with piercing eyes.

"Yeah, okay." He sounds more appeased, but I have a feeling this won't be the last of this guy.

Looking over his head, I find Tenly checking her mail, just standing at the mailbox, glancing over her shoulder at me. The mailman hasn't even come today.

Earl turns around, jerking his daughter by the elbow to follow. Looking at Tenly one last time, I shut the door.

"Paige Adler! Get down here right now!"

I hear her bedroom door open, her feet stomp across the landing, before standing at the top of the stairs. "What?" she groans in a sleepy voice. I wait for her to come down the stairs. It takes her a few seconds to realize I want her in front of me when I call her. It's now that I notice the dark bags under her eyes, and the pale color of her face that's still there from when I saw her earlier this morning. I thought she was sad about Ma's ashes coming today not hungover from a late night of drinking.

"Where were you when I went out yesterday?" My voice snaps, irritated with the way she's standing here with her arms crossed, glaring at me with a 'how dare you wake me up' look.

"Um…" she waves her hand around, her eyes squinted, "here. I was here—you know that."

"Really? Layla's father just came over saying you and his daughter were out drinking yesterday." Her eyes barely widen as she masks her shock and tries to act cool.

"That's why you were in bed when I got home last night!" I came home from being out with Heston and started making dinner for her, but she said she wasn't feeling well and stayed in bed. I had no idea she was drunk.

"I mean, I did drink a little with the neighbor, but come on, Mom, I was in our backyard. I was safe. What's the big deal?" She raises both her hands in the air as if I'm being dramatic over nothing.

"The big deal? Our neighbor thinks you're a bad influence and the whole block heard him say it."

Licking her dry lips, she nods, glancing down. "Well, I can tell you I have a long way to go to catch up to Layla's reputation."

I don't even know what that means, and I don't want to.

"That's enough. Give me your phone." Holding my palm up, I wait for her to hand it over.

"Mom, you can't be serious!" Her eyebrows slip inward, her bottom lip pouting.

"I'm dead serious!" I raise a brow, seconds away from grounding her.

"This is so unfair!" She groans, on the verge of a temper

tantrum. She reaches into her sports bra, pulling her phone out, and slaps it into my palm before stomping up the stairs.

"No more drinking—and I mean it!"

She doesn't answer, but the slam of her door tells me I got my point across. I'm glad she was at home, but drinking with another kid, one I haven't even met, is not okay. Opening the fridge, I lower my head to see if the bottle of wine Owen and Flynn gave me is gone.

And it is.

The little shits.

Slamming the fridge shut, I glance at her cellphone in my palm. She's never acted like this before. I don't even know if taking her phone away is punishment enough. I'm sure her father will have something to say about it, though. I was on a date for a few couple hours with another man. We might be divorced, but he's still a jealous man.

9

Biting my chewed up thumbnail, I look over the room that's going to be my studio. I need to unpack and give things a place—especially my pottery wheel. I might actually even be able to have space for a kiln, instead of trying to do it in my oven. I drop my hand from my mouth, feeling bad about using any more money from my mother's inheritance. This place was expensive, and I should put some away for Paige's education.

The doorbell goes off. I head down the stairs and open it, finding Owen and Flynn.

"Hey, we heard Earl earlier. You okay?" Sympathy fills Owen's voice.

"Yeah, I'm fine." Nodding, I step to the left, letting them in. Both of them are dressed to impress: Owen's tucked in shirt, Flynn's dark green polo and jeans make me remember I'm still in what I slept in.

"Girl, he has no room to talk about anyone's daughter." Owen turns, his hand on his hip.

"My daughter mentioned she might be a little...mischievous," I state.

"That's putting it lightly. That brat broke into our house last year and took our drinking glasses. Her dad made her bring them back and apologize, but she was only sorry for getting caught." He shrugs, folding his arms in front of his broad chest.

"Remember when she left Tenly's house that one night?" Owen makes a face that shows a lot his teeth, as if bringing it up almost hurts.

"Yeah, nobody has said anything about that one. She must have gotten away with it," Flynn adds.

"Wait, are you saying she messed around with Tenly's husband?" Maybe she just broke into their house too, and Flynn and Owen are just assuming the worst.

"Yeah, Tenly was at some yoga retreat and Layla came running across the street barefoot. Why else would she be over there in the wee morning hours?" Owen says, and my mouth drops. It does sound conspicuous. Holy shit. I really don't want Paige hanging out with her.

"The Gradys have ornery twins and a son that's older, but he's not near as much trouble as Layla."

"Wow," I mutter, untying the apron I was using while messing around in my studio.

"What is this little getup?" Owen asks, running his finger in the air, referring to my apron.

"Oh, I was going to set up my pottery station."

"Wait, we have an artist for a neighbor?" Owen bats his eyes, glancing at Flynn before drawing his eyes back to me. Tucking his hand under his jaw, his pinky rubbing his chin, Flynn steps next to him, smirking at me.

"That's pretty awesome. That's a new one."

"Yeah, I like you." Owen raises a brow, as if his acceptance of me is a big deal.

"Well, I don't have anything to show yet. I'm hoping to get it setup soon."

"You better show me when you do!" Owen says with a smile, pawing at the air with his left hand, as if he wants to give me a playful slap, but isn't sure how I would take it. I can't help but laugh. I love how curious they are of my work. The city never gave me that kind of attention.

"I will." I place the apron on the banister, excited to get the room settled.

"Anyway, we won't stay and bother you—we just didn't want Earl running you off. His daughter is a mess. He can't fix her, so he blames everyone else." Flynn's word come out unfiltered and with a hint of irritation. He must really be pissed about her breaking in and stealing their drinking glasses.

Owen opens the front door, letting Flynn go ahead of him. He winks at me before shutting the door behind them.

Wow, these people know everyone's business. Staring through the glass on the door, I watch them cross the street and wonder what they're saying about me.

My phone buzzes on the counter, the vibration causing it to slip closer to the edge. Rushing over, I snatch it up before it falls and see Heston left a text.

Heston: Give me your address, so I can make you dinner?

I shake my head, rereading the text. He really doesn't need to come over here and make dinner for us. I would like to see him, though. Maybe another date?

Heston: Stop overthinking it.

Trying to fight back my smile, I snort instead.

Me: How about dinner at a restaurant?

I counteroffer, nervous to let him come over. It will make things more personal between us, for sure, and I'm not sure

I'm emotionally ready for that to happen. I just lost my mother and am adjusting to a whole new life. What if I really start liking him and he doesn't feel the same way? What if he just walks out of my life? Can I handle that right now?

Heston: See you at six.

My brows furrow with confusion. Wait—what does that mean? Are we going out to eat?

Me: Where do you want to meet?

Three dots pop up then disappear. I sit for a few moments, waiting to see if he begins typing again. He doesn't. My suggestion for a public place must have pissed him off. I sigh loudly, placing my phone facedown. My stomach is twisted in knots. I wanted to see him, and now that he's not talking to me at all, coming over here doesn't sound bad. My brain and heart contradict one another, and it's aggravating.

I glance at my phone one last time, deciding I'll order in pizza and put a movie on for Paige and me. It will be nice to spend some time together after our fight from earlier. Until then, I'll go upstairs and get lost in all things silent art.

Hours pass. I've organized my sculpting tools and checked my phone several times to see if Heston has texted anything. He hasn't. I want to try to fix whatever it is I did, but tell myself to put the phone down and let it be.

The sound of Paige's door across the landing has me looking over my shoulder, waiting to see if she's coming in here or heading downstairs.

"Hey, Mom," she says, her voice tired. Not having her phone must be boring as hell. She swipes a strand of hair from her face and crosses her arms across her Eminem shirt that's so large, you can barely see her cotton shorts.

"Yeah?" I reply, taking my attention back to organizing my paints.

"I'm hungry."

My chest rises, knowing I've waited as long as I can for Heston to text back. I'm going to have to order the pizza.

"Yeah, okay. How about pizza?" I brush my hair from my face to see that she's already nodding. I knew she wouldn't resist.

I laugh, pushing myself to my feet, and stretch. Jesus, I was on the floor longer than I thought. My back is stiff and knees feel heavy.

Grabbing my phone, that I'm pissed at, because it won't magically tell me what Heston is thinking, I head downstairs. Paige's footsteps are right behind me. She sits at the counter while I wash my hands free of clay dust.

"We should do a movie," she suggests, acting like she's didn't just go drinking with the neighbor girl. I'm still shocked by what she did, but she's never in trouble. Would she have lived a normal teenage life, if she didn't screw up once in a while?

"Yeah, I was thinking that too." Drying my hands, I reach for my phone to order dinner, when the doorbell rings. I freeze and look at Paige, who is already glancing over her shoulder at the door.

"Man, we're going to have to pretend we're not here just so the neighbors will stop coming over."

"Paige," I scold. I like the attention. We never had this kind of communication with anyone in the city.

I round the island, looking through the blurred glass, opening the door when I can't make out who it is.

Holy. Shit!

Heston!

"What are you doing here?" I say, my tone higher than usual, excitement and unease swarming through me. "How did you get my address?"

He smirks, a brow raising to complete his cocky ego. He lifts his hand, two grocery bags hanging around his wrist.

"You can't escape my company." He winks. The idea he stalked me down is a bit creepy, but I'm bursting like fireworks to see him. I was so upset when he didn't reply back today. I was mad and angry at myself. But he went out of his way to find me. Is that alarming or romantic?

"So, should I consider this visit a casual psycho-stalking or something more head-over-heels and you couldn't wait to see me?" He lightly laughs, scratching his chin with his free hand.

"And what if it's both?" His eyes take on a look that makes my breath hitch.

"Hmmm. My answer depends on how you got my address." I tap my chin playfully, but I'm serious.

"You told the Uber driver last night," he finally says. Oh...yeah, I did do that.

Feeling like an idiot. I step aside and let him in. His dark green button-up shirt, dress pants, and suspenders are a sight for sore eyes. Inwardly, I wonder where his jacket is, so I can wear it and smell just like him the rest of the night.

"It's you!" Paige's voice holds both excitement and sass as she jokes with him. My eyes snap from his sculpted backside to her.

"It's me!" he says back, placing the bags on the counter. "Care if I make you and your mom dinner tonight? It's the least I can do after crashing into ya."

Paige looks over to me then back at him, her eyes creating a wrinkled valley between her brows, an unreadable expression on her face.

"You like my mom, don't you?"

My face heats with embarrassment. How could she just come out and ask that?

He lowers his head, muttering something to her. I can't

hear him, so I watch his lips, hoping to decipher a word or two.

"…help a guy out?" He glances at me, and I stand there, starstruck. Paige doesn't say or respond in anyway. Instead, she opens the bags and starts to snoop through them.

"What are you making?" she questions, and I'm curious as well. I close the space between Heston and me, but before I can reach the bags, he pulls me into a hug. His hard, warm body against mine causes me to feel secure and not alone. Wrapping my arms around him, I rest my head on his chest. His Amberwood and pepper scent is intoxicating.

"Do you guys like pesto with grilled chicken?" Glancing up, I catch his eyes searching my face for an answer. I look to Paige, who shrugs. "I don't know. Sounds fancy."

Laughing at her response, I take a step back. Feeling Heston staring at me, I shrug my shoulder, my brows raised. "Sounds delicious!"

He slaps his hands and rubs them together, as if he's about to cook up something magical.

"Great, because it's about all I know how to cook." He laughs, and I can't help but find him cute. He's trying so hard.

Stepping up to the bags, which are half-empty from Paige going through them, he pulls out a bottle of wine. My eyes snap to Paige, who is already glaring at me, silently telling me not to bring it up. I won't, but that bottle will be tossed after dinner. I can't trust her around it…and that hurts to say because I've never not trusted her.

Paige sits on the couch, trying to find a movie to watch, while I stand against the counter, watching Heston navigate his way around my kitchen.

"This doesn't exactly sound like a beginner dish. How do you know how to make it?"

He focuses on the task at hand, placing a small number of tomatoes on a cutting board, and begins to slice them.

"Um…it's my mom's favorite. I'd sit on the kitchen counter and watch her cook it while telling her about my day at school." He shares a piece of his life, and it's beautiful. My eyes shift to my mom's urn. I can't help but think about the things she taught me over the years.

"My mom taught me a lot of things. She was an artist," I say. His eyes flick to mine. "You wanna get some water boiling?" He asks, not commenting on what I just shared with him.

"Sure thing." Pushing off the counter, I open the bottom cabinet, pull out a pot, and start to fill it with water.

"Where was your father? Is he much of a cook?"

I turn off the faucet, place the pot on the stove, and turn it to high.

"Um…my dad wasn't really part of our lives," he responds, hurt dipping his voice. Sometimes, I wish Cam wasn't in Paige's life at all.

"My mother was a stay-at-home mom, and my father used to manage a hotel," he shares.

"What hotel—?"

"Find anything to watch?" Heston interrupts, looking at Paige. She turns her head to glance at him then focuses back on the TV.

"How about *The Mummy*—or Mom's favorite movie is on."

Heston walks around the island and stands behind the couch. "What's your mom's favorite?"

"Nooo." I run to slap my hand over Paige's mouth, but she jumps up with the remote in her hand, a sly smile on her face.

Heston laughs and grabs me around the waist to hold me away from Paige.

"Tell me, Paige!" he encourages, and she falls into a fit of giggles.

"I will ground you for life and make you eat creamed corn every night!" I threaten, but she and Heston just laugh more.

He pulls my back against his chest, and I want to keep pretending to go after Paige, just so he'll hold me tighter.

"Tell me all your favorite things, Rain," he whispers in my ear. His hot breath brushes against the shell, and a shiver races down my neck, causing my nipples to press against my bra.

"Mannequin!" Paige shouts, and I suddenly lose the heat simmering inside my body. I internally groan at and lean my head back until I'm looking at the ceiling. Heston lets go of me, and I miss his touch instantly. "I don't know that one." He sounds confused. Thank God.

"It's about a guy who's obsessed with a mannequin—which isn't actually a mannequin. It's a woman who's under a spell." She basically tells him the whole movie, and Heston chuckles at my expense.

"What? It's been my favorite since I was a kid." I cross my arms, my cheeks feeling warmer than usual.

"I've seen it too many times. I'll keep looking," Paige scoffs, sitting back down.

Heston turns around, his backside leaning against the couch.

"So, you're a romantic." His head tilts to the side, his smoldering blue eyes looking through me. "I'm more of a horror movie guy myself." Well, he and Paige have something in common.

"What's your favorite?" I ask.

"Jason," he clips.

"I know it well. A movie where the woman's running and he's walking but still seems to be right behind her the whole time?" I shrug. I could keep going on about the guy. "Paige likes him too."

"Shit, the water." He runs past me to the pot boiling over the top, spilling onto the stove. Turning it down, he grabs the pack of noodles off the counter and pours them in. Following him into the kitchen, I grab two glasses from a cabinet and open the wine. Hints of blueberry and blackberry make my mouth water. Turley is a favorite of mine. Gently pouring Heston and me a glass, I hand one to him.

"Yes. Thank you." He wipes his hands on his jeans and takes it from me. Both of us take a sip, our eyes connecting over the rims of our glasses. I'm so lost in his intense stare, I don't even taste the liquid filling my mouth until he looks away to set his down.

"I wasn't sure if you liked red, but I'm guessing you do." He gestures toward my glass, and I peek down, noticing it's almost gone.

"Yeah, I like it, but I'm more of a Moscato drinker," I admit, setting my empty wine glass down.

"Same," he replies.

"We have a lot in common," I point out, and he grabs me by the hips, pulling me toward him.

"Mmm, seems we do, don't we?" His husky voice and large hands make me want to melt into him. It's been so long since I've been this close to a man that I can barely contain myself. I want to pull my shirt over my head and let him ravish me right here. But, let's be realistic, that can't happen. It's too soon, and Paige is also in here.

"On my way here, I was terrified you'd shut the door on me. Showing up like I did…I haven't done this before," he admits, and I find it charming.

"I'm glad you came." I rest my hand on his shoulder, and he smirks. Fuck, I love that.

"When I looked you up, there were only two Adlers in the area. One, a Cameron Adler, then you. You were pretty easy to find." The way he says that makes me uneasy, but I know he means well.

"Cameron is my ex-husband."

"Ex? As in you're separated but still hook up or you two don't—"

"As in, that boat sailed, sunk, and waters will never be treaded again," I interject, and his brows rise.

"That bad, huh?"

I fill my glass a little more. "Yeah, that bad."

Taking a sip, I turn and watch Paige flip through channels for something to watch.

"Only reason I put up with him is for her," I continue, my hand tensing with anger.

"Well, it's just us now." He brushes my hair from my face, his nose sliding into the crook of my shoulder and neck. He's so touchy-feely tonight, but I like it. I really do. It feels good to be wanted.

Sitting at the table, Heston serves us his homemade dinner, giving Paige and me both a bowl. Steam rises from it, dancing into the air. It smells so good.

We all eat silently. The hot buttery food is the best thing I've had in a long time.

"This is really good," Paige says around a mouthful, her fork holding a tangle of pasta mid-air.

He finishes what he's eating and smiles at her. "Yeah, I never get tired of it."

"Mom hates cooking," she says, throwing me under the bus. *Again*.

Coughing on a noodle, I glare at her. How dare she tell him my flaws. I can't wait until she gets a boyfriend.

He sips his wine and reaches across the table to hold my

hand.

"I don't hate it. I just have to be in the mood," I explain. Paige's eyes land on our hands, her face expressionless. She's never seen me with anyone but her dad. I can't tell if this is too much for her. Not knowing, I give Heston a tight smile and pull my hand away to reach for my glass.

"What did you find for us to watch?"

"*Aquaman* is the best I can do."

"Is that the one with Jason Momoa?" I ask.

"Yeah, I've heard about it but haven't seen it," Heston tells us before taking another bite.

"Well, anything with Jason Momoa in it has to be good," I say. He's hot as hell and can act.

"Is that what you're into? Big, rowdy men?" Heston questions around a mouthful of food, eyes expecting and unreadable.

My breathing catches in my throat. Is he teasing me or being serious?

"Um, I…don't really know what my type is."

"Mom, dating a guy like that? Yeah, right. She's too…shy."

My mouth falls open, and Heston laughs. Paige is telling my business without a care in the world. What the hell has gotten into her? Then again, we didn't really get much company in the city. Not like this anyway. Which apparently made my kid have no manners.

Standing from the table, she wipes her mouth with the back of her hand. I clear my throat, point to the mess she left on the table, and she groans, annoyed at my reminder to take her bowl to the sink.

Shaking my head, I look down at my plate.

"Sorry about that. She's usually not so…talkative."

He sits back in the chair and chuckles, wiping his mouth with a napkin.

"She's great. Really. I wouldn't change a thing about her."

I smile and laugh under my breath. "Yeah, she's something else."

We put our dishes in the sink and head to the couch. I sit in the middle, with Paige and Heston on either side of me. Sometimes, in our apartment, Mom and Paige would sandwich me in while watching a movie, just like this.

Paige leans into the corner, her feet on my lap, and Heston sits up straight, one arm across the back, his other on the armrest. Paige presses play, and the movie begins. It takes me twenty minutes to focus on the movie and not Heston's presence. His smell, warmth, every time he chuckles…

About an hour in, Paige passes out, leaving Heston and me alone on the couch.

Maybe it's liquid courage, maybe not, but I snuggle into him more, and he wraps his arm around me. With my head just under his chin, we watch the rest of *Aquaman*. Honestly, I couldn't care less what's happening on the TV. I become more aware of every breath Heston takes, how he moves, and wonder if me being on top of him turns him on. Why hasn't he made a move? Is it because Paige is in here, or is he not attracted to me like I am him? It has to be because of Paige—and that makes him too damn perfect.

"So, where is your art?" he whispers softly. Goosebumps rise on my arms.

"Upstairs," I reply.

"Show me," he breathes, the dark allure in his voice spellbinding. I gently unfold myself from his lap and stand. Holding my hand out, I help him up. His smoldering eyes bore into mine as he brings my hand to his mouth and kisses it. My whole-body heats from the contact.

10

Quietly, he grabs my mom's gaudy throw from the back of the couch and places it over Paige. Warmth fills my chest, watching him tuck her in. I wish Paige had someone like this in her life. A man to tuck her in at night, play catch, annoy her like a dad should.

He glances back at me with hungry eyes. I hold my hand out for him to take and drag him upstairs. Opening the door, I flip the light on, revealing my mess of a studio. I still have so much to do in here. He walks past me, glancing around the room. He peeks under cabinets and looks at the pottery wheel in the corner.

"That's where I make everything," I tell him, unsure if he knows what it is.

He looks at it for a second before his cobalt eyes are back on me, a wolfish smirk on his face. "Wanna try that scene from *Ghost*?"

My mouth drops before I can stop it. My body pulses with need.

"And here I thought you only watched horror movies," I

tease. Taking a step closer, he tilts his head to the side, the tip of his tongue licking his bottom lip. "It has ghosts in it."

He places a hand on the doorframe behind me and leans in, an edge of darkness slipping over him from the shadows of night filling the hallways. Using his free hand, he tucks a finger under my chin, forcing me look up.

"I'd watch anything for you, Rain," he whispers, then presses his lips to mine. I close my eyes, relishing the moment, the feel of this man against me. I never would have thought this feeling of butterflies and constant smiles would happen again. His lips are so soft and needy, the perfect combination. Inhaling through my nose, I wrap my hands around his neck and pull him closer, sucking his bottom lip between my teeth.

He deepens the kiss, his mouth working against mine, and runs a greedy hand over my hip and down my ass before giving it a squeeze. Damn, that feels so good. Time becomes timeless. This moment is all that exists. The little bit of scruff around his mouth brushes against my face. I grab the sides of his cheeks, feeling the bristles on my palms. My head lolls back, exposing my neck and collarbone. He sweeps in, leaving hungry kisses across my throat. We stumble farther into the pottery room. Slipping my hands up his shirt, I run my fingers over his chest, scratching lightly, and he groans. His hands all over me is too much. Bursts of heat spark over my skin. My core throbs, begging me to take him right here in this room. Sure, we've only known each other for a little bit, but it's a second date—not including the hospital. He makes me feel wanted, needed, and it's undoing every promise I made after Cam.

I swore no more men.

Fuck relationships.

Love doesn't exist.

"Damn, Rain, I haven't wanted a woman this bad in a very long time," he confesses, desire hanging in his every word, snapping the last of my restraint.

"Yes. Yes," I mutter, nearly tearing his shirt off. I jerk it up, wanting his skin against mine. My hands tangle in the material. It manages to get stuck on his shoulders, and we fall into the cabinet holding my tools, some falling to the floor.

Laughing at how sloppy we are, he slaps a hand over my mouth, and I still, waiting for what he wants me to do next as I fall into those blue eyes, cold as ice and serious.

Heavy footsteps on the stairs make me hold my breath.

"Shit!" I whisper-shout, pulling his shirt back down. I brush the hair from my face, then push him away and turn my back, picking up the tools.

"So, yeah, this is where the magic happens—once I actually get this place together—"

"Mom, I'm going to bed," Paige says, her voice sleepy.

I glance over my shoulder and smile. "Okay, hon."

"See ya later, Paige." Heston juts his chin toward her, and she waves before walking to her room and shutting the door behind her. She didn't even look at us.

Thank God.

I fall to the floor, dropping the tools from my hands, and Heston laughs under his breath.

"I'm sorry. We have had so much going on right now and I don't know where she is emotionally and I don't want to present this in the wrong way, yeah know?" I gesture between us.

He takes my face in his hands, his fingers trailing to my jawline. "I get it. I adore Paige. I don't want her disliking me because she thinks I'm trying to replace her dad or something. However, I can only take so much of this." He slaps my ass followed by a firm grip on my right cheek, bringing my body flush with his. A hard bulge in his pants presses against me. My breath hitches in my throat, and I nod. I don't think I could keep doing this either. The constant tease and want will eventually have me throwing caution to the wind and tearing that motherfucker apart.

Letting go of me, he sighs, his demeanor snuffing into the gentleman I know. He presses his lips to my forehead.

"Let's go downstairs before she comes back out," he insists, taking me by the shoulders and turning me around. The fact he respects my wishes and what's best for Paige is not lost on me.

We head down the stairs holding hands while he adjusts his shirt with his free hand, putting it back to normal, and stops at the door. He looks back at me, his eyes hooded, and says, "See you tomorrow, Rain."

The door shuts behind him. I drop my head into my hands, and I can't help but grin like a damn fool while feeling like a damn fool. Nothing has gone as planned with Heston. I wanted to get to know each other more, spend time together, go slow—especially considering I haven't been with another man in years.

Fate seems to be laughing at my plans right now.

Waking up the next morning, I grab my phone from the nightstand. Yawning and trying to wake up, I find three missed texts from Heston and one from Cam.

I read Heston's first.

He's up thinking about me. *2:38 a.m.*

He wants to come over today. *6:20 a.m.*

My cheeks warm. How is this happening? Where did this guy come from?

I text back *get your ass over here*, then turn my focus to Cam's text. He's coming over to get Paige this morning and wants to know why she isn't answering her phone.

Biting my thumbnail in thought, I know I'm going to have to tell him about Paige drinking with the neighbor girl and that I took her phone away as punishment. However, I'll be giving it back to her while she's at her dad's, in case she needs to get ahold of me. He's left her at his house and came back angry drunk too many times for me to fully trust him. Climbing out of bed, the sun splits across the floor. It never did that at our apartment. There were too many buildings blocking the sun from doing what it does best. Taking off last night's clothes, the ones that I slept in as well, because they smelled like Heston, I slip on my favorite pair of lightweight cotton shorts and a white shirt. Today, I'll keep it simple and comfortable. My hair, however, is another story. I slip my fingers through my curly tresses, attempting to tame them. I'm surprised it's silky and not tangled or oily. I guess I'll leave it down. For now.

Heading out of my room, I don't hear Paige awake yet. If I let her, she'll sleep all day. I jog up the stairs and knock on her door a couple times before opening it. She's lying halfway on her bed, the other half hanging at the end of the mattress, reading a book placed on the floor. She's still in her pajamas, and her hair is a clumpy mess from falling asleep in her braids.

"Your dad is coming, get ready."

She inhales audibly and slides off the bed, annoyance clear on her face.

The stairs creak and crack beneath my feet as I walk down them, making me nervous one might break from under

11

Footsteps stomp down the stairway, and Paige comes into the living room before with her arms crossed and her face blank. It's the guess-what-mood-I'm-in teenager game.

"What's wrong?" I ask with a shrug of the shoulder, cramming the rest of my muffin into my mouth, little crumbs coat my fingers, and I wipe my hands free of them over the sink, waiting for her to answer me.

"So, can I have my phone back? I mean, I'm going to Dad's, and sometimes he—" she stops herself and glances down at her feet, embarrassment or hurt shadowing her posture like a heavy storm lurking within dark clouds on a perfect summer day. I hate that I have to share custody with Cam—especially when said child is more of an adult than he is. But there's nothing I can do when the judge doesn't see that side of him. Turning around, I grab a vase and reach in. I slip the phone out and hold it toward her.

"Really, a vase?" She tries to sound angry, biting back a smile. She was probably up looking for the phone all night and never thought of the vase.

"It's dead, so you'll need to charge it." The words barely leave my mouth before she snatches it from my palm, her eyes glued to the screen, seeing if there's any life. "Hey!" I get her attention. "That whole drinking until we're passed out better not happen again. Do you understand me?"

"Yeah, I won't be doing that again. I was so sick yesterday," she mumbles, shaking her head. Man, if I had a dime for every time I've said those words, I'd be rich as hell.

"Good," I clip, rounding the counter.

"How did you and this girl even meet?"

"I heard a dog howling, so I looked out the window and saw her sitting outside. She saw me looking at her, so it would have been awkward not to go say hi."

"Wait, she was howling? You mean like a dog?"

"Yeah. It sounded like a damn coyote on the front porch."

That girl is peculiar for sure. She's young and dressed in black from head to toe, and I don't mean the way I see kids going into Hot Topic at the mall. She gives off more of the energy of a devil worshiper and now she's acting like a dog? Hopefully she doesn't talk Paige into meowing in the front yard. Though…that would be better than getting drunk. Wanting some fresh air and to see if any of the neighbors are out, I walk past the living room, tossing my mom's blanket on the back of the couch, then open the front door. Warm air feathers the sweet scent of the neighbor's tulips right into my house. I step outside and can't help but look at my yard for beautiful foliage. It's bare and in desperate need of something —a lot like the Gradys' yard.

"Hey, Rain!" My eyes snap up, finding Tenly jogging up the road. Just seeing her "early bird gets the worm" energy makes me want to yawn. I look down at myself, brushing away the crumbs from my carb overload, and notice the cool pavement is actually hotter than hell and step into the grass.

Her sports bra and elastic workout pants make her look more like a Nike model than someone trying to stay fit.

"Hey," I respond, and she speed-walks to me.

Out of breath, she still manages to smile that big, white-teeth grin. She inhales, standing a little straighter. "Noticed a handsome man leaving your place last night. I thought you were divorced?" Her eyes rise with concern, but the smile on her face conveys she's up for a saucy secret. Hoping the man leaving my house was there for promiscuous reasons.

"Um, yeah. I met someone. His name is Heston." My brows furrow, and I cross my arms, feeling pushed into an uncomfortable corner. I mean, I don't want her going off and telling people something horrible, so I need to make it known it's someone I'm actually seeing and not a one-night stand. Not that any of this is her business.

"Mmm, does Heston look as good in daylight?" She laughs, and I lightly giggle as jealousy flares inside my chest.

"How did you meet? Was it romantic?" She reaches out, patting my arm for me to spill the details.

"I wouldn't call it romantic." I laugh. I can't help it. "He kind of just crashed into my life."

With her lips closed, she nods as if she understands what I'm saying, but she doesn't because Heston literally crashed into me. I don't know why I don't just tell her, I guess because it's kind of unique, the way we met, and something inside me doesn't trust Tenly when it comes to unique guys.

Her eyes squint, trying to hide from the sun's abrasive rays, and takes a step back like she's leaving.

"You'll have to introduce us sometime. You can't keep him to yourself forever!" She points at me playfully, her grin wide, then turns and crosses the street to her house.

I shake my head, offering a small wave when she does before closing her door. I take the knob in my hand and twist the door open to go back inside. My phone rings, and I dig it out of my pocket. It's the insurance company. Hopefully, they're calling about getting me a rental.

Answering it, I say, "Hello?"

"Hello, Ms. Adler, how is your morning?" a polite female voice asks.

"I'm fine. Thanks."

"So, I have it in our system that we'll be dropping off a two thousand Voyager at the address given to us the day of the claim. We ask that you do not smoke, eat, drink, or have any pets in the vehicle. You are the only one permitted to drive, and you are responsible for any damage. Do you accept these requests?"

"Um, yeah. Sure." I shrug, not really having a choice. I need a car.

"Perfect. If you have any questions, feel free to call us."

"Mmmhmm."

Really? A minivan? I scrunch up my nose as I end the call. I guess it's better than Ubering everywhere, but still. Slipping my phone back into my pocket, the cool floor amongst my bare feet is refreshing than the smoldering concrete outside. Heading into the living room, I see Paige sitting on the edge of the couch with her phone in her hand and the charging cord strung across the room in the wall plug.

"Miss any calls from your boyfriend?" I tease, earning me a scoff. I've never heard Paige talk about boys. Well, beside some guy from BTS.

"I don't know any guys here. Remember we upped and moved? I'm the new kid." Her voice takes on an edge of sarcasm, but anything revolving around school has made her testy since I told her we were moving. I mean, she had a couple friends but no one super close. Maybe she'll get a shot at that kind of friendship here.

Walking past her, I pat the top of her head and go to put the dishes in the dishwasher. An hour later, sitting on the couch next to Paige, the familiar sound of Heston's truck has butterflies fluttering in my stomach. I stand up with a little too much excitement, earning a crooked eye from Paige.

"Really? He's coming over again?" She raises her left brow, sounding angry.

"Yeah, why? Do you not like him?"

Dropping her phone in her lap, she finally focuses on me.

"I mean, he's nice. Are you dating him?" I feel like that's a trick question. We have been on a date, but I wouldn't say we're together, but I don't know what makes a couple have that official status.

"I guess so." I shrug.

Picking up her phone, her focus back on TikTok, she sighs in a way that conveys she's not sure about me dating. This would be new for her. Hell, it's new to me.

The doorbell rings, and I'm there in seconds. Opening the door, Heston stands in blue jeans snug on his backside, and a black simple Hanes shirt that clings to his chest. His eyes light up when he sees me and I hug him hard. I should take it down a notch. I'm acting like we've been together for months. But I can't help it, having someone who wants to be with me and touch me is foreign. His smell alone causes me to involuntarily dig my nose in the crook of his neck and inhale.

"Damn I missed you," he whispers into the side of my head. Maybe I'm not being clingy. He's as excited to be here as I am to have him. If a neighbor happened to look through their window right now, you would think we were a thing for a while now.

"Me too," I finally reply, forcing myself to take a step

back and slip my hands in my back pockets to keep from touching him. He looks around me and sees Paige.

"Hey, you." He gives a wave and smile.

"Hey, YOU," she responds, a little smirk at the corner of her mouth. She likes him which makes me happier about being with him. We all still before deafening silence falls between us, making me feel awkward.

"So, did you have anything in mind to do today?" I ask, gaining his attention and receiving a smoldering look.

"Well, we could finish what we started yesterday." He grips my waist with one hand and pulls me closer. Goose-bumps rise along my arms, remembering how amazing last night was.

"Ew!" Paige interrupts. I remind myself we have an audience and that this is new for her, so I take a step back. "Or you could go get some flowers for the yard," Paige interjects, now standing behind us to head upstairs. Cam and I weren't very intimate the last few years we were together. We met at such a young age that by the time we were married, things started to become cold. Our flame slowly burned out and we did nothing to try and rekindle that spark. The only feeling I got from him touching me in the end were butterflies of fear. There wasn't much to love near the end.

Heston steps back outside and looks at the yard. Crossing his arms, he glances across the street, taking in Tenly's amazing yard. She probably had someone do it for her.

"Everyone has flowers that match their front door. See?" I point to Flynn and Owen's door. But then the house at the end of the block catches my attention. It's empty and darker than the other houses on the block and puts off an eerie vibe. I wonder why a family hasn't moved in and made it a home? Added some pretty flowers, and painted it something more inviting.

"Hmm, they do match. That's weird." He looks over his shoulder at my house. "You have a black door." His nose scrunches.

"Yep. Guess I'm getting black flowers." I shrug.

"Be different—get pink flowers," he suggests, and I bite my bottom lip in thought.

Turning toward me, he rests his warm palm on the right side of my face and the other on my ass, pulling me closer.

"When I look at you, I think pink and delicate, not morbid and dark."

"Delicate?" I nearly scoff. Do I really come off that way?

A roar and squealing tires can be heard from down the road, and I close my eyes, inhaling a staggered breath. Cam.

I'd given up on him hours ago.

Driving way too fast, he slams on his brakes, parks right behind Heston's truck, and turns the engine off. The entire block is now deathly quiet. The birds aren't even chirping, scared away by all the noise he made. He climbs out of the truck, slamming the door behind him. Swiping the aviators from his face, he looks around the cul-de-sac as if he's never seen a neighborhood before. He's big and tall, a red shirt tucked in, with blue jeans and a belt buckle. Heavy footsteps stomp up the driveaway, and my eyes lock with Cam's, sending a shiver down my spine.

"Hello, Cam." I can't mask the unpleasant feeling of seeing him in my tone.

"Why hasn't Paige answered my calls? And who the fuck is driving that? I know it ain't yours. You got a man up in that house with my daughter?" He points to Heston's truck, rage slithering into his tone. I'd think it was jealousy, but it's not; it's simply Cam wanting to control me. It kills him that he can't tell me who I can hang out with now that we're not together, but it doesn't stop him from trying.

I cross my arms, not ready to talk to him about Heston, when he can't even handle a conversation about his daughter.

"Paige got in trouble this week and didn't have her phone, that's why she didn't answer. You could have texted me." Heston walks up behind me, a stern look on his face while glancing over my shoulder at my ex.

"Trouble? What kind of trouble? Why didn't you call me?" Cam's eyes don't leave Heston's, even while talking to me. His sharp brows dip, in an attempt to look intimidating.

"She and the neighbor decided it was a good idea to get drunk."

His focus snaps back to me, his stare hard.

"What? Paige doesn't drink." His beady eyes squinting as he insinuates I have it all wrong.

"Well, she did. She's growing up and going to want to try things, Cam." I swear he thinks Paige is still six. That's the age she was before he started drinking heavily, and everything since has been an abyss into the bottom of an empty bottle.

"Don't act like I don't know that she's growing up!" he sneers, and I'm furious that he is trying to play attentive parent today. The man is only around when it suits him, not Paige.

"Oh, I'm sorry, I didn't realize you were sober today," I jab, and his upper lip twitches with anger.

"Where the hell were you while she was doing this, Rain?" His eyes flick back to Heston. "Were you with this guy? Huh?" His face turns red, and with his shoulders tight and a snarl on his face, he tries to step around me.

"That's none of your business." Panic fills my chest. I shove my hands into his chest to push him away, but he just walks through me like I'm of no obstacle.

Heston straightens to his full height, his left brow raised as he watches my ex-husband become the Hulk.

"You fucking my wife? You trying to play Daddy to my little girl?" He jabs his finger toward Heston, and I rush to step between them.

"That's enough!" I shout. Cam shoves me to the side, throwing me off balance. I stumble to the ground, my head jerking up at the sound of crunching bones. Cam's hands shoot to his face as he howls, blood pouring from his nose. Heston steps away, his fist unclenching as he reaches down to help me up. Before I can get to my feet, Cam tackles Heston to the floor, tearing him away from me. Stumbling to my feet heavy grunts, and spewing hate pursue between the two men. Brushing the hair from my face, I see Heston with his arm wrapped around Cam's thick neck, using his free fist to punch him in the ribs. Cam wheezes and knees Heston right in the chin, his skin instantly splits and bright blood dribbles down his face. He reaches up and touches the cut, looking at the blood with wild eyes, his face slowly rises, and I know he's going to retaliate. An ominous whisper fills the air, a shadow taking over Heston's handsome face, and I can't help but be taken aback by it. It's chilling and nothing like him. He roars like a monster, making me jump where I stand, and tackles Cam to the ground like a linebacker. Now on top of Cam, he uses both of his hands to grab and squeeze him by the throat. The sweat on my body suddenly grows cold when Cam's feet begin to kick out, as if he really can't breathe.

"That's enough! Stop it!" I clap my hands at them, working to get their attention, but neither of them listens. Tears fill my eyes, and I look around the neighborhood, needing help.

"Heston?" Paige's voice rings out, seizing the chill-biting wind. Everyone stills. Heston, who is still on top of Cam, looks over, finding Paige staring at him with wide eyes. The terror on her face makes her look pale. Cam shoves Heston off of him. Rolling onto all fours, he coughs then spits, looking at me with more hatred than when he arrived, if that's possible. Heston stands next to me, and I fight back tears. "Was that necessary?" I mutter. He looks back at me without a word. Cam rubs his neck then brushes the grass off of his jeans as he stands.

Shoving past Heston, he walks over to me. "You'll never replace me, Rain," he says, so only I can hear. A string of dark memories fill my head landing on a particular time when he pinned me to the trailer floor and yelled I was unlovable. He was so loud I couldn't hear for two days. Blinking the past away I fight back my tears and glare at him as he takes Paige to his truck. They both get in, and he peels out, driving off like a bat out of hell.

"So, that's your ex?" Heston asks, brushing grass and dirt off his shirt, his chin covered in blood. His face is lighter, his inner monster back in its cage. He smiles, as if his question was meant to be funny. There's nothing funny about what just happened. I imagined some pushing, maybe a few scathing words thrown, but Cam really got under his skin, showing me a scary side of Heston. I can feel eyes peeking through blinds, and I become jittery, unsure of what to say or do.

"Look, I'm sorry," he begins to apologize, his tone soft and calm, like nothing bad happened.

"I just…I don't want anyone hurting you. When I saw him throw you down like that…I snapped," he explains. His words wrap around me like a shield, making me feel safe for the first time in a long time.

"I'm sorry. He was so late I didn't think he was still coming today, and I'm sorry for putting you in that position—"

"No, don't apologize. I'm glad I was here," he interrupts, swiping a tear from my cheek with his thumb.

Taking my face in his hands, he makes me look up at him.

"Are you okay?" he mutters. My bottom lip quivers at the care in his tone. My stomach warms as much as my heart does, this feeling of affection from a man so unfamiliar.

"Yeah. I just lost my balance." Acid threatens to burn my esophagus at my attempt to cover for Cam.

"No, that was a bitch move." He growls. "You don't put your hands on a woman. Especially the mother of your damn child."

I scoff. "Cam used to hit me *while* I was pregnant. He didn't care. I guess he missed the class about having morals." I remember the shock that riddled my heart when he pushed me after announcing we were expecting. He wanted to watch the news and I didn't, so I got up to do something else. He didn't like that.

Heston inhales a large breath, his chest rising as if the mere thought of it causes him pain. Reaching out, he pulls me into him, wrapping his arms around me.

"The world is full of monsters. The only way to beat them is to become like them," he breathes into the top of my head.

"You okay, Rain?"

My head whips to the left, and my eyes lock on Flynn, standing at the end of his driveway, his arms crossed, biceps bulging, stance wide. How long has he been watching?

"Yeah, I'm okay." *My nerves are a trainwreck, though.* I raise my hand, waving him off as my pulse quickens. I bet the whole neighborhood just watched what went down.

Looks like I'm the guaranteed entertainment.

12

Heston sits on the toilet in my bathroom, looking up at me while I dab a wet towel on the tip of his chin, the blood staining the fabric. I feel his eyes on me while I work on his cut, the sound of his subtle breaths making it hard to concentrate.

"We need to put something on this." My voice light.

"You mean a band-aid?" There's laughter in his voice.

"Unfortunately, I think that's all I have?"

He takes the rag from me and stands to look in the mirror. "Nah, it doesn't need anything. I'm good." Dropping the towel in the sink, he rests a hand on the counter and looks at me with hooded eyes. "You have the softest touch."

I feel that down to my bones.

"Well, I have a tomboy for a kid, lots of scrapes and cuts," I say.

"That's not what I mean." His lips rise at the corners, giving that playboy smirk I love.

"Oh," I whisper. Turning away and leaving me wanting more, he stops at the doorway.

"You coming?"

Both of us get into his truck and head to get flowers. Hopefully, we can get them in the ground while the sun is out because storms are on the way tonight. Heston has a new truck already, and just sitting inside I can see down into other cars passing by. The leather seats are polished and new give off the new car scent that everyone loves, and his steering wheel doesn't look close to the one in his other truck.

"Do you want to go to Lowe's?" he asks, shifting to his side, so he can see me better.

"Um…actually, I was thinking about checking out a place called Olive's Flowers. It's a smaller shop here in Fairview. I don't really want to go to the city." I express more emotion in my reply than I meant, but I can't help it. You could compare my feelings for Charlotte to as a cold biting fear, reminding me I'm alone, no matter where I go in that damn city. I imagine my mother waiting in line for coffee and cussing under her breath. I can't even pass someone asking for spare change because my mother would always give what she had in her purse. She's everywhere there. I can't go back without her. It's not home anymore. It's a reminder of everything I lost. Her.

"Their supply will probably be limited. Are you sure?" He raises a brow, the reflection of the clouds through the windshield swimming in his blue irises.

"Yeah. It's fine." I shrug with a smile. He reaches over his massive console, grasping my hand, and I can't help the hard breath that rushes through me from his soft palm. With Luke Bryan's "Kiss Tomorrow Goodbye" on the radio, the sun caressing the windshield, spreading warmth across my face, and the most handsome man I've ever met holding my hand in his brand-new truck, I can't help but feel like this is all too perfect.

Pulling up to Olive's, I can't help but admire how simple

and cute it is. A one-story brick shop with glass windows and a matching door propped open by an old tin watering can. Wooden barrels filled with flowers sit under the awning with fairy lights hanging above them. I inhale. Wet earth with a hint of sweetness fills the air.

An older woman comes through the door, her shoulders hunched, her hair once black but graying. Her green apron and bright yellow rain boots grab my attention, standing out like a daffodil in a dirt road.

"Hello. Can I help you find anything?" Her voice cracks with old age, but her eyes are bright emeralds, making her seem younger.

Heston looks to me, and I clear my throat.

"I'm just looking—"

"She needs pink flowers for her front yard," Heston interrupts. His smile irks me, and I realize I'm scowling. He's hellbent on me getting pink flowers, and I don't want them. I mean, they're nice, and he's right about the color softening the image behind what's living beyond our black door, but it's not what Paige and I talked about. Our new house is the beginning of new memories and that night we picked the color was the first of many. I hope.

"Hmm…does your yard get a lot of sun or is it mostly shaded?" the old lady asks, staring out at the flowers as if one will speak to her.

"It's mostly sun." *I think.* I've only been there a couple days, so I don't really know.

"I have one you might like." She walks past us, her speed surprising me. The ol' gal still has some pep in her step. As I follow her, I can't help but notice some deep purple flowers that almost look black. Stopping, I look over at the cup-shaped blossom. Placing a dark silky petal between my thumb and index finger, I feel it, staring at its luscious green foliage. A tag hangs from the pot and I have to tilt my head sideways to read it. Queen of the Night tulip.

This one feels right. There's a bond between us, and it dawns on me, this must be what

Anthophiles experience. It's like a life breathing through your touch and rooting itself in your chest. It's a motherly instinct.

"Rain!" My eyes snap up at Heston's voice, finding him on the other side of a flower booth.

"This is the one," the old lady says as I approach them, holding beautiful bright pink flowers climbing a stake.

"Wow," I mutter, rubbing the petals between my fingers.

"It's a Bougainvillea. A vine-like shrub. It longs for the sun and will grow bounties of beautiful flowers."

"Do I put it in another pot or plant it in the ground?" I ask, mesmerized by how pretty it is. It almost looks fake.

"These can be big babies when they're transplanted. They like to plant roots and stay for the long haul. They don't take change well, so I'd cut the sides of the pot for it to grow and plant the whole thing."

"Sounds easy enough," Heston adds.

Shaking my head, I snap out of my daze.

"I'll take them."

13

Ominous clouds loom over the horizon. Droplets splash against the windshield as I round the bend, nearing my house. A shadow is in my driveway. A black van.

Who the hell is that?

As we pull into the driveway, the license plate cover comes into view, and I breathe out, remembering the insurance company was dropping off a rental. I pull my cell out of my bag and check it.

Right with Us Insurance: Vehicle is parked in driveway. Key is under the mat.

"Someone's in your driveway, Rain." Concern laces Heston's voice, his face hard and serious. A dark, protective energy radiates from his pores, almost scorching me. He's always on edge, ready to go to war. Something made him this way, and I want to know what.

Reaching across the console, I take his hand in mine and give it a squeeze. He flicks a hard glare my way.

"That—is my ride until my claim is processed."

"That?" He points. "That's your van?"

I nod, and a grin takes over his features.

He belts out a chuckle that turns into a laugh, and I playfully slap his arm.

"It's cute," I defend. *In a soccer mom kind of way.*

"You wanted the 'burb life—looks like you're getting the whole experience." He puts his truck in reverse and pulls in next to the van. I unbuckle and get out, rounding the bed of the truck. Heston meets me on the other side, grabbing the two shrubs.

"Shit!" I drop my head back, then palm my face. "I don't have a shovel." We lived in the city, where there was no digging of any kind.

"I got you covered." Heston hands me the flowers and pulls a shovel from the bed of the truck, slinging it over his shoulder. Heston gone construction worker is definitely a turn-on and now I wish I bought every shrub Olive had.

He strikes the rich soil with the pointed tip of the blade, lifts his foot to the kickplate, and thrusts the spade into the ground.

"Here good?"

"Let me look." Placing the plants down, I hurry to the middle of my yard, looking at my house and where he is.

"Hmm, a little more toward the door. I want them on each side of the walkway." I point my finger for him to move inward about two feet.

"Here?"

"Perfect!"

He tugs the shovel from the ground, leaving a disrupted pile of dirt, and steps over two feet, right where I told him.

He thrusts the spade back into the ground and tosses the dirt to the side with ease. For a man who lives in the city, he knows his way around with a shovel pretty well. Grabbing the pots, I drop to my knees in front of the overturned earth and eye the side of the plastic container, looking for where I should cut it for the roots to grow.

"Here, use this." Heston drops a pocketknife next to my foot, before moving on to dig the next hole. I lift it, immediately noting its weight. Caressing the hard black handle, I run my thumb underneath, looking for a way to open it. Feeling the liner lock, I press into it, and the blade swings out. The stainless steel is shiny and intimidating, making me flinch. Swallowing the lump in my throat, I throw a prayer to God that I don't cut my finger off and press the edge of the blade to the plastic pot. It slices through like butter, without any pressure. I do it again on the other side, then to the other pot next to me.

Heston falls to his knees, grabs the shrub, and gently lowers it into the hole. Forcing the blade back into its place, I hand him the knife.

He slips it into his pocket, then uses both hands to grab the loose dirt and fit it around the plant. A low crack booms from the sky, followed by a low tide of rumbles. The clouds are near black. The sun has been swallowed whole. A raindrop falls on my hand, then another on my head, instantly soaking me.

"Shit, we better hurry." Scrambling to stand up, I hurry to the next hole with Heston right behind me. Placing the pot into the hole in the ground, I position it just right. The rain comes down heavier. A flash of lightening illuminates the sky. We scoop the dirt and throw it in the hole, covering the roots as it turns to mud in our hands.

"That's good!" I yell over the storm. We run to the front door and dart inside, both soaked with mud on our hands and arms. Mother Nature is angry—and she's taking it out on anything within reach. Turning around, back against the door,

Heston stares at me, his eyes hooded. His wet hair drips onto his face. His shirt clings to his chest and outlines his toned stomach. I know that look. The way he's standing. Taking a step forward, he rushes me, grabbing the side of my face. His thumb just under my chin, he turns his head to the side and presses his thin lips along the damp skin of my neck. The cool air kisses the droplets slipping down my spine, heightening my senses. My muddy palms slide to his face as dirty water drips down his jaw, making him come off sexier. A low heat burns in my core. I moan into his mouth, running my fingers through his thick hair. Soft curls coil around my fingertips. He grabs the hem of my shirt and pulls it off, leaving my hair to fall into my eyes. His head falls between my breasts. His tongue slides along my skin, licking up the beads of rain. It feels so good. Too good. I cradle his head, feeling him lick and nip the valley between my boobs. My nipples harden as my lower half pulses.

We stumble back onto the stairs, my elbows on the third step, my knees spread. Heston kneels between them and grabs the nape of my neck, his eyes almost black.

"Wait—should we—"

I shake my head. "No, don't stop. I can't get pregnant." Hearing me say it out loud hurts as much now as it did the day I was told that very thing. I had to have an ovary removed because of a tumor and the other one was so scarred, they said it would be a one in a million chance. I predict my scarring is from Cam. All the times he would hit and kick me in the stomach had to land somewhere and I think it was my ovary. Thunder cracks. A flash of lightening brightens the whole house. I sweep my hands under his wet shirt and pull it over his head, running my hands back down his chest and abs. I dig my nails in, and his eyes clinch shut. I grip his hips, my damp hair framing my face and falling into my eyes, as I lean in to nip just above his belly button. He presses his hands into my hair as my lips explore his happy trail. I stop at the button and zipper of his jeans, and look up him, meeting hooded, blue eyes sharp with desire. I tug the wet denim down his legs, and he helps kick them off with his shoes. Pulling back his briefs with my finger, his lengthy cock springs free, almost hitting me in the face. It's skinny but long. I flick the tip with my tongue, and his knees wobble. He likes it.

"You don't have to do that." His voice is low and husky.

"But I want to." My breathing heavy, I slip him into my mouth. His soft skin glides along my tongue, filling my mouth with the salty taste of his skin. I close my eyes, taking him as deep as I can before I gag and pull off. My eyes teary, my mouth watering, I watch him stroke himself with the spit I left behind. He suddenly drops to his knees and unzips my shorts, jerking them down to my feet. I step out of them, my shoes still on, and he grabs my hips, flipping me to where my stomach is now facing the stairs and my ass is up in the air. I grasp the step above me, shuddering at his warm hand caressing my left butt cheek that's peeking out from under my white lace panties.

"Damn, you have a perfect ass." He growls. I toss my hair out of my face and peek over my shoulder at him. I was sure I lost my ass after I had Paige but to hear him say it makes me feel better.

He smacks my ass, the sound filling the room seconds before I feel the sting. My head snaps up, and my eyes roll back. Every touch, look, and kiss take me closer to the edge nothing but impulsive thoughts to lead my next move. The only thing I can think of is his cock inside me. He gently hooks a finger on each side of my panties and slides them to my knees, leaving my core practically dripping with need. He unhooks my bra, loosening it and causing it to slip down my arms until it rests at my wrists. I feel heat along the skin of my back as his chest claims by body, his hand slipping underneath kneading my breast. It feels so good to be touched, to be wanted. My whole body pulsates. I push myself into him, telling him exactly what I need. Getting the hint, he positions himself right at my opening. On my stomach, staring at the dusty stairs, Heston finally thrusts inside me. My mouth parts on a low gasp as he stretches and fills me. I'm so tight, it almost hurts, but it feels so good at the same time. He pulls out then drives back in, and a moan escapes my lips. He grunts, grabbing my breast harshly as he fucks me faster and faster, taking me to the brink of ecstasy. I try to fight it, not wanting it to end so quickly, but warmth blossoms in my core, telling me I'm about to free fall.

"Shit." He growls, pumping faster and tensing up. He's about to come too.

"Do it," I beg, so we both get what we so desperately need.

One hand on my shoulder, the other on my hip, he becomes more and more aggressive, and my whole body detonates. The sounds of me coming are his undoing. He follows seconds later, jerking inside me, our breathing louder than the storm abusing Fairview just outside the house.

He steps back, and I notice for the first time how sweaty I am. I flip over, so I can face him. He stares back, his cock hanging fully erect, his chest rising and falling. He doesn't speak, and neither do I. Instead, I pull my panties up and search for my shirt, snatching it off a step.

. . .

Thunder shakes the walls, and the windows rattle. I stand up, looking out the window. Rain penetrates the ground, splashing the freshly disturbed dirt onto the flowers.

I cross my arms, feeling suddenly cold.

"So, what should we do now? We have all night." Heston smiles, now leaning against the kitchen counter. His unbuttoned jeans are slung low on his hips, showing his briefs. His chest is shirtless, allowing every outlined muscle to be admired.

"Food," I say, walking toward him, my stomach nearly growling.

"Worked up an appetite, did ya?" He scans the length of my body. "Fuck, eat, sleep, repeat? Sounds fun."

I roll my eyes and lean against him. He wraps his arms around me as if we do this every day. His warm burgundy and pepper scent wraps around me, and I close my eyes, never wanting to move.

"I'm sleepy too," I mutter into his chest, his chin resting on top of my head.

"Me too. You want me to feed you and then sleep? Or nap first?" I look up at him, smiling. The idea of him taking care of me, as if I'm someone special, makes my heart flip-flop in my chest. I was nervous he'd fly out the door after we did the deed, never to be seen again—until the next time he wanted another taste. Which…I think I would be okay with. Regular sex without a man invading my space? There are worst things.

"Your mom teach you another recipe?"

"Mmm, I can usually throw something together. I'd have to see what you have, but I think I'll find something." He looks down at me, waiting for me to accept his offer. Pulling out of his hold, his hand reaches for mine and our fingers link together, as if we have to constantly be touching in some way.

"I'm really glad you're here," I admit, barely above a whisper. Our eyes lock. Losing my mother has been hard. Without Heston here, filling my time, taking my mind off her, God only knows where I would be. Maybe I do want more than just a booty call.

"Me too," he mutters, and I wonder if I'm imagining the desperation in his words. I've never had someone long to be in my company—not the way Heston seems to. I can't help but doubt I'm enough to entice such a need in someone. Not even sure what he sees in me.

"I don't like being alone," I admit, hoping it will an entice him to tell me why he wants to be here. As if a piece of me longs for him to say the same thing.

"Neither do I. Lately…I haven't found comfort in anybody's company but yours." I'm taken aback by that, my eyes widen for a split second before I mask it with a smile.

"So, you're saying I'm special?" I say, my attempt at being coy.

"Yeah, special ed." He pops me in the forehead, and I freeze, surprised he actually did that and then start giggling again. I love that we're getting more comfortable with each other. When I'm around him, my chest is full, butterflies swarm my stomach, and I smile so much, it hurts my cheeks. But deep down, there's a pit in my stomach, something dark and bleak, whispering, "This is too good to be true." I refuse to acknowledge it, burying myself in the here and now.

Heston cooked us up some hamburger and noodles, along with peas and cheese, all in a pot, and it was amazing. Now, we both lie in my bed, waiting for sleep to take us. He's spooning me from behind, one arm under a pillow, the other thrown over my waist. His breathing is soft and shallow. If I

14

I open my eyes. Light spills across the room. The sun is so bright, you would never know how bad the storm was mere hours ago. I blink, clearing the sleep from my eyes, and roll onto my back. Heston yawns, stretching his arms up into the air. His eyes open, casting clear blue irises, similar to the sky outside.

Covering my mouth with my hand, I tell him, "Good morning."

His brows furrow.

"What are you doing with your hand?" he asks, a laugh on the tip of his tongue.

"I have really bad morning breath."

He grabs my hand and lowers it into my lap. "I don't even care."

"Really?" I take a risk at letting him smell how bad it is, and he shrugs.

"I don't smell anything."

Raising a brow, I put my hand across his mouth. "Well, yours smells."

His eyes widen as he barks out a half laugh in surprise. I

chortle, and he rolls me underneath him, tickling my sides. I kick my feet into the hair, my hands slapping and grabbing at him to stop.

The doorbell rings, and he stills. My laughter fading as I try to catch my breath.

"I better get that."

The bell rings again as I slide off the bed, grabbing my robe from the back of my door and leaving the room. Dried mud crunches under my bare feet, and I make a mental note to mop. A bright pink outline comes into view, blurred by the glass. Unlocking the door, I open it, and Tenly's head snaps in my direction.

"Morning!" She beams like a kindergarten teacher with too much energy. I imagine her breaking out into song at any moment, waving her hands around.

"Good morning, Tenly." I pull the sash to my robe a little tighter and muster a sleepy smile.

"I was checking my mail yesterday and saw the commotion—are you okay?" Her brows furrow with concern.

"Yeah. Everything is fine. My ex came to pick up my daughter. He and Heston didn't hit off."

"Is the boyfriend here?" she whispers. She points down to where we're standing, reminding me of when my mother would yell at me to get over here right now.

"Someone say my name?" I look over my shoulder. Heston stands behind me in just his jeans and a smirk. His hair is tousled, giving off a fresh bedhead vibe.

"Yeah, I was just telling Tenly about the disagreement between you and Cam and how everything is fine."

He silently nods, glancing at Tenly for a moment before focusing on me again. "I'm going to make us some coffee."

"Oh, yes. Everything is on the counter."

"Nice meeting you, Tenly," he says before walking away.

The man is all charm.

Tenly looks over to me, her eyes wide, her cheeks painted pink.

"Wow. He's really something, huh?" Raising her hand, she rubs the nape of her neck. Her reaction to Heston doesn't sit well with me. She's too eager and interested in him. I clinch my jaw to keep from making a fool of myself and spewing something hateful. I might just be jealous and reading her wrong, but deep inside I have my eye on her.

She's married. Why is she so infatuated with Heston? Maybe she's not happily married and on the prowl. I do remember Owen and Flynn saying something about her husband cheating on her.

"Anyway—" she shakes her head from whatever dirty daydream she conjured up, "—I stopped by to tell you about the party our block has at the end of the summer. Everyone gathers in the street. There's food, music, games…The only thing is everyone is required to bring a dish to pass."

"Oh, okay. Sounds great." Her lips roll onto one another, her expression unreadable.

"Okay. And the rule is that it can't be store bought."

"Got it." I grab the door with my right hand and start to slowly close it.

Her face scrunches, as if she has something to say but isn't sure she wants to. I stare back at her, waiting for her to spill whatever's on her mind. Silence falls between us. Just as I open my mouth to tell her goodbye, she holds up her index finger.

"Rain, you know what I was thinking? Maybe you should do a pie." She suggests with a coy voice and perturbed look on her face as if my cooking is horrid. Biting my cheek, I keep myself from spewing some colorful language. I hate cooking anyway.

"A pie, it is."

Standing uncomfortably, her gaze travels over my shoulder, gawking at Heston. Jealousy rears its ugly head and anger mounts inside my chest. I want to remind her she's married and to stop eye-fucking a man I have in my house.

"Okay, thanks for stopping by. Bye Tenly," I say briskly, and shut the door in her face. With my hand on the doorknob, I lower my head and take a deep breath.

"Neighborhood princess?" Heston asks. I turn around to get a cup of coffee.

"She definitely has an opinion about everything. Based on her yard, I think she's part of the HEA, so I have to play nice. I don't need to make enemies while settling in."

He shakes his head. "Used to have one just like her in my building. So, you're going to bake a pie?" he asks with humor, and I resist the urge to cringe. The fact that I can't buy one from a store makes this a chore, but the party sounds fun and having community is exactly why I moved out of an apartment, where the closest thing you got was stomping on the floor and shouting for them to turn their music down at eight in the morning.

"Hey, I can do it!" I smile. "It just might take me a couple tries."

He laughs, stepping away from the coffee and coming to me. With his arms on my shoulders, he looks down at me with soft eyes.

"You should do a cherry pie. Everyone loves cherry." The song "Cherry Pie" plays in the back of my head at his comment.

"I was thinking apple." I shrug.

"No, do cherry. Trust me." His tone takes on a sharper note, and I can't help but furrow my brows. "I'll look into it."

He smiles, pleased by my response, and then drops his

hands to his sides. Not sure what that was all about, I shake my head and change the subject. "How was last night?"

A sly smirk pulls at the corner of his mouth, and I can't help but reciprocate. "Amazing."

I laugh, heat blooming across my cheeks. Having him in my bed, with his arms wrapped around me, made me feel whole, safe, secure—things I haven't felt in way too long.

He grabs his cup of coffee from the counter, and with his phone in his other hand, he winces and looks up at me.

"I gotta head out. I have a house to show this afternoon. Can I come by after I'm done?" I roll my lips, contemplating. If I say yes too fast, he'll think I have nothing better to do than wait on him—which you don't want a guy to think because he'll freak out and think you're moving too fast or are clingy—thank you, Cosmo magazine, at the checkout line. But if I say no, it could really put us back in our relationship, and I don't want that either. I like having him here. His company soothes me, making me feel less alone.

"Yeah. If you feel up to it, come on by," I answer, my voice relaxed and casual. He takes a sip of his hot brew while looking over the black ceramic at me. Swallowing, he places the cup in the sink and asks, "Will Paige be here?"

"Yeah. Cam usually drops her off before dinner." Usually. There were a few times I had to go get her because he didn't feel like it.

"Nice. She's a good kid, you know? Having her here makes the house feel…full, like an actual family." He stops at the door, his jaw tight, eyes serious. "Family is what shapes a person into who they become as an adult." His right brow rises. His Adam's apple bobs. He's telling me so much without telling me, yet I can't read between the lines. Something life changing happened to his family that much is clear; I just wish I knew what it was.

"Yeah," my voice cracks, "family is everything." I couldn't agree more as I think about my mom and how she had always been there for me.

"All right, I'm off," he states, his tone back to normal. With a wink, he shuts the door behind him.

Two hours, one shower, and a muffin later, I look at my shrubs. Some petals lie on the ground, dry mud creating a cast over them.

"Shit," I mutter under my breath. Bending down, I hold one of the flowers in my palm. It took a beating, bit beneath the mud, it's still bright pink and full of life. No matter the storm, it made it through and will grow into something stronger. Kind of like me, I've swam the waters of abuse and grief but I've come out on the other side where love and friendship surround me.

My head lifts at the rev of a loud motor barreling down the street. The hairs on my arm lift, and my stomach drops. Standing, I wipe my hands on my jean shorts and start walking around the white fence to meet Cam. He parks at the curb and shuts off the engine. The passenger door opens first, and Paige's Converse hit the ground. She shuts the door, sees me, and instantly smiles. The sick feeling I had vanishes. Just seeing her makes everything else seem small and redundant. She's the one thing I've done right. She has her hair in Dutch braids, a tie dye shirt on with some boyfriend looking jeans on.

"Hey, baby!" I shout with a grin. She walks right up to me, and I hug her tight, missing her.

"Hi, Mom," she mumbles into my arm, and I realize I'm suffocating her as well as embarrassing her.

Letting go, I say, "Check out the flowers I picked out." I point toward the door, and she walks over to look at them.

"Where's your boy toy? Get enough of you after one night?" Cam's rancid voice has me slowly looking in his direction. Hatred rattles in my chest, trying to block his insult, my heart already dented and scarred from his never-ending harassment. His mental attacks are unmatched. He's a ghost I can't lock behind any door. Reaching up, he tugs his red ballcap down on his head a little tighter, and I can't help but notice his dirty shirt and ripped jeans. He sticks out here, looking like a man clinging to his high-school days. Not to mention, his loud ass truck and the cowboy attitude he brought with him yesterday.

"I cannot believe you yesterday!" I sneer, ready to fight this out on the lawn and give Tenly something to come over tonight and talk about. "How many sluts have you had on your arm and I never said a thing? But I have a guy over and you act like some jealous teenager? Why? For what? You don't want me, you made that clear, so why the hell would you pull something like that?"

He steps closer, a scowl on his face, a cold shadow beneath his feet as if the reaper has attached itself to him. I feel small, the insecurities I harbored while married to him growing inside my chest. I refuse to let him see how much he still affects me and stand tall.

"I choose who's in my daughter's life." He points to himself, his teeth clenched. Is he serious? He does not get to dictate who I see!

"No, Cam, you lost that right when I left your ass."

I turn on my heel, starting toward the house.

"Right, because how many times were you on the floor

15

I sit on the couch. The room is dark except for the lamp letting off a soft glow and the low hues illuminating the TV screen. My eyes heavy with sleep, I stare blankly at the screen, completely zoned out. Paige put on a show called *Bates Motel*, but I'm exhausted from finishing up my pottery room the rest of the day and can't focus on what's happening. At least it's finally done and everything has its place. But now the room is crying for me to hide inside it and pour every emotion into my work. I can't wait to see what I create after everything that's happened recently.

"Mom, I think I'm going to go to bed." Paige's voice snaps me from my mind. I sit up with a deep inhale.

"Okay, babe. I'm going to stay up a little longer." My eyes sweep to the kitchen, where the stove reads ten thirty.

"Dad got me up at the crack of dawn to go fishing. I didn't catch anything, and he drank and told stories about how his dad never took him. It was boring and exhausting." God, I don't miss those stories. They were all so depressing.

"Mom, you look tired. You should go to bed too." She stands there with droopy eyes, her arms at her sides.

"Heston said he might come over tonight. I don't want to lock him out if I go to bed. I'll just wait a little longer." I sound like a teenager waiting for a boy who never intended to call back, and it makes me sick. Have I succumbed to needing a man's attention? Am I this eager for another person in my life to disappoint me? No, I'm not doing this to myself, and I sure as hell don't want my daughter seeing me waiting up for a guy and thinking this is what she's supposed to do when she's interested in one.

"Actually, I think I'll go work in my studio for a bit," I say, stretching my legs out. I don't mind staying up a little longer because I feel like I do my best work at night, but I'm not sitting here waiting and looking at my phone every five minutes.

She crosses her arms in front of her chest, her face unreadable. "Is he staying the night?"

I don't answer. She's old enough to know she doesn't want that answer because she already knows what I'm going to say. Her eyes shine with curiosity, but whatever she's thinking, she doesn't say out loud. Turning around, she runs her hand along the back of the couch, heading toward the stairs.

"Night, Mom."

I stretch my arms above my head and yawn, trying to wake myself up. Standing, I fold the blanket Paige was covered up with and place it on the back of the couch. Maybe I should dust or wipe the counter before Heston comes over. No, I don't really want to do that. Looking at the stairs that lead to my studio, I think about my pottery room. My fingers itch to slip into the clay and let everything I'm feeling but won't say into my work. Screw it, even if I just get some supplies out to start something another day, it will keep me awake for a little while longer. After climbing the stairs, I open the door and flip the light on, the room glows from the one fixture above, giving off a barely-there white light. Turning on my floor lamp that hangs over my shoulder illuminating my space, I grab my apron from the back of the door and slip it over my head, tying it behind my back. Opening Spotify on my phone, I put on my playlist and sit in my low wooden chair that's behind the wheel. Taking a deep breath, I grab a box of clay next to my foot, and some water from the jug on my art cart and start kneading them together. My foot presses the pedal and the wheel starts to move the chunk of clay in my hands, helping me transition it from nothing into something. Closing my eyes, letting my hands do the seeing for me, I listen to "You Give Love a Bad Name," and go into a deep state of relaxation. I needed this so badly. My mom passing, the accident, moving…it's been a lot. I feel spread thin, trying to keep my head held high, especially in front of Paige.

Suddenly, a chill runs down my back, causing the hairs on my arm to lift. Like the feeling you get when you're being watched. Uneasy, I open my eyes, and find Heston standing in the doorway, his arms crossed, staring at me with a smoldering expression.

Losing concentration, my piece begins to wobble and fall to the side. I release my foot from the pedal and let out a breath. Shit, I didn't even get to see what it was becoming.

"I didn't hear you come in," I say, unaware he let himself in. I thought he'd text when he was here or knock, so finding him already in the house is surprising. I'm attracted by the gall of this man.

He doesn't say anything, just struts farther into the room, his shoulders square and his eyes prowling, as if he's an animal hunting in the dark. His intense gaze has me all hot and bothered and my lips part as he grabs the back of my chair and slips one of his legs behind me. I scoot forward until he's sitting behind me, my ass now halfway on the edge of the chair and his lap. Reaching for my phone, he puts on "Unchained Melody" by the Righteous Brothers, the song from the movie *Ghost*, then sets it back down. I want to laugh, but I bite my lip, reining it in.

His hands cradle my elbows. His fingertips, soft as silk, slip down my arms. My breath hitches and my core pulsates from his touch. His hands cup mine around the piece of clay I was trying to inspire life into. Pressing my foot back on the pedal, my hands glide up and down, renewing its shape. He leans in closer, his breath hot on the nape of my neck. I close my eyes, feeling, listening. His heat on my back. His large fingers slipping between mine as the wet clay dances beneath my palms.

His lips press against the dip right under my ear, and I can't help but sigh and lean into him. He shuffles beneath me, his hard length against my ass. I circle my hips, so it rubs my clit just right. Heavy panting fills the room, our hands still working the pottery. I release my foot from the pedal and turn in his lap, until my legs are straddling his, our faces inches apart. With my hands caked with clay, I grab both sides of his face and kiss him hard, need burning inside me. I lick his upper lip, and his tongue returns the gesture, flicking my bottom lip before sucking it into his mouth until our tongues touch. His hands slide up my back, untying my apron. I pull it over my head and toss it across the room. The light now shining right in my face, he raises his hand and turns it off. He stands, my legs squeezing his hips, so I don't fall, and we walk across the room. Holding me up with one arm, he uses the other to turn the lights off and shut the door. Slowly, he drops to his knees and lays me on the floor, his hands on either side of my hips. I arch my back, needing friction, his touch, something. Lifting my shirt, he leans close, his lips leaving butterfly kisses on my stomach. My hand falls to his head, running my fingers through his hair. He devours my body, his hands all over me. Moonlight streaming through the room, soft music crooning from my phone lead to sex so powerful, it depletes every one of our senses until we both go languid, our bodies imprinting on one another, binding us into something stronger than just friends.

Laughter and pots banging in the kitchen cause me to stir awake. Naked and hiding under the soft sheets, I fight the intrusion and try to go back to sleep. Giggles and a male voice have my eyes snapping back open.

Paige and Heston must be in the kitchen.

Tossing the covers off me, I grab my robe from the door, tie it tight, and make haste to see what they're doing. Turning the corner, I look over the living room and kitchen and find Heston standing in front of the stove in jeans and no shirt, his feet bare. He holds a pan in his hand, hovering it over the stove top as Paige, in her pajamas and Dutch braids, stares at him, happiness in her eyes.

"I'm going to laugh so hard if you miss!" Paige says, not seeing me standing here watching.

"You're the one who says flipping them in the air makes them taste better."

"It does. It makes them more fluffy or something."

Shaking his head, he gives his ass a little wiggle to prepare then tosses the pancake. We all watch with bated breath to see where it lands. It flips twice, then free falls back into the pan.

"Oh my God, you did it!" Paige squeals, her arms in the air like he just made a goal.

"I was nervous it was going to hit the ceiling for a second." Wrinkles form across his forehead. Using my favorite red spatula, he slides the pancake from the pan and places it on a plate. I enter the room. "Wow, first try and no casualties." My crack at being funny has them both turning my way. "First time I did it, the thing landed in a potted plant," I say.

"Hey, you!" He lights up and sets the spatula down to walk over, wrapping his arms around me. "Hungry?"

"Starving, actually," I reply around a smile. One I can't seem to stop. Who can blame me? Paige hasn't acted this happy in a long time either.

"I've got you." He winks and walks back to the stove. I grab a cup of coffee and sit at the table across from Paige. She stares at her phone, blindly stuffing her mouth with her breakfast.

"So, who said pancakes taste better flipped in the air? Was it you?" Heston asks me, pouring batter into the pan.

"My mom." I let out a small laugh. "She said it as far back as I can remember." Memories of standing on a chair next to my mom in a kitchen over an old green stove warm my chest. God, I miss her.

"Hmm." He focuses on the pan, as if lost in thought, and I immediately feel bad for bringing her up. The way he acts when I talk about my family…the tension, looking away, not saying much, makes me think he doesn't get along with his folks.

"What about your parents? How were they?" I ask, probing.

"Um…when I was younger, my parents were close. As I got older, my dad became more absent."

"Oh," I mutter. "My father was out of the picture before I was two," I tell him.

He glances at me with an unreadable expression then focuses back on the pancake.

"I'd love to meet your parents sometime. See the people responsible for the pancake-flipping expert. Maybe they can teach me," I tease, then take a sip of hot coffee.

His shoulders tense. A tic in his jaw destroys his beautiful mood. And I suddenly feel like an idiot for the joke.

"That's going to be kinda hard when I don't even see them." His tone is grim, darkening the kitchen. I set my cup down and press my fingers against my temples. "I'm so sorry. I didn't mean… I mean…I was—"

"It's fine. Don't worry about it." He shakes the pan, silence spreading between us. This is why I've stayed single. I'm just as terrible at dating as I thought I would be.

"Don't forget to flip!" Paige reminds him, still staring at her phone, oblivious to what just went down. Heston shakes his head, as if wiping away a bad memory, and his lips lift into a smirk. He widens his stance, shakes his hips, and flips it into the air. The pancake goes rogue, and Paige laughs, covering her head with both hands. My eyes on my breakfast, I watch it flop onto the kitchen island behind him.

He glances at me, his eyes wide, and I nearly spit coffee laughing.

Holding his finger up, he says, "Let me try that again."

"Bet he misses again?" I whisper across the table to Paige. She peeks over at him then back to me.

"Bet."

Five minutes later, he made it in the pan.

"I gotta get to work."

"Will you be over tonight?" Paige asks. Their time together this morning must have paid off.

Heston looks to me for an answer. "I mean, if he wants to, sure." I shrug, like it's no big deal, but deep down, I want to yell, "Stay!"

"Sleepover?" Heston asks, his eyes barely masking the heat between us. Paige stands up, her chair scraping across the floor.

"Eww, I'm out," she mutters, stomping up the stairs to escape to her teenage paradise of a room. The moment she's out of view, Heston reaches for me. Grabbing the sash of my robe, he pulls me to him.

"Do you want me to come back over?" His voice is low and throaty as he unties the knot of my robe. My breath quickens, and my nipples perk at the sudden intrusion.

"Yeah, I do," I whisper with a heavy breath.

"Then I'll come over." Letting go of the robe, he kisses me on the mouth, rubbing his thumb over my cheek.

God, this is too perfect. Where did this man come from? He pulls away, stepping back, his eyes brighter than ever.

"This morning has been the best. Feels like a real home with family in it."

A chill runs down my arms, and I can't help but feel like I need to shield myself from the uncomfortable feeling enveloping me. Crossing my arms over my body, I

nod, not sure what to say.

"I have a change of clothes in the truck. I'mma grab them and change for work before I'm late." He grabs his stuff from his truck and heads to the bedroom and I finish my coffee, making a note to check the pottery Heston and I created last night. A few minutes later, he's back in the kitchen anxiously adjusting his tie.

"Does this look okay?" He glances up at me with worried eyes. The three-piece black on black suit and green tie look really good on him. "You look professional."

"Professional,' he whispers, smoothing down the silk. He's nervous, and it's cute. I wonder why.

"Big client today?" I prod.

"Hoping to close on a house. Walk me out?" he asks, and I nod, opening the front door. The morning sun is hot, ready to sweep over the state with a mid-summer smog. The air is so thick, you can hardly breathe.

"I should be back around dinner, unless things fall through, then I'll be back by lunch," he says, walking fast.

"Rain, dear!" I look past him to see Flynn and Oliver heading toward us. Oliver's dressed to impress, despite the rising heat, in a white-collared shirt with a cardigan thrown over his shoulders, his better half standing taller and tanner, in jeans and a fitted tee. Owen eyes Heston, waiting for me to introduce them.

"Heston, this is Flynn and Oliver. Guys, this is Heston."

"Hi, there!" Flynn extends his hand to shake, and Heston reaches forward to accept.

"You going to a wedding?" Flynn asks, his eyes squinted as he looks Heston up and down.

He glances down at himself. "Uh, no. I'm closing on a house. It's kind of big deal for me," he says around light laughter. I can't help but smile with him.

"Wait," Flynn says, holding his hand up for Heston to stop talking. "You're going to persuade someone to buy something looking like a salesman?"

My brows furrow. Wouldn't you want to look the part?

"What are you suggesting?" Heston hesitantly asks, just as confused.

"First, take off that tie." Flynn rests one hand on his hip, the other gesturing toward Heston.

"Uh…" Poor guy doesn't know what to do. I have to bite

back my reaction. My gay neighbors are styling my boyfriend.

"Then that topcoat and vest need to go." Owen points to everything on Heston's upper half.

He glances at me, questions in his eyes.

"Do it. Listen to what they have to say and see if you like it." I shrug.

Okay," he mutters, taking off the tie and handing it to me, the fabric silky in my hand. Next, the coat and the vest are in my arms, weighing me down, causing me to sweat in this heat.

"Okay, what now?" Lines form around his eyes. His hands fall and slap at his sides, reminding me of a little boy asking his mom what to try on in a dressing room.

"Here, let me help." Owen steps forward and loosens the collar on Heston's black button-up, undoing one or two buttons. Grabbing the bottom of the shirt, he pulls on it slightly, so it's not so snug on his body but still tucked in.

"There. Done." Owen claps his hands and takes a step back to admire his work.

"Yeah, now you look good. You don't look like you're trying so hard but it's still respectful," Flynn adds.

"Yeah, I guess I do feel more comfortable," Heston admits, his eyes trailing off, landing on the house at the end of the cul-de-sac.

"Hey, what do you know about that house? How long has it been up for sale?" We all look to the house. I haven't seen anybody there since I moved in.

"Been for sale for a while. Probably will be for a while still."

"Why? What happened?" I ask, curious myself.

"It was quite scandalous. A guy cheated on his wife with the woman who used to live in your house." Owen points just behind me. "The husband was taxed with rage and he killed the other husband that slept with his spouse."

"Like, murder?" I ask, my eyes wide with surprise. No wonder nobody lives in it. Just thinking about the man who used to live in my house being deranged with jealousy, to the point of taking another life, makes me feel uneasy. Why didn't the damn realtor say something to me about all this? Probably because nobody actually died in the house.

Ringing sounds from Heston's pocket. He pulls his phone out and glances at it.

"Shit, I'm going to be late." He kisses me on the cheek and waves to the guys. "Thanks, I owe you one." Climbing into his truck, he backs out and drives away. I feel Owen and Flynn staring at me.

"Where did you snag that snack?" Owen asks.

"He wrecked into me," I confess, turning until I'm facing them both. Owen squints from the morning sun, his left hand fanning him from the harassing heat. Flynn crosses his arms, smirking.

"Girl, you better hold on tight to that one. Men like him can't do monogamy." Owen's tone is serious. "Like, they literally cannot."

His words hit the dark pit of my heart, where the whispers and roars tell me Heston and I won't last.

"I guess we'll find out because I can't not be with him. Having him here makes everything feel better—it makes me feel better."

"Hmm, are you in love with him or his company, darling?" Owen asks the million-dollar question. All I can do is stare back at him.

Do I really like Heston or do I just like not being alone?

16

The week goes by, and Heston has slept over every night except tonight. He has to network with some big wigs over coffee in the morning, so here I am, staring at the vase I just made. It's bulbous and looks different than my normal work. I can't help but wish my mom was here to tell me what I'm doing wrong, to talk to me. Not having another adult in the house is depressing. The silence is deafening. It makes me think about everything I don't want to. Feeling frustrated, I grab the rag off my cart, wipe my hands, and head downstairs. Laughter streams through the front door, and I pause, trying to listen. I open the door carefully, hoping it doesn't creak, and find Paige sitting with Layla—the girl she got in trouble with or drinking. Anger heats my cheeks. My mouth opens to yell for Paige to get inside, but then I see Layla laughing. Her smile reaches her eyes. Her face is bare of dark makeup and black lipstick. She's wearing one of Paige's shirts—a maroon American Eagle tee—and is looking at my daughter like a big sister she's always wanted. Closing my mouth, my brows furrow as they go on about how clueless boys are at their age. I was worried Layla was a bad influence on Paige, but it looks like my daughter is rubbing off on her. Brightness peeks through the darkness that surrounds Layla, and my daughter is the sun.

Gently shutting the door, I head to my room to shower. Taking my clothes off and kicking them to the corner, I grab my phone to turn on music and see a text from Heston.

Heston: *It feels weird not being with you.*

Me: *Then come over.*

Heston: *Coming.*

After showering, I head to the front porch. Paige is long gone and up in her room by now. I sit down, wiggling my toes on the warm asphalt beneath my feet. Owen and Flynn's front porch light comes on, and they step outside, talking and in their own world. They're cute together. Funny even. Owen looks up as if he feels me staring and waves.

Getting Flynn's attention, they start my way. The anticipation of them coming over makes me shift. I don't know what to say or do. I have seriously been lacking social experience.

"Please don't tell me you're out here waiting for Heston," Flynn says, turning his head to the side. I stay quiet. He said not to say it.

"Couldn't even make it a night." Owen laughs, and I can't help the smile pulling at my cheeks.

"Remember when we were like that?" Flynn nudges Owen, and they give each other that look—the one of love and memories. He's right though, I've become obsessed with Heston. I miss his mouth, his eyes, and laughter. Some would even go as far as saying I've become obsessed with the man.

"Well, if he has you out here waiting on him like this, he must be good in bed," Owen says conspiratorial. I can't help the laugh that escapes.

"Jesus," Flynn scolds. Owen rolls his eyes.

"Well, we won't keep you, but you better come over tomorrow and spill the details!" Owen points to me.

"All right, all right. No need to be pushy," I tease, and Owen swings his hand like he's flipping his hair.

"That's all I do, babe."

I watch them go back to their place, bickering and flirting, and can't help but want that for myself. I've always been the one to sit back and watch others be happy. I'm not upset right now. If anything, I love seeing them together.

Lights flash across my face, and I squint to see who's pulling into our little nook. It's Heston. I stand up as he turns his truck off and gets out in only his boxer briefs and socks. He didn't even take the time to get dressed. Rushing to me, he nearly knocks me over, crashing his mouth to mine.

"I'm here. I couldn't get here fast enough," he says between kissing me, his fervent energy wrapping around me, hugging me.

"Never again. You can't leave," I mumble against his lips, both of us stumbling inside the house and into my room. The isolation suffocating me moments ago now taken over with love and adoration. The way I'm falling for this man is unhealthy and I know that, but I can't stop myself from craving his touch. He was mine and I was his.

Falling into the doorway he fucks me on the stairs, my nails chipping and breaking from gripping the stair above and railing to keep from face planting. It occurs to me that this unhealthy obsession I have is like a drug, and in the end our story won't end well.

The next morning, Heston leaves for his meeting, but my body remembers his touch very well. I told him not to ever leave me here alone again and he promised. I think that means he's moving in. My hand on my face, I breathe through the nerves making me want to laugh and cry at the same time. I know what I'm feeling, but what the hell am I thinking? Moving in together already? This is just crazy, crazy beautiful. Getting out of bed, I dress in jeans and a white tank, throw my hair up out of my face, the thought we might be moving in together still playing out in my head. I need some fresh air. Rounding my doorway I open my front door and inhale the dew on the grass and summer blowing through the trees.

"No! The birdbath is fine—and you know it!" Owen shouts from his yard, gaining my attention. Tenly stands in jogging pants and a sports bra, pointing to the little birdbath, her face bunched in anger. "It's going to bring more animals to the area!"

"So what? They're part of nature bitch!" Owen sneers, stepping in front of his concrete yard ornament.

Stepping off the porch, I make my way over to see what insight I might be able to offer. I mean, they're always in my business…

"Seriously, Tenly, do you have to do this now?" Flynn asks, standing in buffalo checkered pajama pants, sounding nearly half asleep.

"Hey, guys. Everything okay?" I ask, walking up to them.

"No, this devil bitch hates nature and wants me to take my birdbath down." Owen doesn't back down, ready to fight Tenly over this, his red robe flying open behind him.

"It's just a birdbath." I look between them, not understanding. It's not like a bear is going to come wash its face.

Everyone quiets. Tenly snaps her eyes to me. I don't give in to her silent threats.

"See?" Owen gestures toward me. Flynn holds his head, ready for this to be over so he can go back to bed.

Silence falls onto our shoulders. Tenly crosses her arms.

"If it's overlooked and someone else does it and says, 'Oh, you let them do it,' then it's my ass! I'll double check with the HEA. If they agree, it comes down, Owen." Her voice is lighter, more accepting than the screaming match they were just in.

"Looking forward to it," he snaps. Tenly huffs and jogs away, leaving me with the guys.

"Are all mornings this entertaining?" I ask. Flynn grins.

"With Owen and Tenly, we could open a ringside attraction."

Laughing, I look to Owen. He closes his robe, shaking off his anger like a cold chill.

"She has it out for me and you know it, Flynn," he says sternly. "So, I would ask how last night went, but the whole neighborhood heard how well it went."

My mouth parts in disbelief. My face fuming with embarrassment. Is he insinuating he could hear me having sex?

"No," I gush, praying he's just teasing.

Flynn shakes his head. "He's just messing with you."

My shoulders deflate in relief. I glare at Owen laughing his ass off at my expense.

Game on.

17

SIX WEEKS LATER

"Woman, do you hear me?" Owen's high-pitched voice cuts through my thoughts. I blink a few times to clear my head. Sitting out back at Owen and Flynn's, I sigh in frustration, as I perch my pink toes on the edge of a metal patio chair. I *was* listening until he started getting excited about Heston possibly proposing, then I zoned out. My first marriage didn't work out, why would I tread that path again? Then again, Heston and I are moving fast so the thought of marriage isn't preposterous. In the last six weeks, he sold all his furniture and put his place up for sell. He's even been helping Paige with her pitching a softball. Something her dad was supposed to be doing but fell short. He always promises her things and then ends up with some excuse why he can't follow through. She used to buy whatever lame reason he gave but now that she's older she knows he's a liar and doesn't expect much from him.

"I hear you. I just think you're wrong." Looking over my shoulder, I bat my eyes with a close-lipped smile, knowing that disagreeing with him will rub him the wrong way. He stares back at me before lifting his hand to inspect his cuticles. Oh, how I love his drama queen tantrums.

"He's right though, I think Heston is going to propose. Even if it's only been six weeks, you should see the way he looks at you," Flynn adds, resting his elbow on the table. I think back on the 42 days and how great it's been. Showering together, working in the yard, and fucking until we can't breathe. I feel a blanket of security having him here. I feel safe and cared for, not just for myself but for Paige too. In fact, when he leaves, I start overthinking all the things: what if he doesn't come back? Am I truly in love with him? Is he in love with me? Then I start talking to my mother's urn, asking her the same crazy questions and wishing she could tell me when she knew she was in love? It's like I can't move on without her, the idea of her being gone sinks into the pit of my stomach where I'm deeply afraid I'll be alone for the rest of my life.

"Like an obsessed little boy with a new toy." Owen scoffs, and I roll my eyes at his absurdity.

"Look how protective he is over you and Paige. No man would act that way without good intentions," Flynn adds, and I sigh just thinking about it. I swear in the last six weeks, I've had to become a referee between Cam and Heston. If they cross paths, there's always some kind of physical altercation. Heston says he can't help it because he can't stand the way Cam talks to me. That Paige and I deserve better. If it were up to him, Paige would never go to Cam's, but the fact that Cam's her father and he does try, even if he's not the most reliable.

Red finches fly around Owen and Flynn's birdfeeder, quickly landing, only to take to the air again when a mockingbird decides to land next to them. "How lucky they are to just be able to up and fly away to wherever they please," I say, my voice thick with envy.

"Yeah, but some landings take you straight into the cat's den."

"True," I mutter. I don't know what I think about Heston proposing. We burn so hot, moving through the steps of a relationship too fast. I'm happy with him, but I don't know if I should marry him. I know this is what happy couples do so I shouldn't be surprised but I'm not ready. I'm not sure I'll ever be ready.

The wind shifts from the south, blowing a hard, hot breeze. I close my eyes and ease back as the smell of cut grass and sweet purple azaleas surrounds me. The birds chirp. The wind rustling the leaves of the big oak trees behind the property line. As the breeze wanes, I open my eyes, feeling calmer. Owen and Flynn have been my neighborly therapists for a while now, so much so that I don't know what I'd do without them. Standing, I stretch my arms above my head.

"Well, boys, I need to get home and take over playing catch, I forgot Heston is waiting for a call back about work today." I wave as I walk toward the side of the house to cross the street back to my house.

"Bye!" they say in unison. As I reach my front porch, I'm left wondering how long I've been gone because Paige and Heston are no longer where I left them. Opening my front door, Heston is sitting on the couch in khaki shorts and no shirt.

"Where's Paige?"

"Her room, I think. I threw a ball a little fast and she tried to catch it with the hand that didn't have a glove." He winces. "I think it hurt a finger or two, but nothing's broke."

"Oh, man, are you sure she's okay?"

He nods, a weak smile on his face. "Yeah. She punched me in the arm before calling it quits."

I sense something is wrong. Plopping down next to him, I place my elbow on the back of the couch and rest my head in my hand.

"Babe, what's wrong? Something's bothering you." Sighing, he pushes my legs off of him and heads to the kitchen.

Looking over the couch, I rest one arm on the back and look at him. "Tell me!"

His back rises with a deep breath, then he turns, putting his hands flat on the counter with his head drawn low.

"I just found out before you walked in that the house didn't close. The buyers backed out. My boss is pissed. He's putting me back on smaller properties." Pushing off the counter, he jerks the fridge door open and bends to grab a soda before slamming it shut. I don't understand real estate. I haven't even met his boss or any of his clients, and I can't help but wonder if he's new to this kind of profession and he's still learning the ropes.

"Well, that's not fair. It's not your fault the owners wanted so much for it."

"Yeah, maybe. I won't be making as much, though. Don't you have an art show coming up or something? How much do you make at those?" His question about my work comes out of the blue. I'm concerned about where he's going with this.

"A couple hundred." I shrug. "But you don't need to worry about money. I have some if we get in a pinch. You should focus—"

"That's not the way it works, Rain. If I'm going to live here, I should help!" His voice rises, and a chord in his neck strains as he scowls at me. A peak of his dark side lurks behind his charming smile, and romantic gestures. At first a seed but not it's a full stalk of nothing but thorns.

"I understand, you're the man of the house and want to support us." I honestly have never seen a man want to be the one working; men like that don't exist in my life, so this is both surprising and refreshing.

"This money you have, I'm assuming it's from your mother?" He shakes his head. "You need to save that and get a job."

I feel like I've been slapped in the face by his comment, so much so that I sit with my mouth open and my throat cinched up, unable to respond.

"I'm going to go take a shower. Cool off," he mutters, looking down at his soda before walking off.

Sulking, I burrow myself into the couch and sigh. I feel bad he was demoted, but I'm sure we'll be fine. His questions about how much I make though, doesn't sit well with me. It's something Cam used to always bring up and then follow it up with an insinuation that I don't contribute enough. I mean, sure it would be nice if I could make way more on my pottery, but it takes time to get to that level. Defeat settles in my chest as I stare at the dust motes that float in the sun beaming through the blinds from window. This hobby of mine seems to really bother the men I'm with; they act as if the money I make from my art doesn't matter and is somehow lesser than what they do. Why does it matter though? I have money who cares where it came from? Money is money! I don't think I would have won today's argument if I tried, it all results back to one thing. Me getting a real job with steady income.

18

Feeling hot and sweaty, I flip my pillow, searching for coolness, but as soon as I lie my head back down, it warms. Huffing, I kick the blankets off of me and reach for Heston, wanting to feel his body, to know he's still in bed with me. Especially after our fight yesterday.

My hand swipes cool, empty sheets. Raising my head, I look to see that Heston is gone. My brow furrows, and I look around the bedroom.

"Heston?" I call out. When no one replies, I get up, grab my robe from the back of the door, and pad down the hall. The living room and kitchen are dark and quiet, but there's a slight hint of coffee in the air. Where is he? It's not like him to leave the lights off. I go into the kitchen to find the coffee pot mostly full and a note left in front of it.

See you at dinner. - Heston

I scoff, turning the note over for more of an explanation. We usually wake up together. The fact that he didn't get me up and left a half-assed note upsets me.

Grabbing my phone, I text him.

Me: *Why didn't you wake me?*

Heston: *I don't know.*

Biting my bottom lip, angry with the impersonable message, I look at the clock on the stove. Ten. Man, I really slept in. I just don't get why he left without waking me up, and his explanation doesn't give me any answers. Fuming, I make myself a cup of coffee, slamming cabinets and growing more pissed by the second. I need a neighbor therapy session. Exiting the front door, I walk across the street and head to Owen and Flynn's. I go around to the back door, finding them sitting at their patio table with fresh fruit and juice. Slumping into a seat, I grab a strawberry and bite into it.

"You okay?" Flynn asks, scratching his chest.

"I don't know," I mumble.

"Spill it," Owen demands, rubbing his eyes.

"It's just…Heston didn't wake me up this morning, and when I asked him why he didn't, he said he didn't know. Like, what does he mean, he doesn't know?" I vomit my feelings all over their breakfast, watching Flynn's brows rise and Owen eat up everything I'm giving him.

"So, you're mad he didn't wake you up? Don't you have an alarm on your phone for that?" Flynn asks, totally not getting it.

"No, it's not that. It's the fact that we wake up together every morning; we talk, have sex, and share some laughs. We get up and make coffee and start our day together. We've done it for weeks now. He even said it was his favorite part of the day, and then for some reason, I wake up today and he's gone. Then I ask him what happened and he just doesn't know. How is that his answer? What the hell?" My voice rises as I continue to explain, my heart hammering against my chest.

"The honeymoon phase faded fast, baby girl," Owen says, reaching for some fruit.

"Honeymoon?" I ask, unsure what he's talking about.

"Yeah, you're starting to settle down and become a couple," Flynn answers for him.

"That was just an asshole move honestly." Owen raises a brow.

"Yeah, I know. Maybe it's from our fight yesterday," I mutter, thinking about how upset he was over our finances.

"That fire burned too hot and is snuffing out," Owen adds. A lump forms in my throat. I love the butterflies, the touching, missing one another when we're apart. The way Heston's been acting recently, though, hasn't been pleasant, and I don't know what to do about it. What do I say—I don't like you, so please change?

19

ONE WEEK LATER

I grab my robe laying haphazardly on the dresser and slip it on. Tying it while walking into the living room and finding Paige and Heston already up. It's a nice surprise to see him home, instead of working to make up his big loss. We could use some time together. Every day this week, I've wakened up alone. No kiss on the forehead, no whisper that he loves me. It's as if I'm just a pair of socks on the floor that he doesn't remember having.

"I wonder what his job is," Paige says, staring out the living room window.

"Who are you talking about?" I ask.

"Tenly. Layla texted me that her husband is home. I guess it's a big deal because nobody ever sees him," Paige informs me, her breath fogging up the window.

"I haven't met him," Heston says from the couch, tapping his chin with the remote.

"Yeah, me neither," I mumble. Pushing Paige out of the way, I glance out the window, checking out the SUV parked across the street. I should go over there and knock on her door like she does every time something new or unexpected happens to any of us. I bet Owen and Flynn are staring out their blinds too. My eyes shift to their house. Finding the curtains moving in the window, I can't help but smile. My nosy friends are the best. Standing up straight, I let Paige go back to gawking and head toward the coffee. I open the fridge, reach for the pitcher of cold brew, then turn toward the counter, smacking into Heston's hard chest. The coffee splashes, nearly spilling onto the floor.

I let out a squeal of surprise. "Oh my god, you scared me."

He takes the pitcher from me and sets it on the counter behind him.

"Babe, I want to apologize. I've been having a hard time at work and I took it out on you."

I tuck hair behind my ear and cross my arms, suddenly feeling vulnerable.

"I mean, you moved in here Heston, so it's not fair for you to tell me to get a job because you felt like you weren't making enough."

"I know, I was just in a bad mood that day." But that's not the truth, he's always snapping or saying things that come off wrong.

Chewing on the inside of my cheek, I look away.

"You should do your pottery thing if it makes you happy." He smiles, and suddenly everything is right in the world. I'm in his arms, he's looking at me like he used to, like I'm the only thing he wants in life. It's unnatural the way he moves on so quickly, it makes me think he's Bipolar.

I place my hand on his smooth chest and smile up at him. Having him close feels good. I missed us being like this.

"I don't have to worry about money. My mother made sure Paige and me were taken care of, so I could build my portfolio."

His chest lifts with a large inhale, and he shakes his head. "My mother had two jobs, and my father had a career that had him tied to a desk seven days a week. Money is just a reminder that I don't want to be like that."

"Wow," I mumble. All of that sounds horrible, like they were surviving not living.

"So this is new to me is all, I'm still learning…how to be with someone." He places his hand on mine and I look into his eyes, the color of the sky just before a storm. He's told me he's had girlfriends before me, which I expected, but they never lasted more than a week because he didn't feel a connection with any of them past sex. It didn't turn me off because when we first met, I wasn't looking for anything serious. We just kind of happened.

The front door opens, and I pull the sash to my robe tighter. I see a flash of pink and muscles sprint by me into the foyer. It's Owen with Flynn beside him.

"What are you two up to?" I ask, walking toward them.

"Did you see him?" Owen asks, fanning himself after running over here in the midsummer heat of South Carolina. Flynn stands coolly, lifting his hand and smoothing his hair back.

"See who?"

"What do you mean, who? Tenly's husband! Duh!" Owen shouts.

"What's the big deal about this guy? I don't understand why everyone's acting like this." I laugh. Watching everyone squirm is like watching drunk people when you're sober.

"Are you serious right now?" Owen looks to Flynn. "I can't tell if she's joking." Flynn just smiles, and Owen tosses a hand at him in dismissal, before looking back at me.

"It's Asher Mathew, the plastic surgeon." He looks at me like I should know who he's talking about. I stare back, still clueless. "Celebrities and deep-pocketed fat cats seek him out for secret augmentation," he continues.

"Tenly said he had a show before he got tired of all the fans trying to unmask who he was working on—which affected his clientele, of course," Flynn adds.

"When Layla said he was famous, I thought he was an actor or something," Paige says, still looking out the window.

"Baby girl, being an actor isn't a big deal nowadays—not when you can get so much more attention doing other things. Cooking, blogging, playing video games!" Owen schools her. And, I mean, he's not wrong. We lived in the same building as a YouTuber. He was five.

"Maybe I can get him to make my lips bigger." I pucker my mouth and look to Owen for his critique.

"Girl, go suck on a shot glass, it's cheaper."

I bust out laughing, and Flynn chuckles at his witty partner.

"Guess I have to hide all the shot glasses now," Heston chimes in from the kitchen.

"I don't know, it might enhance her skill at sucking other things." Owen crosses his arms, waiting for everyone to react to his statement. Stunned, I glance over my shoulder at Heston. He stands there holding the top cabinet doors open, his face stoic.

"And I'm going to my room…" Paige announces, her eyes wide, like she's been traumatized.

Owen looks to me with flushed cheeks.

"My oops." But he's clearly not sorry.

Amused with himself, Owen laughs and walks to my front window. "So, are you going to go over there and see if you can get acquainted?"

I bite my bottom lip, thinking about it for a second, curious who her superstar of a husband is. But if he's been gone this long, I'm sure he and Tenly are doing things I don't want to walk in on.

"No, I'll let you two busy bodies seize the opportunity."

"Very well. Your loss." Owen's contemptuous tone causes me to nearly snort. I didn't know me joining him in his morning gossip charades was so important.

Flynn gives me a respectful nod and then holds the door open for Owen, shutting it behind him as they leave. Looking out my window, I watch them head over to Tenly's place and knock on the door. Nobody answers, so they knock again.

"Did they really go over there?" Heston asks.

"They did." Turning around, I head into the kitchen and wrap my arms around his waist, his back to my face. He smells like his bergamot body wash. Sliding my hands up his fit stomach, I kiss his back gently, ready to have him touch me and make me feel good. There's nothing worse than being alone when you don't have to be.

Running my hand up his collarbone and around the nape of his neck, I deepen the kiss. A deep growl vibrates his chest.

"Someone's ready to make up," he says.

"Yes." I nod, my voice husky and full of desire.

Reaching for my hand, he kisses it tenderly, then turns around, grabbing my face. His lips press against mine, and I breathe him in, my fingers scratching his chest as he delves into my mouth. Grabbing me under my left thigh, he hikes my leg up and pushes his length against me. My mouth parts in desire. My eyelids flutter.

"I think I need to oversee how well you suck things and taking my cock into your mouth is better practice than any shot glass, my dear." Holy fuck that was hot.

Smiling like the devil, I slowly go to my knees, taking his khaki shorts and briefs with me. Placing his clothes under my knees to stay off the cold, hard floor, I fist the length of his cock and pump my hand, flicking the tip with my warm tongue. His hand falls to my head as he guides himself into my mouth. Salt coats my tongue, the taste acquiring. I hollow out my cheeks, nearly suctioning my mouth onto him. His knees wobble, fueling me on. I slide my mouth back and forth, spit dripping down my chin, becoming messy, just how he likes it. He whimpers and grunts like he's close, the simple sounds he makes a siren of a man's undoing. I twist my hands along his shaft and continue to bob until his body shudders and his cock jerks in my mouth, spilling his cum down my throat. I swallow, milking him for every last drop, then look up at him. He's breathing erratically, his eyes cast down on me. He holds his hand out to help me up, and I take it and stand. My knees are sore, and my jaw aches from holding it open for so long. But a caress of satisfaction that I got him to cum makes me feel high. I've read online not many girls can make their man come with their mouth.

"Jesus, you got a gift, babe." Wiping my mouth with the back of my hand, I smile.

"Guess I don't need to practice on a shot glass after all?" My brow rises in triumph.

He laughs, grabbing his shorts and underwear from the floor.

"I guess not."

After getting dressed, he opens his arms wide, and I take the bait, going in to hug him. He kisses the top of my head, and I'm feeling nothing but bliss at the moment. "Maybe I should put a ring on that mouth of yours, make you mine forever?"

I tense and look up at him. A heavy feeling spreads over my chest, making it difficult to breathe. It's too soon. We still have to figure out how to settle down with each other.

"Just a thought." He winks, giving off that Ryan Phillippe

vibe again. He grabs an apple from the counter, bites into it with a crisp crunch, and heads to the bedroom, leaving me swirling in emotions and thoughts.

Holy shit, Owen was right.

He's going to propose.

20

NEXT DAY

Sitting on Owen and Flynn's back patio, I eye the cloudless sky, while Owen fills a glass of lemonade for me—his specialty when I come over for our little visits.

"So, he actually said he should put a ring on it?" Flynn asks. I nod in answer before taking a drink.

"I told you!" Owen chirps. "I knew he was going to ask you."

Sighing loudly, I set the glass down. Tension in my neck makes my shoulders ache. I can hardly relax in this chair.

"So, if he does, indeed, ask you to marry him, what will you say?" I can feel their eyes on me, watching every time I blink or swallow, sizing me up.

"My mother used to say doubt causes chaos, so I shouldn't think so much into my own stubborn doubt, and go forth, if he does happen to ask me." I can practically remember my mother saying the words to me when I was scared to move forward with my pottery and not get a "real job."

"What doubt do you have?"

"My experience with marriage makes me feel as if I'm an

animal only available for mating rather than a person of my own mind and beliefs."

"If that's so then I agree, you shouldn't concentrate on the past, but rather more of what the future holds." Flynn coincides, my eyes swiftly move to his. His fingers interlock into a fist under his jaw. "The past will always be there if you don't move on, babe."

"I see why Owen likes you. You're a romantic," I say. I do have a lot of baggage from my first marriage and I know I often dwell on it. It's a part of my life that scarred me, questioning everything and turning me into the indecisive person I am today.

He smiles, and Owen grins back at him, as if they're having their own private conversation with just one look at each other.

Taking another sip of the bitter, sugary drink, I decide it's best to change the subject.

"So, did you guys get to meet Tenly's husband?"

Owen rolls his eyes, finally sitting in a chair next to Flynn.

"No, she didn't answer the door, and you see his car is gone today."

"Yeah, I noticed that."

"How the woman can live without the caring and comfort of her partner at least a few days a week is beyond me." Owen's face wrinkles in bewilderment, almost insulted that Tenly didn't invite him in and tell him all her dirty little secrets.

But, pondering his feelings on a woman being away from her husband so often does make me wonder how she does it. I'd go stir crazy if Heston was gone that much because I wouldn't feel connected to him and our relationship would suffer from it. We have to be able to have sex. We could be silent all day, but when we slip into bed and into each other's arms, our bodies do all the talking. It's how we communicate.

"Sharing your life with someone is more than just carrying their last name. It's setting the bar for everyone else in your family. You should marry your best friend for passion and the desire to be together as much as possible, nothing else," Flynn adds. I'm jealous of how a buff guy can have such a big heart.

"I can't help but wonder if Tenly is with the hotshot doctor for other reasons," Flynn says.

"Like, what? Money?"

"Or free plastic surgery," Owen mumbles, looking off at the birds flying.

"I don't know if that's true. She wants a kid with him. Then again—that would mean more money," I add, making everyone ponder.

My phone dings.

Heston: I have a surprise!

Curiosity has me place my hand on my collar bone, and anxious.

"I better get going," I tell them.

"Bye, Love!" Flynn hollers. I start walking around their house, the grass tickling my ankles. "You better get this mowed before Tenly sees it."

"I'm not drunk enough for that," Owen teases, but the way his face stays serious, I suddenly don't think he's joking.

Coming around the other side of their place the cold shadow of the murder house swallows me whole, as if the sun doesn't exist in its presence. Gobsmacked, I swallow and stare at it, wondering what exactly happened. Did the wife see it coming? Did the husband make it fast? Now I see why Owen and Flynn haven't mowed on the side of their house, being over here is fucking creepy. Someone special is going to have to move into this house to turn it around for the neighborhood.

"Do you think anyone will move into that house?" I ask out of curiosity.

"Probably not. I mean, not anyone with a conscience. Then again, I didn't think anyone would move into your place." A chill tickles down my spine. Ever since I found out the husband that used to live in my house murdered the man in this very house , I've been paranoid. Like the dark energy that walked through the very hallway I do is still attached and waiting to pounce on my family at any moment.

"Flynn, the new Bridgerton show is on!" Owen snaps his fingers, his face glued to his phone.

Walking across the street and into my house, the cool air-conditioning kisses my skin, soothing away the blistering heat. Taking a deep breath, I await for Heston to rush out with something exciting, but instead he's pacing the living room floor with his phone to his ear. Feeling let down, but hopeful there is something that is going to make me happy I head to the kitchen for a snack, snatching a muffin from the cupboard, I lean over the kitchen island and peel back the paper wrapping, trying to hear what Heston is talking about.

"Yeah, I'm not doing anything." He laughs gleefully, making me raise a brow. I expect a man to sound like that only when he's talking to his mother. Am I actually going to get to meet her?

Pulling the phone away from his ear, he looks to me with bright eyes and smile.

"What?"

"That was my boss. He invited me to play golf." I can't help the detached expression that masks my face. I was not expecting him to say that. I thought he had something romantic planned or was naked ready for a hot quickie. Not kissing ass at his job.

"I didn't know you played." I say with an exhale.

"Uh…I don't really. My dad and I would sometimes on the weekend, but that was it."

Another tidbit about his father—the man who left him as he got older.

"Yeah? Was he any good?" I ask, making conversation. I feel stupid to think he had something planned for us, this whole proposal thing has me distracted.

Heston is silent, my question falling on deaf ears. I don't press him, not wanting to push, but I wish he'd tell me more. Walking to the closet I usually store throw blankets in, he opens it and reaches inside, tugging out a blue Callaway bag. Golf balls fall everywhere. I slightly remember him having a golf bag when he moved in, but must have overlooked it.

Sinking my teeth into my muffin, I watch him pull out his drivers and inspect them.

"I could come with you. Maybe the idea of a family man would make an impression," I offer.

He stands up straight, rubbing his head with one hand, the other on his hip as if he's thinking.

"No, I better do this alone. I have some ass kissing to do. I can't let you be a victim of seeing that."

I laugh, licking my lips.

"All right. I guess Paige and I will order pizza and watch a movie tonight."

He nods, like he's going along with what I'm saying, but not really hearing me. He's nervous, and I find it cute. He really cares about his career, and I can respect that.

He hurries off to our room, and by the time I'm finished eating my muffin, he's standing next to his bag, wearing blue chino pants, a blue-collar shirt, and clean white shoes I've never seen before. He fits the stereotypical golfer perfectly, and I have to keep myself from laughing. On second thought, I'm glad I'm not going. He would probably have me in a plaid skirt and one of those damn hats with a green see-through bill.

Dusting my hands of crumbs, I come around to kiss him goodbye.

"Alright, I think I have everything," he mutters, before looking up at me with a heavy exhale.

Rubbing my hands up his chest and onto his shoulder, I give him a reassuring squeeze and look into his eyes.

"You got this babe, relax." He nods, blowing out another calming breath.

"You're right. I mean, if he's invited me to go golfing with him, it has to be for a good reason. It would be awkward to fire someone on the green then keep playing," he says out loud, like hearing himself say it gives him strength.

"Exactly!" I chirp, trying to do my girlfriend duties.

Leaning in, he presses his lips to mine. His hand slips behind my head, turning a simple goodbye kiss into something passionate. Closing my eyes, I relax into him, his need slipping from his mouth to mine.

"Love you," he whispers, our lips brushing. My chest feels like it's been struck with lightening, the two words that everyone woman lives to hear has just been said.

"I love you too." I've felt that I was falling for him but wasn't sure if it was too soon to say something.

Pulling away, he winks, grabs his bag, and heads out. Lifting my hand, I touch my mouth where we kissed, my lips still wet and tingling. I swear, I'll never get used to his deep kisses.

21

TWO WEEKS LATER

In my studio, I look over a piece I made a week ago, unsure of the eccentric decor on its side. My style isn't normally so outlandish, but I felt like I needed to expand my horizons and do something off-kilter. There are spikes along the top, and deep waves covering the sides. Thinking about the blue green colored I could paint it excite me more than it should.

"Hey, I've got something for you," Heston says. I turn around, finding Heston standing halfway in the doorway in a white button-down and my favorite pair of torn jeans.

"What is it?"

He smiles, and my curiosity piques. Eagerly taking my hand, he leads me down the stairs. All the lights are off, allowing only the glow from dusk to brush into the room.

"Close your eyes," he says, cupping his hands over my face, blocking my view.

"Wait—what are you doing?" I nervously laugh.

Taking a shaky step forward, my hand fumbles, my body longing for the house to whisper where I'm walking. Heston chuckles at my clumsiness, and then the recognizable squeak from the front door opening fills the space right before the heat of the night washes against my skin. His hand remains on my lower back as he guides me where he wants me to go. We walk a few more steps, and my feet feel the familiar cracks of the walkway before we move down the driveway and toward the street, I think.

"Ready?" he asks, his voice smooth as silk. His hands lift from my eyes. With my sight a little blurry, I blink a few times. The neighborhood comes in to view, everyone standing in the street with candles in their hands. Paige stands a few feet in front of them in a white dress, her feet bare, cradling a candle. The ember glow from the flame caresses her face, reflecting in her chocolate eyes. She looks down, and I follow to see what she's looking at.

Will you marry me?

Is written in colorful chalk on the street.

Gasping, my hand snaps up to cover my mouth in surprise. Oh my God!

"Will you marry me, Rain?" he whispers into my ear, the question leaving a trail of goosebumps down my neck. Lifting his hand in front of us, a black box with a shiny princess cut diamond greets me. It's sharp and dazzling, like a siren luring you into matrimony chaos.

"Oh, Heston…" I breathe heavily, my heart beating in my chest so fast, I feel faint. "It's so beautiful." Tears well in my eyes. It's too soon, but it's so beautiful and sweet. I don't know what to say.

"I know how much this neighborhood means to you, so I thought the best way to propose was with the people you care about most, in the place you love most."

Looking at the chalk dusted into the ground, I think about how far Heston and I have come. The way he's blanketed me with his love and protection. The role he's played in Paige's life these short months. I know this is what people do—they fall in love and take the next step—I just hope this doesn't change things between us. That's what happened with Cam and me.

No. Like Owen and Flynn said, if I keep living in the past, that's what my life will always be. I have to move forward. Plus, everyone is out here watching, how could I even ask for time to think about it? Heston makes me happy. He is who I want tucking me in at night and going on adventures with me, for as long as he'll have me.

"Yes," I answer, my impulsiveness making me giddy.

"Really?"

Turning toward him, I nod. "Yes! Yes, I'll marry you!" He pulls me into his arms, kissing me all over my neck and face. I giggle, and he turns us, so we can look at everyone together.

"She said yes!"

They all cheer, clapping hands and whistling as Heston takes my hand in his and places the ring on my finger. It's a little big, but we can worry about that later because I'm not taking it off. Tenly pushes through everyone, her blonde hair in perfect waves, her purple summer dress looking flawless. Beaming, she grabs my hand to look at the ring.

"Oh my God, I'm so excited for you!" She looks up at me, her eyes bright with delight. "You know, if you're looking for a bridesmaid, I have taken on the role with honor six times!"

"Oh, wow!" I laugh.

"Are you excited to plan the wedding? Flowers, cake, your dress?" She becomes giddy. Butterflies nosedive inside my stomach. I have to plan a wedding. I'm actually getting married again, after I said I never would. I look at Heston, who is talking to Owen and Flynn, nerves taking over. Cam's destructive words sear through what's supposed to be a happy moment.

"Nobody will marry you. You should feel lucky I even did!"

"So, what's your last name going to be? I don't think I've heard Heston mention it," Tenly continues, prodding.

Through the roller coaster of emotions, I say, "Um…Thayer."

"Rain Thayer. Interesting." Her grin morphs into a presentable smirk, but I can't overthink what she means by it because…I'm already unraveling where I stand. The fly-by-the-seat-of-my-pants' era is over, and now we make it official. Realization sets in. I'm agreeing to give another person my heart, when I haven't even fully healed from the first time.

I'm terrified of, once again, becoming attached to someone else's life, just so they can fool me and leave me without any friends or family. Cam and I were fine until we signed those damn papers. They're like a bad omen, signing away your soul.

My chest feels tight. I can't breathe through my nose. I open my mouth, pulling in fresh air.

"Mom!" Paige's voice breaks through my PTSD, her cheeks red from the heat, her skin glowing against her ivory sundress. Holding my arms out, she rushes into them and hugs me, and I kiss her on top of the head. "Did you know about this?"

She looks up at me, freckles on her nose like the stars in the sky.

"Yep. He told me this morning."

I rub my thumb over her cheek, and she pulls away. Too much physical contact. I'm embarrassing her, I'm sure.

"So, you're okay with this?" I ask her.

She shrugs, looks at Heston for a second, then back to me.

"I just want you to be happy, Mom. If you're in a good place, we're in a good place, ya know?" She's right. When Cam and I were at our worst, Paige felt it. Seeing me at my best makes her relaxed and content. I'm second-guessing things—which is normal for every couple, even the ones who stay married for life. Having this ring on my finger means I'll never be alone again. I'll always have his love until the day we die. I don't have to worry that a fight will end in a break-up, we'll work it out and move forward.

Everything is going to fine.

We're fine.

"Yeah, I'm starting to." I smile.

22

The next night is uneventful. I find myself sitting on the couch, my legs tucked under me, leaning against the arm, scrolling through social media while listening to Bridgerton in the background. Owen seemed pretty excited about the show, so I thought I'd give it a try. Looking at flowers and wedding dresses on my phone causes a tension headache to form. It's all so overwhelming. The smell of pepper and soap fill the air while Heston takes a shower in our room. I think about joining him, knowing my body craves an orgasm. Standing up and headed that way, tires squeal outside, causing me to freeze and look out the window to see what is going on. Owen stands in the driveway with Flynn peeling away in their blue smart car. Owen throws his hands up and marches back inside, where he slams the door. I don't think I've seen them angry at one another, let alone an actual fight. It must be serious. Sitting back on the couch, I grab my phone and text Owen.

Me: *Everything okay?*

It shows that he's seen it. Time stands still while I wait for him to reply. Maybe I shouldn't have made it so apparent I was spying out the window.

A swoosh sounds, alerting me to his reply.

Owen: Fine. Flynn's being cranky, and me having a soul and feelings conflicts with his emotionless heart.

Light laughter fills my heart at Owen's insufferable need for drama.

Me: *Let me know if I need to bring wine over!*

Owen: ***Save it for Friday when we come over to gush over you and that ring on your finger.***

Raising my left hand, I look at the ring, my stomach still uneasy. I was hoping the nerves would pass and my fear would diminish. They haven't. There's something about that piece of paper that changes people and I don't see why we need it to be together. I can wear the ring, have a small gathering, and be just as happy. But I'm not sure Heston will see it that way. He was already talking about churches and catering last night.

Dropping my phone in my lap, I look at the TV, trying to get my mind off of marriage and everything it entails. I have to watch 'til the end. I need to know what the Duke decides. My phone dings again, and I glance down.

It's Tenly.

I bet she saw Flynn speed off.

Opening her text, my brows furrow.

Tenly: *I went to see what that noise was and saw your daughter with Layla going down the alley between you and the Gradys' house. I didn't know if you knew or if they were being mischievous.*

Mouth parted, I listen for Paige moving around upstairs, but the only thing to be heard is the show I'm watching.

"Paige!" I yell, hoping she replies. Seconds tick by, and

my stomach cramps in frustration. *Please don't be doing anything horrible. I want to trust you.*

Me: *Thanks. I'll look into it.*

Taking the path around the house, I peek between mine and the Gradys' property. A narrow entry creates an alley, where their air conditioning units are. I catch a glimpse of black as Layla tosses her hair over her shoulder. I walk closer, the smell of skunk gets stronger.

Weed.

I know the smell because of the neighbors who lived next to us in our old apartment building. They smoked it every Saturday night at eleven o'clock on the dot. I might dabble in the recreational use from time to time as well, but nobody knows about it. Certainly not Paige.

Walking closer, I finally see Paige. She's in her bright orange crop top and jean shorts. Layla is dressed in her usual black attire with a striped shirt and black jeans that are so ripped, you can see her black fishnets underneath. They couldn't be more opposite. Paige hands Layla something and shakes her head, coughing. Layla laughs and easily takes a puff.

"Excuse me, young ladies!" They both snap their head in my direction, the color draining from their faces. Getting closer, I inspect Layla's hand, smoke creeping between her fingers.

"Hand it over. Now!" I hold my hand out, summoning her to give it to me. Rolling her eyes, she lifts her hand, and I take the rolled-up joint.

"Follow me, ladies." I walk out the alleyway and stop at the edge of their yard. I so want to go to his house, pound on the door, and accuse his daughter of corrupting mine like he did to me when the girls were out drinking. My eyes fall on Paige. She nearly has tears in her eyes. Wait, they could just be bloodshot. Her arms are crossed defiantly, and she won't look at me. As unhappy that I am about her smoking weed, I can punish her myself. I don't need to embarrass her in front of Layla.

"Layla, go home." I jut my head to the side, conveying that I want her to leave.

"What?" she asks, her tone surprised. I'm sure she thought I would drag them both to the front door and tell on them to Layla's father, but for the sake of my daughter starting a new life, I won't.

This time.

"Go home before I change my mind!" Narrowing my eyes, she turns abruptly, nearly tripping on her own two feet as she rushes away.

I turn my head, and Paige's eyes finally meet mine.

"Your dad is going to have both our heads." I sigh deeply. "Go to the house." She marches away, with one heck of a chip on her shoulder. That teenage rebellion seeding through her and making its grand bloom.

Once inside, I slam the door. Heston shoots up off the couch, his face alarmed.

"What's wrong?"

"Paige was smoking weed with our lovely neighbor, Layla," I inform him, not sure what to do. I don't think it's good for her to be smoking at such a young age, but everyone swears by its medicinal use.

"Where did you even get this?" I demand.

"It doesn't matter, okay!" she yells back. Her mouth is wrong. Her attitude is wrong. She's so grounded!

Heston stands and comes over to me and Paige, staring at her with a thousand swords in his eyes.

"Does this family mean so little to you that you think you

can run around doing trashy things like this?" he shouts, while Paige looks the other way.

"Answer me!" He grabs her by the chin, forcing her to look at him. Her face turns red, eyes welling with tears.

"Heston, let her go!" I hiss, shocked he would ever dare touch her.

Paige grabs him by the wrist and shoves out of his hold.

"You're not my father!" Turning, she stomps up the stairs, and I look at Heston, wondering what the hell he was thinking.

"You don't have the right to put your hands on her." My voice cracks with emotion, the familiar ache in my chest from when I was with Cam, rearing its dark head.

"Someone needs to teach that kid discipline. You obviously don't." He raises a brow, accusing me of not punishing her to his standards. "Think about that," he clips before opening the front door and slamming it behind him.

Hot tears slide down my cheeks. I knew Heston had a temper—we all do—but his is darker, more ominous, and seems to peeking its head out of the shadows more and more.

Feeling the weight of the world on my shoulders, I climb the stairs with a heavy heart. I knock on Paige's door then open it. She's sprawled across her bed, lying on her stomach, her feet kicked up behind her. Her face red, eyes glossy, she stares at her phone, ignoring me. Closing the door behind me, I step over a pile of clothes and sit at the end of her bed. The moon filters through the curtains, lighting up the room in glowing streaks. I place my hand on her back, her shirt damp with sweat, the smell of weed reeking from her clothes. I want to ground her, yell at her some more, until we both break down and talk about it, but Heston grabbing her like that…I don't know what to say or do.

"Babe, talk to me."

She doesn't respond.

"I'm sorry about what Heston did. It wasn't right."

"You think?" She sniffles, and I can't help but wonder what my mother would have done if she'd caught me smoking weed at thirteen. Maybe she'd have beat my ass. Then again, she was the chill artsy type and would probably join in. It's hard to tell what she'd do.

"Whose weed was it? Where did you two get it?"

"She had it. I don't know."

"Okay, well that's a big no. You don't know this girl well enough to take drugs from her. What if it was laced with something?"

"We got it from a guy on the next block, so she didn't really know either."

"I thought you said you didn't know who she got it from?" My voice rises, catching her in a lie.

"I panicked! I didn't want her to get in trouble."

My brows hit my hairline. Two girls out causing trouble and experimenting together. "So, who is this guy?"

"I don't know, just some guy!" She sucks in a sharp breath, her tone on the edge of hysterical.

Scooting back, she sits up, wraps her arms around her knees, and rests her chin on top of them.

"And I know Layla. I trust her." She stares blankly ahead. "I talk to her every day, whether it be on the phone or at her house." I guess I've been so deep in mine and Heston's quarrels, I didn't even know about her and Layla's friendship together.

I reach for her, grab her shoulders, and pull her into my

lap. My fingers undoing her ribbons, then redoing her Dutch braids.

"You're reaching that age where you want to do things—"

"Mom, that's not—"

"Let me finish. What I'm saying is, we aren't always going to see eye to eye, but I want you to tell me things, to talk to me, to promise to never hate me when I have to be strict with you." I want to be her friend, but I have to be her mom first. It's going to be hard to define that line. But if she's not honest with me, I can't protect her.

"Mom, I would never hate you," she mumbles, as if the notion is ridiculous. "Are you disappointed in me?" she asks.

My head instantly shakes no before I can form the words.

"Honey, I'm not disappointed. I just want you to be safe." My words are dipped in understanding, needing her to know I have no intention of being the bad guy, but sometimes, I'm going to piss her off if it means keeping her safe.

Done with her braids, I kiss the top of her and stand. "You're still grounded, though."

She scoffs, looking up at me with angry eyes.

"Mom!"

"Now, go take a shower. You smell like a skunk." I ignore her outburst, gaining an eye-roll.

The front door slams. Heston is back.

"Might want to make sure your new husband is okay," she sneers, and my lips thin with frustration over the entire situation. I open then close her door behind me. I might baby Paige, but I don't agree with putting my hands on her like Heston did. Heston is to be my husband and that means we'll have to parent Paige together. We'll have to come to an agreement on how to do that moving forward. Because physical discipline is not an option!

Heading down the stairs, my hand sliding along the rail, I

can hear him in the kitchen opening drawers and cabinets. Rounding the foyer, I spot him behind the kitchen island, his face and chest sweaty as if he just went for a run. Placing his hands on the granite, he slowly lifts his head until our eyes lock.

"I'm sorry," he grovels. Exhaling, I drop my arms and walk through the living room until I reach the other side of the kitchen island.

"What made you think that was okay?" I assert, my nostrils flaring. His silence pushes me to continue, "You need to remind yourself that you aren't her father!" I slap my hand on the granite, but he doesn't even blink. In fact, he seems unfazed by my anger.

"Got it." His monotone makes me sigh. Pressing my elbows on top of the counter, I reach for his hand and hold it.

"Just, don't do it again, Heston. She's going to test you, us. That's what kids do and it's up to us to keep a clear mind and redirect. We're partners and when one of us gets too frustrated then the other needs to step in."

Lowering his head, we stand in silence for a few seconds before he looks back up at me.

"You're right. I just don't want the neighborhood painting Paige in a bad image when I know how amazing of a kid she is. Kids need discipline. They have to have it to become civilized individuals."

His hand squeezes mine, and I look up at him.

"I love you." He smiles.

My grin freezes on my lips, the corners of my mouth turning down and I façade a smile. He keeps saying he loves me while hurting me over and over. A game of chess played by the devil that I'll never win.

23

A FEW DAYS LATER

"Love you!" I kiss Paige's head, and she runs off toward her dad's truck at the end of the driveway. My eyes lock on Cam's, the tension buzzing in the air between us. Breaking my stare, I turn around and head back inside, the sound of Cam's truck filling the small space between the houses as he drives away. Shutting the door behind me, Heston claps his hands, then rubs them together, looking over the spread he created on the kitchen island. Pepperoni, ham, four different sliced cheeses, and crackers. Simple but amazing. A lot of people asked about the wedding date and wanted to see the ring, so we thought a get-together to hang out would be perfect, so we invited all of our neighbors over, including Layla's mother, Melanie. I don't think she'll come though; she stays inside with the twins every day. I know nothing about her beside the fact that she cleans, cooks, and tends to four children.

"It looks good. You did amazing." I wrap my arms around him, and he kisses the top of my head, his hand rubbing along my bare back, the dark blue romper leaving the skin exposed.

The doorbell rings, and I pull away from him to greet our guests.

"Hey!" Tenly beams, her arms open wide for a hug.

Laughing at how excited she is, I accept her embrace, then we both head inside.

She instantly spots the food. "This looks so yummy, guys!"

"It was all Heston. If it had been left to me, we'd be having chips and store-bought cookies."

"Mmm, I bet." She tries to act as if she's simply agreeing with me, but there's more behind her words. A shadow of criticism. I'm starting to see why Owen always wants to fight with her. "You know what? I have a girlfriend who does these for her Instagram. She always adds a piece of fruit to the spread to give it a burst of color!" She flicks her fingers out like she's miming an explosion.

I place my hands in my pockets, and Heston's eyes lock on mine, silently conveying that he wants to tell Tenly to fuck off but won't.

The door opens, and Owen and Flynn's voices fill the house. Owen, in his white shirt with a salmon-colored sweater over his shoulders, steals the attention from Flynn, who is more casually dressed in a green button-up and dark blue jeans, his loafers as clean as can be. They both carry a bottle of wine, still arguing over which one should be brought to the get-together.

"Hey guys!" I attempt to interrupt. Owen finally looks at me and smiles joyfully.

"Honey! I brought you some red wine!" He does a little dance, his demeanor doing a 180.

"I brought white because of the occasion," Flynn adds, gaining an eye roll from Owen.

"You guys, thank you. Bringing two bottles means I get to

drink more!" I joke, hoping to lighten the mood. Heston takes both bottles and places them next to the spread.

"Tenly, nice to see you." Owen purses his lips.

"Mmm, same," Tenly says quietly. "Oh, Owen, while I have you here, you need to limit your bird feeders down to one."

"What do you mean? We've had four bird feeders for months," Owen snaps, his cheeks turning red.

"According to the HOA, they're bringing in unwanted guests like squirrels and raccoons—like I said they were," she presses, and I cringe inwardly. Why is she doing this now?

"You can tell the HOA, they can kiss my—"

"Thanks, Tenly. We'll figure something out," Flynn interrupts, stepping between them, motioning for Owen to let it be.

"So, Rain, I heard you invited Melanie Grady to this little shindig." Resting one arm on the counter, her sharp brow raised, Tenly says, "I've invited her to every event. I can tell you now, she never attends."

"How come?" I get that she's a busy mom, but the idea that she doesn't ever come to a celebration is perturbing. Is something wrong with her? Does she not like it here?

She scoffs, taking the glass of wine Heston just poured. "I think she has some illness or something."

"I think she's pregnant again," Flynn says.

"Pregnant?" I ask, turning toward him, alarmed at the thought of Melanie having another baby when she already has her hands full.

"Enough about Melanie, let me see that rock again," Owen says with a growl, like we're looking at hot men parading around my finger. I hold my hand out, and he lifts it, inspecting my ring with one eye.

"Damn, that's pretty. You did good, Heston."

Tenly walks over and takes my hand, turning it left and right.

"It looks too big. Does it fit?"

My eyes snap to Heston. He looks back at me with worry riding the tide of his ocean blue eyes.

"Is it okay?" he asks nervously, grabbing my hand to inspect it. I didn't want to say anything because I know he worked hard picking it out and the little wiggle room is fine.

I open my mouth to say just that when Owen cuts in, "Girl, after he knocks you up with three kids, it'll fit fine." At a loss of words, I just stand in front of them with my mouth wide open.

Flynn laughs, and I can't help but join in. Slowly pulling my hand from Heston's, I place it on his shoulder.

"Oooh, are you guys going to try?" Tenly asks, rubbing her chest, her bright eyes looking between me and Heston. It kills me. She wants to be a mom so badly, and every cycle that passes, still no positive test.

"Um…it's come up, but we haven't really said we're ready for that," I sputter out. Looking at Heston, who is staring back at me, we both silently watch for each other's reaction. I stay silent and hope he can tell them better than I that us conceiving is not in God's plan.

"I wouldn't mind a few extra kiddos running around," Heston tells the group, and my eyes widen. I can't have kids, I've told him that! Does he want to have a baby and he's stayed silent this whole time? Besides, we can't even agree on how to raise Paige, how the hell would we be with a baby?

"So, Tenly, how's everything for the block party going?" Flynn asks, and I'm thankful for the change in subject.

"Great. I think Asher is going to be able to make it!" Her face glows, talking about her husband.

"Yes! That would make it that much sweeter!" Owen

starts to fangirl, and I catch Heston quietly slipping off into the other room. I wonder if he's okay. Did I say something wrong about having babies? Ridding my head of the thoughts, I tell myself he's just going to the bathroom and it's not him running away. We're engaged now; he's proven he's here with me and in it for the long haul. I should go join him in the bathroom. I'm not saying sex will fix whatever is going on, but it will calm me down. Plus, everyone being here is reckless and even more of a turn on.

A loud rumble from outside silents Owen and Tenly's chatter, all of us looking to the windows to catch a glimpse of what's making that unfamiliar sound.

"Is that a motorcycle?" Flynn asks, perking up in excitement.

"Nobody has a motorcycle I know of," Owen says, a confused look on his face. Flynn opens the door and walks out. Owen and Tenly follow, and I lag behind. A matte black Harley follows a moving truck, the rider's, whose long black hair flows freely behind him, is wearing jeans and a black tank that shows off his dark tan skin and his tattooed-covered arms.

"Looks like someone's moving into the murder house," Owen mumbles.

"You think he knows about the killings?" I ask.

"He has to, they have to tell him before he buys it," Tenly adds.

"Maybe he's into that sorta thing." Owen lifts his chin, crossing his arms. Two things pop into my head, devil-worshipper or one of those people who investigate haunted houses.

Two movers get out of the truck as the guy on the Harley pulls in behind it, shuts the bike off and dismounts, before walking over to talk to them. Tenly looks down the street where he came from, and I raise a brow.

"Is it just him? Where's his family?" Tenly questions.

"I think it's just…him," Flynn says. A single guy who looks like that buying a house in the suburbs? Why?

"I don't like that. This is where you raise families." Tenly shakes her head.

"Oh, I'm sure he's willing to make babies," Owen flirts. I laugh, and Flynn rolls his eyes.

"Right, because murder houses scream American dream," I jab. Owen laughs and glances over his shoulder at me, his face telling me *good one*.

"What's going on?" Heston asks, coming outside.

I gesture toward the end of the road, where all the commotion is. "Someone's moving in."

He looks around me, his face hardening, sharp eyes darting back to me.

"What?" I ask, curious as to what has him so irked all of a sudden.

"Thanks for coming, everyone," Heston dismisses, and my brows rise to my hairline.

"Wait—what? What are you doing?" I whisper to Heston, embarrassment flushing my cheeks. He snatches my hand, retreating backward. Ignoring my question.

"Heston, tell me what is going on!" I demand, my nostrils flaring. This is supposed to be our party, to celebrate us. Why is he's suddenly ending it?

"I said it's over!" He snarls, but in a whisper, so only I can hear it. His eyes piercing with anger, making my breath hitch in my throat.

"Already? The party is just getting started!" Tenly objects, her eyes now on us.

"Yeah, I'm not feeling well," he lies, and I blink slowly.

This is actually happening; he's ending the party without even telling me why.

"Um…yeah, thanks for coming, you guys." I follow his lead, my voice laced with confusion. We were having a good time, what the hell happened? Heston tugs me inside, slamming the door behind us.

"What is going—?"

He grabs me by the shoulders and presses me against the back of the door.

"Really? Everyone is here to celebrate our engagement and I can't even leave the room for five minutes without you gawking at another man from the front lawn?"

My mouth drops open, but nothing comes out, shock and surprise swallowing every word I want to say. I finally force myself to say something. "W-We were all looking Heston, it was a new neighbor." My voice wavers, on the edge of an emotional break down.

"You're taking my last name, and I forbid you to smear it with slutty behavior," he sneers, his words stabbing me in the chest, allowing my heart to fall onto the floor.

"Excuse me? How dare you—"

His open palm smacks across my cheek, and my head snaps to the side, my hand instantly raising to cover the spot that was hit.

"Dammit, Rain." He rubs his neck, regret pinching his features. Placing his hand on my now red cheek, he cradles my head. "I'm sorry. It's just…you mean so much to me. The thought of losing you is too much to bear."

I stare ahead, my eyes on my mother's urn. She saw everything, and I would do anything to hear what she had to say. To have her comfort and wisdom, when clearly my mind is at war with my heart when it comes to Heston and me.

"Do you accept my apology?" He steps into my view, and

I finally look back at him, blinking. All I see is Cam's face, yelling at me and raising his hand up like he's going to slap me if I don't answer fast enough. Closing my eyes, I will the image to disappear. Why is this happening again? Why am I with another guy who hits? Heston is so sweet and gentle, I can't help that the problem is me. I'm unraveling him, making him let a monster rise.

"Rain?" Heston waves a hand in front of my face, breaking me from my thoughts. The pain in my face fuels my anger, as I pinch my lips and cast a glare in his direction.

No, this will not happen again. I will not alter who I am and what I do just to please a man. Adrenaline rushing through my veins, I shove him away from me.

"No, I don't. Get out!" I point to the door, tears streaming down my face because I want to slam my knuckles into his face, but it will only make this worse, and possibly dangerous.

"Rain, come on, you're being crazy." He holds his hands out as if he doesn't understand why I'm angry. Opening the door myself, I grab him by the shirt and begin to tug him in the direction of the doorway. He plants his feet and won't budge. Using my backside and knees, I shove with all my might, wanting him out of my sight and out of my house right now, but he doesn't go.

Screaming at him, I give up and step away from him.

"Get out!"

He's looking at me like I'm a crazy person and it douses my anger and makes me question what if I really am losing my shit. I don't even recognize myself anymore. I'm losing my mind.

I step past him, my legs wobbly and my heart broken. I walk down the hall to our room in a stupor, my stomach queasy, thinking about what just happened. My hand trails the

24

"Good morning, beautiful." Heston's soft voice wakes me up. He didn't sleep in our bed last night, but he obviously didn't go far. The day before comes into mind, and all I want to do is hide. He stands beside the bed, my favorite cup in his hand. Sitting up, I take it, the smell of the delicious hot brew invigorating my senses.

He smiles, but it doesn't quiet reach his eyes, our fight lingering between us.

"I'm not going anywhere, Rain." My head looks up from coffee, our eyes meeting. He promises he won't go anywhere and that seeds through my heart blooming in comfort. I never want to be alone again, but I'm pushing him away. Should I work this out with him? Am I going overboard over one slap? "You said you would marry me and that means we are together forever." That last word battles what I was thinking seconds ago. He doesn't sound romantic and passionate. He sounds like a madman. That no matter how dark it gets, we are bound to one another even if we're only engaged.

Sitting down beside me, he grabs my hand and places it in

his, interlocking our fingers. My brows furrow at the contact. All I see is my hand entwined with the one that hit me.

Lifting our linked palms, he kisses my knuckles, peering up at me, his eyes kind, remorseful.

"I'm so sorry about yesterday," he whispers softly. I inhale a harsh breath. his small step into apologizing causing me to inhale. I want him to be sorry, but there is something in me that won't forget what happened. No matter what he does. What happened, happened.

"I really think we need some time apart, Heston," is all I can muster. All of the dark moments Heston has showed here and there are coming together, and I don't know how much worse he'll get.

"No," he clips, and tears fill my eyes.

"I've never done that before, hit somebody I'm with. You just do something to me, Rain. You and Paige are my life. The thought of losing you undoes me," he explains, my emotions battling a sea of anger and love. The urge to be angry at him swims against a current of affection. All the times we laughed, touched, simply laid next to each other and heard one another breathe and exist, reminding me how much I love him. I swear I have a gift making men into monsters because Heston was anything but not a bad man when we got together.

"My mother hit me a lot. Even as an adult, she would put her hands on me if she felt moved to do so. I always swore I'd never be like her, but here I am." He stares blankly ahead as he mentally revisits the painful memories. This bit of information about his mother is new to me, pushing me into thinking about a little boy with blond hair getting smacked around by a grown woman. It tugs at my heart strings, and I feel bad for him, but I can't help but be concerned this will happen again. This is how it started with Cam, a smack or push here, until I started wearing bruises and excuses as my daily outfit.

"Hmm," I softly say to him, and his eyes snap to mine. I don't want to show him I feel bad for him, to encourage him that his behavior is justified. I don't know, maybe he's right about sticking it out, my being so quick to run away from our problems isn't how relationships work. I've read he is my better half and I am his.. That's how we become a whole. Closing my eyes, my mind screams that this is bullshit and I need to demand him to leave but I know he won't go. Literally he won't leave. His words ammo to my anger. I want to work things out; I do, but I'm scared. I'm scared he'll he hit me or Paige, but I'm also terrified of being alone. I come with baggage and he's dealt with mine. I should deal with his, right? It sounds like Heston has PTSD, maybe some therapy would help. Thinking about being rational versus headstrong, I fixate on the glass end table, the top scratched from drinks, phone cords, and the lamp being shuffled back and forth along it.

"I want you to go to therapy," I finally say, sniffling back the snot and looking at him. "Or couples therapy even."

"Therapy?" he scoffs, as if I just asked him to see a witch doctor.

"Yeah, if what you're telling me about your mother hitting you is true then you are suffering from something deeper than you and I can fix."

His shoulders lift and he rubs his chin in thought.

"If it means I get to keep you then yes."

A sigh escapes my mouth and my whole body feels lighter, a weight lifted from my shoulders. The feeling making me dizzy. It seems I'm either angry to the point of no return or overly excited with this man. Is he making me this way? Is he making me crazy or have I always been this way?

"What did Owen say about it? Did he tell you to leave me?" He assumes I already texted Owen and Flynn about what happened, but I haven't.

"I didn't tell him, actually. It's not a light I want to paint us in. I'm embarrassed and even more humiliated about the entire situation, Heston. Also, Owen would come over here with a wine bottle and beat the shit out of you." I raise a brow in his direction, and he nods, knowing it's true.

His Adam's apple bobs.

"I think it's for the best. Owen gossips too much. The entire block would think I beat you within an inch of needing an ambulance." The way he says that unsettles me, it comes out so easy and without concern. He looks up and smiles, my apprehension lifting.

He's right; Owen is a drama queen. Which is one of the many reasons he's my best friend, but I don't want everyone looking at Heston and me and trying to fix us. The therapist will tell us one thing and then the neighbors will give their two cents, which may cause us to derail before we even have a chance to fix things. It occurs to me that I might care about what the neighbors will think of me too. I've been doing that since I moved here. I might love the houses, the freedom, and the companionship, but I've been living my life by the book of living in the suburbs and not how I truly want. I want to check my mail in my pajama's and make a sculpture for my yard. Things I couldn't have in the city, but could have here if I just stop thinking what people would think of me.

"How do you feel now?" Reaching forward, he tucks a piece of hair behind my ear, and I flinch. Our eyes lock.

"You don't trust me?" Disappointment is thick in his voice. My trust in him was slapped out of me yesterday and I don't know if he can gain it back. Do I want to trust him again?

"Can you blame me?" Silence falls between us for a few seconds that seem like hours.

"No, not at all. I'll show you that you can depend on me, Rain." He promises and it makes my bottom lip tremble with emotion. Wanting to change the subject and move on with the day, I ask, "What do you want to do today?"

His eyes take on a deeper shade of blue. "You," he replies, and I swallow, crossing my legs at the knees.

"I'm on my period," I lie, and he exhales.

"Really?"

I nod, and he stands up from the bed. "When is Paige coming home?"

"Noon. That's what Cam said anyway." I roll over and reach for my phone to see what time it is. Eleven.

"I'll wait until she gets home before going to work then," he informs, his tone casual, as if we're magically fixed. Heston steps into the bathroom, and I raise my hand, looking at the ring on my finger. I still want to get married, but I also don't. He's convinced me it's the thing to do—people fall in love and get married—but the conviction is missing. The belief that it's really what we need as a couple is not quite there, and after what happened yesterday, I want to run far away from any altar.

The faucet turns off, and Heston comes out, wiping his face with a blue towel.

"You like it?" he asks.

I glance at him, then back to the ring, knowing what I'm about to say might be the end of us. "I think we should wait." The words come out softer than I intend. I hoped to be strong and confident when telling him.

"What?"

Dropping my hand, I sit up on my elbows and look at him.

"I don't like the idea of getting married right now. It's too soon. We have so much to learn about each other. And besides, it's just a piece of paper. It doesn't change anything between us." He swallows, looking at anything but me.

"You're saying you don't want to be with me anymore, Rain?"

"No, I'm not saying that. I just don't want to marry you. I mean—look at us!" My voice rises, along with the pounding in my temple. Adrenaline shoots through my veins at such a high rate, my heart can't keep up.

He slides his hand through his hair, slicking it back. His eyes cast down to the floor, and I bite my bottom lip.

"You aren't even going to give my going to therapy a chance?" His words hit me in the chest, and I feel bad. "After you have been going for a while, let's see where we are. Maybe without the added pressure, we can get back to where we were and move forward."

Without another word, he opens the dresser drawer, pulls out the ring box, and tosses it on the bed next to me, before walking out of the room.

Pulling the ring off my hand, I take one last look before placing it snugly back inside. Why do I feel like the jackass here?

25

Drying my hair from the shower, I walk into the living room. The TV is on, the blinds open, and Heston is standing at the kitchen island with a piece of toast. He glances at me, tension and fresh-cut pain filling the space between us. I sit on the couch and pull my legs up beneath me. I want to say something, to try to smooth things over, but it's a weight hovering above me I can't get out from under. Maybe this is it for us. And if it is, I definitely chose the right path. If we truly love each other, this shouldn't set us back that much.

Cam's muffler sounds from the driveway, and I stand up. My eyes lock with Heston's for a split second before I look away and go to open the door. I lean against the jamb, crossing my arms, watching Paige get out of her dad's truck. Her eyes are red-rimmed like she's been crying. When she sees me, she quickly looks down. Her usual happy-to-see-me look isn't there, instead it's replaced with one of sorrow. Instantly, I look at Cam for an explanation. He doesn't look any better. His face is red, shoulders tense, hands clenched in fists.

"What is going on?" I finally ask.

"Where is he?" Cam barks, stomping up the walkway.

"What is going—?"

"Who the fuck does he think he is putting his hands on my daughter!" he yells loud enough for Heston to hear. I press my hands against his chest, pushing him back, playing referee once again.

"Do you mind?" I hiss. He finally looks down at me, that look of darkness I know so well deeper than ever.

"I heard you're marrying this prick. What do you even know about him?" Cam tries to push past me again, and I grab his arm, trying to keep him from barreling through me but he's stronger than I remember.

"Will you please knock it off!"

"Did he hit you? Has he put his hands on you, Rain?" Cam's eyes widen, his sudden urge to protect me baffling. I open my mouth to reply, but nothing comes out.

"What's going on?" Heston asks, walking out to stand beside me.

I become rigid, my muscles tensing. "Heston, I have it handled."

"You put your hands on my daughter again, I'll fucking kill you!" Cam jabs his index finger in the air as if shooting a bullet.

Heston juts his chin, making direct eye contact with Cam, as if he's ready for a challenge. And that look alone stirs something in me that makes my stomach feel sour.

"She needed discipline—something this family lacks because there's been no man to take care of them."

My mouth drops open at Heston's words.

"You motherfuck—" Cam pushes past me, throwing himself at Heston, fists first. The sound of knuckles hitting bone is so loud, I'm sure the whole neighborhood heard it.

Snapping out of my shock, I run after them, both now on the floor in the house, throwing punch after punch.

"You guys, stop!" Paige hollers, tears streaming down her face.

Stepping over Cam's legs, I grab him by the hair and pull him back before he kills Heston.

Cam roars and falls back on his ass, causing me to fall into the doorway. Frustration and pain squeeze at my chest, making me feel like I can't breathe. I'm fed up with this shit. I can't take it anymore!

"Get out, Cam," I heave, out of breath. He stands on wobbly legs and points to Heston.

"Something ain't right with him, and I'm going to find out what it is," he promises, his tone wrapped in thorns.

"Cam, go!" I scream, my eyes swollen from tears.

Glancing at me one last time, he turns and stomps back to his truck. His motor revs, and he acts like a jackass pulling out onto the street.

Heston stands, dusts off his hands from the dirt, and turns his attention to Paige.

"You're stepping on the flowers." His tone is light and airy, instead of irritable and angry. It's completely abnormal, considering what just happened.

Her face pulls down, tears streaming down her cheeks. She turns red, trying to keep it together, but sobs wrack her chest. Heston thumbs his bleeding lip and walks into the kitchen. He's calm and quiet, like what just took place didn't happen. It's scaring the shit out of me. Is he bipolar?

I push myself up and straighten my shirt. Heston is…off.

Whistling, he walks around the island and grabs his briefcase by the couch. Paige shuffles back as he walks toward us, and I just stare, like I'm watching a monster climb out from under my bed and make himself at home. Stopping in front of me before he walks out, he kisses me on the forehead.

"I'll be home soon."

After he leaves, I look at Paige. She stands frozen. I can't possibly yell at her for telling her dad what happened. He deserved to know. I didn't tell him because I knew this would happen.

"Come on, honey. Let's get you settled." With my hand on her lower back, I usher her to upstairs.

Stepping into her room, she sits on her bed, her eyes swollen and red.

"Mom, I'm so sorry. I didn't know Dad was going to do that!"

"What did you tell him?"

"That I got in trouble and Heston grabbed my face and told me not to disgrace the family."

Sighing, I sit next to her, placing my hand on my cheekbone. I wonder what Cam would have done if he knew what happened yesterday. Wait, why do I care about that?

He and I may not see eye to eye, but we share something that pulls us together and makes us care about one another to a point, I suppose. We may not be together, but he will always see Paige and me as his; he always has and always will. When we were together and someone disrespected me, he would make a scene and even hurt whoever said or did something, which made him a hypocrite because he hit me behind closed doors.

After talking with Paige, I walk back outside to inspect my flowers that got trampled. They look rough, the bright pink petals already dark and trying to close. Squatting down, I hold one in my hand. Poor things. Something moves out of the corner of my eye and my head snaps upright. It's Tenly. She's wearing a white summer dress and sandals, and her is hair down. I don't think I've seen her wear anything outside of athletic gear. I notice she's carrying a pan of food in her hands, walking down the road in the direction of our new neighbor. I squat back down, like I'm looking at my flowers, but I keep a watchful eye. She's now at his door knocking. When he opens the door, my eyes widen in awe. He's shirt-less, wearing shorts that sit just below his hips, showing off that V thing healthy men have. His big frame fills the doorway.

He smiles and nods, taking the plate. Tenly twirls her hair around a finger and looks down at her feet. That's a first. Shoving his door open wider, Tenly walks past him into the house. As he moves to close it behind her, his head snaps up, and our eyes meet. I hold my breath, snapping my attention back to my flowers. I'm breathless, flustered even, not knowing if I should play with my flowers, go inside, or text Owen. The man has moved into the house of horror and has every woman on the block ready to sin.

26

THREE DAYS LATER

Laying in my bed, I look at the dark ceiling, the moon blanketing the room in a low light. Heston sleeps beside me, letting out a little snore every few minutes. Things have changed drastically between us the last three days. I don't know if it's because I called off the engagement or because I suggested therapy, but we haven't had sex or held hands, and there's a negative energy hanging between us. The kind that brews in the sky right before a hurricane. I don't know what we're trying to salvage at this point; it's clear we're done. This is over and one of us is going to have to admit it. Knowing him, it'll have to be me. Huffing, I stand up and walk to the window, my eyes sweep the moon and the houses that sleep at four in the morning. The murder house lights turn on, catching my attention, so I cross my arms and watch. A woman with dark hair rushes out the front door in a small top and jean shorts. Getting into a yellow beetle, she leaves with the headlights turned off. That car looks familiar. I've seen it in the neighborhood. He's been here days and already sleeping his way through the neighborhood. I can't help but wonder how he's living in that house?

Maybe I should introduce myself? I'm drawn to this man, curious about him more than I should be. I've come to notice an increase in my pulse just thinking about him. I want, no, I need, to know more about him.

Next Morning

Grabbing my robe, I throw it around me and go in search of coffee. Feet stomping down the stairs causes me to stop and look up. Paige is coming down with her phone in hand, not paying any attention. Sensing me, she finally picks her head up. "Hey, Mom, Layla's brother just got home from college and their family is having a BBQ. Can I go?"

"Uh…you're grounded—and you and Layla can't be alone together." I pull my robe tighter.

She rolls her eyes.

"Oh my God, please! I'm so bored!" Her right foot does a light stomp. "Her parents are going to be there."

Biting my bottom lip, I stare at her, thinking. It has been really rough around here lately, and her getting out would be good for her, but Layla is a kid on the road to self-destruction and Paige is riding shotgun. And I can't let that happen.

"I need to talk to Layla's mother and make sure she's okay with babysitting you."

Paige texts Layla, asking for her mother's number and reads it off to me.

"No, I want to meet her, Paige," I clarify and she snaps her head up with a pale color taking over her glowing face.

"Mom, no." Her voice is soft and filled with embarrassment.

"Yes, I haven't met her and would like to." I turn around

to get dressed, leaving Paige staring at me with a gaping mouth.

Dressing in a simple shirt and shorts, I walk over to their house with Paige in tow.

Pointing at her, I say, "I swear Paige if you do anything stupid!"

"I won't!" She groans.

Their front yard is bare of any character or personality, a sun-faded basketball lying next to a small tree that has no leaves.

Stepping up to their house, it's quiet, no sounds of kids playing or the TV blaring. The smell of bacon still fills the air from what I can only guess was for breakfast. Knocking, I step back and cross my arms. I glance over at Paige, who purses her lips, not thrilled with me coming over.

The door swings open and there she is, Melanie Grady. She's wearing a loose shirt and sweatpants, her dark hair pulled into a messy ponytail. Despite her lazy attire, she's pretty, her face clear of any blemishes, her eyes wide and beautiful.

"Hello?" She acts as if she doesn't know me, which I find odd, seeing as how the whole block is always peeking out of their blinds. Maybe she's just putting on a front and acting like she hasn't seen me walking around because it would come off creepy.

"Hi, I'm Rain, Paige's mom." Smiling, I look to my daughter and then back to her.

"Oh, hello!" Her face brightens, a smile that hits her eyes. She goes quiet, which I find slightly awkward. I can tell she's not used to talking to people or entertaining guests.

"Paige said something about a BBQ?" I press for her to talk to me.

"Oh yes, we would love to have her!" She nods, crossing her arms, not saying anything else.

"Just make sure to keep an eye on her, she can be trouble sometimes." I laugh, trying to imply I'm joking, but I'm not.

"If she's anything like our Layla, I bet, but she'll be in good hands." She tucks a stray hair from her face behind her ear, and shifts her weight onto her left leg, clearing a space for me to see into the house. It's a mess with toys, juice boxes and furniture covered in kid blankets.

"Perfect," I reply. Hopefully my threat to Paige will keep her ass in check, because I'm not sure Melanie can handle her rogue moments.

"Come dear, the twins are almost up from their nap." She waves Paige inside, and I get the feeling she's ready to end this conversation. This is way more socializing than she's used to if Tenly is right about Melanie never leaving her house.

"Alright, have fun!"

Going back home, I rub the sleep from my eyes, remembering I haven't had my coffee yet. Inside, I find Heston standing in the kitchen. I thought he was long gone for work; I didn't even notice his truck.

"Are we really going to let her go over there?" he asks, without looking up. Something bitter inside me wants to say, "We? You mean, am I? She's my daughter," but I don't.

"I know it's probably not the smartest thing, but she'll be with Layla's parents, how much trouble can they get in?" I'm just trying to pick my battles with her at this point. All the fighting and anger is exhausting.

"Has Cam followed up with his detective work to figure out who I am?" The sarcasm is clear in his voice.

"Not today," I mutter. "Last I heard, he was talking to one of his cop buddies about looking you up." Cam is serious about finding skeletons in Heston's closet, but luckily, he's found none so far.

"The man's insane," he casually implies, not seeming affected by the fact Cam is trying to tear him apart any way he can. Speaking of insane.

"How's it going looking for a therapist?"

"I gotta go show a house, be home for dinner," he says, ignoring my question and pouring out the rest of his coffee. I can't help the sigh that leaves my body. I really wanted to talk about our relationship today, but of course, he's leaving. It's like he knows what I'm going to say and is avoiding it as much as he can. He doesn't stop to tell me he loves me or give me a kiss on his way out the door. We're practically roommates at this point. My phone dings in my hand, with a text from Owen.

Owen: Met the new neighbor. Tenly beat us there, of course. He is BIG, girl. I haven't seen anything like him around here.

Biting my bottom lip, I can't help the longing inside me, whispering for me to go see what the big deal is with this guy. I know Heston would get jealous if he found out; he doesn't seem to have a high regard for the man. But he's not home, and I could use some fresh conversation. I never got to invite someone to a neighborhood before, and I'd like to do just that. I'm also curious why he's living in a place known as the Murder House. Where's his family? What's his name? He's just not the type of person you'd expect to see in such a place. He definitely stands out in this picture-perfect suburbs. But what should I bring him, everyone brings something when someone moves in.

Texting Owen, I ask what he brought.

Owen: *A plant. We were out of wine.*

With a smile on my face, I put my phone back down and turn around to look through the cabinets. A fluttery feeling in my stomach just thinking about going over there. A feeling in my heart, telling me not to go over there, but my head is telling me something else. I'm riding on impulse and tingles, which often means this is risky or not the right thing to do, but somewhere inside of me I just don't care.

Chewing on my inner cheek, I search through the kitchen for something nice to give him. I'm definitely not cooking, so I need to see what else I have around here. Surfing through another shelf, I find a mason jar with a yellow ribbon tied around the top: a jar of honey. I got it at the farmers' market last week, from a local farm. A chunk of comb swims in a thick golden nectar, and just looking at it makes my mouth water.

Settled on what to bring, I go in search for something to wear. I don't want to show up in my robe. I mean, I'm not going to dress up or anything, just something casual because I'm just being a nosey and welcoming neighbor, nothing more.

I change into jean shorts, a maroon blouse, and my brown slip sandals to complete the outfit. My head fantasies about what could happen when I show up at his door with a jar of honey. Closing my eyes, I will myself to calm down. I don't understand why I'm so caught up in this guy, pulled to him like a demon is to the devil. Shaking my head of the thought, I grab the jar of honey and head out.

Walking across the street, I feel eyes on me, my neighbors watching and probably wondering why Heston isn't with me. I haven't told anyone about our troubles, so with my head down, I take a deep breath and trudge forward. To my surprise, he's not inside. He's crouched down on a blue milk crate working on his bike. His hair is pulled back and anyone would take notice of his shirtless chest, allowing him to display an array of tattoos all over his upper body. He's extremely attractive already but something about the board shorts and brown sandals he has on makes him that much sweeter. I catch him sneak a glimpse of me, but then act as if he doesn't see me coming.

"Hi." I smile as I approach him. He turns his head away from his bike and looks me up and down, his mouth tipping into a smirk. Wow, his skin is a beautiful golden, peachy brown, like a native American. His dark and silky hair looks much healthier than mine.

He stands, the little bit of hair under his belly button catching my attention.

"Um…honey…" I fumble over my words then let out a nervous laugh, my cheeks heating. "I mean, I brought you honey." I hold out the jar toward him.

He lifts his right brow. Pulling a red towel from his back pocket, he wipes his hands.

"I like honey," he simply responds. His promiscuous tone and hooded eyes cause me to hold my breath. An exciting feeling rushes through me and I glance down.. He takes the jar, and I can't help but look down at his hands, grease staining his skin and nails. His knuckles are swollen and cut, like he's been in a fight recently.

I clear my throat. "Right…well, I just wanted to come say hi and introduce myself. I'm Rain. Rain Adler." I slip my hands into my back pockets.

His eyes remain on the jar as he spins it in his large palm. "Rhodes. So, tell me, Rain Adler, where is your husband and daughter?" His tone is rough and scratchy, and his question takes me aback. He's been watching me close enough to know I'm with someone and have a kid. He'll fit in well with this block and our tendency to spy on each other.

"What do you mean by that?" I tilt my head to the side.

"Just curious why a man would let a woman like yourself around a man like me alone?" His vainglorious attitude a major turn-on.

"Well, my boyfriend—errr, fiancé, is at work." He raises his brows, his curiosity piqued at my stammering. Lowering the jar, he crosses his arms, one of his hands rubbing at the dark stubble on his chin.

"It's complicated." I look down.

"Doesn't look complicated to me if you're here, darlin."

Wow, talk about arrogant! Who does this guy think he is?

"Excuse me! You're being rude!"

His eyes light up, soft laughter spilling from his curt mouth.

"I was trying to be nice and welcome you to the neighborhood, but I have enough assholes in my life so…" My brows lift to my hairline, my pulse drumming in my neck out of frustration.

"Now who's being rude?" He tilts his head to the side.

My head snaps up. He's mocking me. Turning on my heel, I walk away, a slew of words to spew at him blistering on my tongue. The last thing I need is to deal with another jackass.

He laughs, and my nostrils flare. I should have listened to my head, instead of my heart about coming over here. If I see a dick, I just need to walk away because all I seem to be drawn to is jerks.

Walking away, he says, "Where you goin'?"

I don't reply.

The rest of the night, I stew on his crassness, and what I should have responded with. The way he looked and talk to me, it pisses me off and makes me want to go see him again all at the same time.

"Time to eat!" Paige announces, and I stand up from the couch, biting my nail. I didn't even know someone was making dinner. Hell, I wasn't even watching TV, I was thinking about him, Rhodes. His crassness and beautiful skin. What I should have said to him, what I want to say.

Sitting at the table, my knee bounces with a sinking feeling in the pit of my stomach.

"Mom?" My mind goes blank and I look up, finding Heston and Paige both looking at me with concern.

"Yes?" I clear my throat and grab my fork, digging into the spaghetti.

"What did you do today?"

I almost laugh at the question. Pushing the food around on my plate, I think about how I should answer. I know I can't say what I want to, even though talking about it would definitely help. Instead, I lie. "I was in my studio." They both nod, bored with the same answer I give almost every night. Heston goes on to talk about his day, but I can't focus on anything he's saying because my mind keeps going back to Rhodes. The way Heston keeps looking at me, I feel like he knows I went over there, or at the very least, knows I'm hiding something. I can't help myself; I can't stop thinking about the neighbor who stands out like a villain in a fairy tale.

"You look good," Heston says, complimenting my summer dress and flats.

"Thanks. I thought it would be nice for brunch," I reply, glancing at his polo and khakis. "You look great too."

He scoffs, grabbing his shoes from under the bed. "I'm sure Owen will tell me how I could have made it better."

I laugh. He's probably right. Owen and Flynn invited us over for brunch, and Heston didn't try and run for the hills. It occurs to me that we're having casual conversation. It's crazy how we can slip into something normal when we're anything but. We're broken and unrepairable. I see it and feel it. How can he not?

"Hey Heston, after Owen and Flynn's, I really want to sit down and have a talk," I tell him, my finger tapping my chin, waiting to see how he'll respond.

"Yeah sure, I'm home for the day," he replies on an exhale, his tone not giving away that he's worried about anything. I don't understand him. How can he not feel how severed our love is? We're a butterfly that has a wing clipped, unable to fly and flopping around fighting and hoping we can still keep going.

He reaches for my hand as we cross the street, and I immediately pull away and smooth out my dress. Avoiding eye contact, I act like I'm unaware that he wants to hold my hand. Why would I try when he won't even go to therapy like he agreed? Hell, I would have gone with him and did couples' therapy, but we're way past that now. Reaching Flynn and Owen's walkway, I ring their doorbell. Heston rubs the back of his neck, seeming tense. He definitely knows I did not want to make physical contact.

The door opens, and Owen squeals in delight, ushering us inside.

"Come in, come in. We're all out back!" he says, their perfectly clean house is decorated in modern-day earthy tones with lots of plants. Their gray couch looks soft and plushy, a

Sherpa tan and white throw over the back, and on their coffee table is a statue of an English bulldog on a skateboard. Stepping through the glass double doors and onto the porch, Flynn's eyes light up.

"Hey, guys! Glad you could make it."

Then I see him. Rhodes. Sitting next to Flynn, a beer in his hand. My smile drops, and my heart beats a little harder.

"Have you and Rhodes met yet?" Flynn questions.

"No, I don't think I've had the pleasure."

Rhodes' eyes become hooded, his lips pulling the tiniest smirk at the corner of his mouth, as if he likes that I lied, and wants to be my dirty little secret. The overwhelming feeling of wanting to hide weighs on my chest.

"Nice to meet you," I reply, making sure to come off polite and as if we've never met. I didn't tell the truth because I'm afraid of how Heston would react. Just the thought of him getting worked up and physical makes my hand tremble. I fear he'd hit me again.

A knowing smile brightens Rhodes' eyes. "Yes, happy to meet you. Been meaning to come over and say hello, but been busy." His voice is like honey, and I ignore the fluttering in my stomach, and the desire that sends goosebumps down my back. Forcing a tight-lipped smile, I nod and look away. I refuse to see the delight in his eyes, knowing he affects me.

Taking a seat, Heston beside me, I try to avoid eye contact with Rhodes.

The back door opens and Owen steps outside with a pan of bagels topped with bacon and tomatoes and little green garnishes on the side.

"Who's hungry?" he asks, looking around and waiting for someone to jump and plead for the food he's slaved over.

"Wow, it looks good, Owen," I compliment, wanting out of the circle Rhodes and Heston have put me in.

"Well, you definitely get the first one," Owen says, pursing his lips, almost offended no one else is pleading to be the first one served.

"And this is why I love you more than everyone here," he snips, sliding one onto my plate.

"Hey," Flynn protests, and I can't help but laugh. "Help me get the mimosas out and I'll see about bumping you to the top," he says, a little too seriously. "Do you need help getting the mimosas out?"

I nod a little harder than needed, but I need liquid courage right now.

"Yes! That sounds amazing!" I add and feel Heston tense beside me. He doesn't like the idea of us drinking. He raises his hand and I close my eyes and quickly shift away from him.

"Hey, can I get two of those?" He points to the bagels, and it occurs to me that I just flinched. I thought he was going to hit me, but he just wants bacon. Clearing my throat, I situate myself back into place and look around to see if anyone caught my reaction. My eyes lock with Rhodes, his face hard and jaw clinched as he stares right through me. Tearing my gaze from his, I look at Flynn and Tenly, who are lost in conversation. The only person that saw was Rhodes, great. Placing my head in my hand, I start thinking about how I'm going to explain what he saw if he asks.

"Rhodes offered to BBQ for the end of the summer bash," Tenly announces to everyone.

"Oh, that'll be nice." Owen's eyes smile.

"Rain is making an apple pie," she informs, and I inwardly cringe. Great, now everyone will know the burnt apple pie belongs to me.

"Good luck, she hasn't even started trying to figure out how to make one." Heston raises a brow and shakes his head as if I'm behind as usual. I roll my eyes. Tenly pushes forward, changing the subject. "Flynn, have you guys decided what you'll do to contribute?"

"Um…we're still thinking. But I'm sure it'll be great whatever it is," Flynn replies, looking at Owen, who gives him a reassuring smile. Owen must be beside himself with what to bring. I'm sure he's got four ideas and is stressing which one would bring the most attention.

We eat, making light gossip and laughing. I can't help but sneak a peek at Rhodes, here and there, and find him looking at me every time. Finished with my food, my plate in hand, I squeeze through everyone to take it inside. The cool air caresses my arms as I shut the door behind me and lean back, inhaling deep, taking in the silence and cooling my overheated skin. Pushing off, I make my way to the sink to rinse my plate, focusing on the sauce that doesn't want to come off.

The sound of the glass door opening and shutting has me sneaking a glance at who is coming in. It's Rhodes. My breath quickens, being in here all alone with him. He's tall, a black shirt and ripped jeans, his brown worn boots not normally seen around these parts. Fantasizing about what we could get up to in here, I look back down at the plate, trying to act casual. Why does he affect me so much? My body acts on its own accord when he's near, the strong desire I have for him surpassing anything I felt for Heston when we first met.

He stands behind me with his plate, his arms crossed, and I feel as if I'm holding him up.

Turning the faucet off, I finally turn around and face him. He's so close, I can smell his cologne and feel his body heat. Notes of orange laced with a wooded vanilla smell caress my senses. My cheeks warm and my throat thickens from arousal. My mouth parts and his eyes land on my lips, the way he's looking at me heightening my awareness. This isn't right, the way I feel around this guy especially when Heston and I are having problems. Looking down, breaking the connection, I clear my throat.

"Thank you for going along with—" I wave my hand toward the door. He steps beside me, putting his plate in the sink. "Why don't you want him to know we met? Did he not want you to?"

My nostrils flare, and I rest my hand on the counter, my nails picking at the granite.

"Well…" he takes a deep breath, "he's smart, trying to keep you all to himself."

"I guess," I mutter. He turns, facing me.

"Maybe it's just me, but you look like you're more afraid than in love with your boyfriend…or rather fiancé?"

My head snaps up, eyes wide. Embarrassment heating my ears, I fumble for a response, completely dumbstruck.

Reaching forward, he brushes his thumb along my cheek bone, the same side Heston hit me, and I jerk away.

"No, I just—" I have no idea what to say. Is he referring to me flinching or has seen or heard us fighting? Not wanting to say one thing and it be the other, I walk away. Large fingers wrap around my wrist, halting me. I spin toward him and freeze, his moss green eyes pinning me in place. With our chests inches from one another, we stare into each other's eyes, my stomach fills with butterflies, like it used to do with Heston. The feeling is both exciting and arousing. "By the way—no cherry pie. Do apple."

My brows furrow. "Why?"

"Because the apple is forbidden." My breath hitches. Jerking my hand from his, I go back outside, sliding into my seat beside Heston. He reaches for my hand, tangling it in his, but I can't feel it over the tingling Rhodes left behind. Leaning in, Heston whispers, "Everything okay?" His grip on my hand tightens, and it takes everything in me not to react to the pain.

"I'm fine," I grit, looking straight ahead, acting as if Heston isn't hurting me under the table.

Fighting through the pain, knowing bruises will form by tomorrow, I grab his fingers with my other hand and dig my nails into them. He shoves me away, the table rocking, and my breath hitches in my throat, scared everyone saw what just happened. Glancing around, the only one who staring is Rhodes. His brows furrow and his rocky mountain green eyes pin me where I sit. He definitely knows Heston and me are not okay.

As we walk back across the street, the sun is resting on the horizon. I'm over wanting to talk like a rational adult with Heston. After what he just pulled, I'm ready to fight the asshole. No more putting off this conversation. It has to happen now because I'm done; I can't do this anymore. "Heston, I need to talk to you. Now!" I demand, shaking my sore hand as if the pain will just fall off from him hurting me.

Walking ahead of me, he doesn't respond. He's ignoring me, acting as if whatever I have to say is of no importance to him. As soon as we're both in the house, I slam the door behind me.

"Things have been different—I feel different." I press my hand to my chest, making myself calm down, ensuring I speak rationally. I don't want to be by myself, but having him here, without us being the way we were, is the coldest isolation.

"What are you trying to say?" His brows inch inward, his jaw tensing. "Wait—are you breaking up with me?" His question is sharp, making me feel small.

"I'm sorry, it's just…you put your fucking hands on me and my kid!" I finally shout.

"But we went over that and made up. You accepted my apology, Rain. Why are you bringing this up again? Do you not get enough attention? Is that it?"

My mouth opens, then closes. How the fuck is he turning this on me?

"I acknowledged you were sorry and felt bad, that doesn't mean it was forgotten."

"It does. You fuck up, you say sorry, you move on!" he yells back. Warm tears slip down my cheeks. My hand covers my mouth to hide my quivering bottom lip. He might be right, but I don't feel the same about him, not like I did before he put his hands on Paige and started hurting me.

"We aren't working out anymore, Heston," I finally say, "This isn't us, we bring the ugly out of each other and we're to the point of hating one another.

"You hate me? Is that what you're saying?" He raises a brow, waiting for me to respond, a challenge in his voice. I don't reply, I'm too scared to do so.

"I sold my place! I have nowhere to live! You want me to sleep on the couch?" he sneers. My eyes fill with tears, I'm never going to get this man out of my life, am I? Grabbing his keys off the counter, I throw them at him as hard as I can.

"No, you can sleep in your truck!" I seethe hysterically. I'm trapped. Like a sheep shut in with a wolf, I have nowhere to go and nowhere to hide.

27

Heston slept on the couch last night, despite me telling him to go to his tuck, and we haven't spoken today. I feel like a stranger in my own house. I should have called the cops—I should have ended it then and there. There is no saving this.

In my pottery room, I count the pieces I have finished, nervous I won't have enough to fill a booth. I need variety, more colors and sizes. I tap my chin, contemplating. A knock at the door has my head snapping in its direction.

Paige stands in the doorway with worry lining her forehead, her phone clasped in her hands.

"Hey, everything okay?" I ask.

She shakes her head like she doesn't understand something, looking at me with sorrow-dipped eyes. "Dad was supposed to pick me up an hour ago," she starts, frustration in her voice. "He won't answer me back either." *Damnit Cam, not this shit again.* When he's a no call, no show, it usually means he landed himself in jail.

I grab my phone, looking at the time. Two-thirty. No texts or voicemails either. I raise my brow, looking at Paige.

"When did you last talk to him?"

"Um, I'm not sure. Couple days after the fight, maybe?" She shrugs. I rub my temples, trying to think. It's not my job to go chasing him down at some dirty bar anymore, but the weight of him still being Paige's father has me putting my art aside and looking for my keys.

Paige rides with me into the city, and we check Cam's place first. The one-story house has seen better days. Paint chipping, shutters hanging off, weeds overgrown, taking over the dry-rotted porch. Paige knocks, and I try to look through a window. It's scummed over with nicotine and dust, the dark curtain blocking the view. Jesus, and I let Paige come over here.

"He's not here," I mutter.

Paige turns, pointing to the driveway.

"His truck is here, though."

I bite my bottom lip. If he went on a bender, he would've taken his truck. The entire time I've known him, he's never had a sober driver come get him. A bad feeling fills my chest. My forehead starts to sweat. Grabbing my phone, I look through our mutual contacts and text his sister and his fishing buddy, asking if they've seen them.

"Come on, let's go sit in the van while we wait for someone to text me back." I press my hand on Paige's back, ushering her to come and rest. Reluctantly, she goes, sitting in the passenger seat, her legs kicked up on the dash. Climbing into the driver's seat, my back is slick with sweat, so I turn the van on for the air conditioning. A black bird flies over the house, circling it like it's roadkill, ready to tear it apart until nothing is left. It caws and flaps it wings, and I can't help but wonder what it's really going off about. Tapping my phone on my thigh, it finally dings.

I read aloud, so Paige knows what was said.

"Hey, I haven't been able to get ahold of him for a couple of days."

Sighing I glance up at Paige, who is biting the inside of her cheek.

"Wait, his sister wrote back. Aunt Liz says I don't know." I scoff, wow that was helpful.

"Mom, where is he?" Paige's voice wobbles, and I shake my head. "Let's head back and I'll make some calls." I try not to sound annoyed, but Cam has done this so many times, it's hard not to get pissy.

"No, do it now!" Paige pleads, fear clouding her eyes, and I see just how scared she really is.

"Alright, calm down." I place my hand on her shoulder.

I phone the hospital, but he's not there, as well as his favorite bar, but nobody has seen him. I don't know who else to call. Sitting back in my seat feeling defeated, I say, "I have one place left to call, the jail," I tell Paige, and I'll be honest, I'm getting nervous myself. Where is he?

Waiting on the station to pick up, I remember having to do this several times when I was married to him, but I always found him within an hour. But something in my gut tells me this time is different.

"This is the sheriff speaking," she answers.

"Yes, I'd like to report a missing person."

Coming back home, Heston's truck is parked in the driveway. Getting out of the van, I notice Paige's shoulders slumped, so I wrap my arm around her shoulders, pulling her in for a hug. "They'll find him," I assure her. Her lips pull into a tight-lipped smile before she slides out of my hold. As she walks into the house, I inhale a deep breath, tilting my head back against the headrest. I swear, if Cam is high in some abandoned house or trapped in a basement for unpaid

28

"Yes, this is what I needed," I mutter softly. My mouth fills with a hot earthy tone, and I savor it. Smoke instantly begins to circle around and drift into the wind. I love the taste of weed. I kept the joint I took from Layla and Paige, needing it tonight more than ever. I look up at the full moon as it hangs brightly in the sky like a lantern. It's quiet out here, except for the air conditioners' soft humming and I somehow find peace in the noise, wanting to fall asleep right here. It would be safer than in my own house, since Heston still won't get out and I was preoccupied with finding Cam and keeping Paige calm today rather than starting up another fight with that asshole. I'm going to have to actually do something rather than say something to get him out. For him to see that we are done, that there is no saving this relationship. He's a blind man living in a fantasy world. Exhaling, I look down at my phone for any missed messages about Cam. Still nothing.

A tiny voice inside me tells me I'm wasting my time, that Cam isn't our responsibility. He's a grown man who makes his own choices. But I wouldn't be able to look Paige in the eye if I didn't do everything I could to bring him back to her. I place my phone down and run a hand through my hair. I'm so fucking stressed I could smoke two joints tonight…with wine. I've never been one to smoke weed regularly, but I've done it a few times in my life. Even with my mom. You know what, I should grow a small plant or two. I lightly laugh at the thought. I could only call them tomato plants so long before Tenly figured it out. God I'd love to see her reaction to finding pot plants all over my property.

A bright light flashes in my eyes, causing me to squint and raise my hand in an attempt to block it. A tall shadow stands in front of the moonlight, making it impossible to identify who it is.

"You been smoking weed, ma'am?"

My shoulders relax, and I blow out a puff of smoke, coughing. "Jesus, you scared me."

Laughing, Rhodes sits down next to me and turns the flashlight off, the smell of his cologne, mint, orange, and woods, drifting over the weed.

One hand on his knee, he twists to look at me.

"That smells like shit. Don't put that in your body." He takes the joint from my hand and tosses it to the ground before stomping on it. My mouth drops open, pissed that he just ruined by high. It might be shitty, but it was all I had.

"Here." He reaches into his pocket and pulls out a thick blunt. Gazing at his hand, I can't help but wonder what his palms would feel like on my skin. My eyes widen at the thought, my cheeks warming, as if Rhodes can read my thoughts. He runs the blunt under his nose, like he's smelling a cigar.

"Here," he offers. Taking it from him, I place it in my mouth, and he flicks open a Zippo, lighting the end. I puff, trying to get it started. The red cherry illuminates his face in orange and red shadows as I pull it to life.

"There ya go," he whispers, closing the lighter.

I take a lengthy drag, and my lungs resist. I exhale some, and my eyes water, my body wracking with the urge to cough. Unable to hold it any longer, I bark out, my lungs burning like hell.

He pats my back.

"Easy, girl."

"Holy shit," I croak, handing it back to him. His fingers brush mine for a split second, and our eyes meet. His pine-colored irises darker than ever and watching me.

Silence falls between us, the moon highlighting certain features of his face. I lick my bottom lip, still searching his face, committing it to memory.

"Do you want me?" he asks, and my eyes widen. Thinking back on all the times my body reacted to being near him, I begin to sway into him. Jerking myself back, I mask my desire with laughter. Hoping he can't see how much I'm into him.

"Excuse me?" I say, biting back a smile.

"I meet pretty woman all the time. I can always see lust burning in their eyes, but you…I can't read you."

"Maybe because I'm with someone," I say, pulling the boyfriend card—I mean, I haven't successfully kicked Heston out yet.

"Nah, that's not it," he replies, his eyes narrow, looking down at his hands. I forget he knows Heston and me are not a happy couple, so my lack of jumping in his bed right away seems to really confuse him. Not wanting to divulge what I'm feeling, especially when I'm high, I decide to have some fun with him.

"Do I keep you up at night?" I whisper. Maybe it's the

weed, or maybe I really want to know, because he keeps me up. I'm always thinking about him and his smart-ass mouth.

He smiles, the grin on his face as sharp as a knife. "Answer my question, and I'll answer yours." He raises a brow, playing games with me.

Biting my inner cheek, I think for a second. My thoughts slower than before, my body feeling relaxed, I say, "Yes, you're hot. I just do my best to restrain myself and act like a lady. How am I doing?" I bat my lashes at him.

He takes another drag, blowing it into the air.

"To answer your question, I don't think about you."

Well, damn. Okay then. I begin to laugh, and his smile fades. Clearly, he was hoping I'd be distraught by his answer. He carefully pulled me in so he could get off on being an ass in the end. He better get in line behind the other two men in my life if he wants a reaction.

My head feeling too heavy, I rest it on his shoulder. It's strong and warm, and his cologne divine. My body caressing his for his warmth and touch. He's so full of muscles but his skin is so soft. Pulling my hand up, I trace the crucifix tattoo on his lower arm with my index finger. I want a tattoo, but what would I get?

"You good?" His voice echoes, the melody so soothing that I close my eyes and lean into him a little more. The feeling of being safe and not alone is a lullaby I've missed recently. I could lie here all night, but being in his arms comforts me more than I'm aware, and I become sleepy.

"I'm definitely high." I laugh.

"You sure you're alright?" he asks, his voice rough but smooth at the same time. Like an old country song. His hand brushes the side of my face, the sound of crickets, frogs, and him slowly drifting into nothing.

29

My mouth dry and throat parched, I shift, nearly falling. Opening my eyes, I find myself in my bed. How'd I get here? Last I remember, I was on the porch with Rhodes. Did he bring me in here?

I throw the blankets off me and rub my hands over my face. God last night…There was definite flirting, and my restraint was hidden under a haze, allowing me to admit I find him attractive.

Getting up, I grab my robe and put it on. Last night replays in my head so loudly, I almost don't hear the racket from the kitchen. My vibe is quickly extinguished because Heston is still here. Today is the day I make Heston leave for good. No more distractions. No more twisting my words. I'm not trying to leave Heston and jump right into Rhodes' bed, but there is something between us for sure, and I can't sleep at night knowing I'm feeling the things I am for the guy while still being bound to the monster in my kitchen. I may be a lot of things, but I won't be a cheater.

Heston stands in the kitchen, his hair washed and slicked

back, an unbuttoned shirt hugging his shoulders, revealing his chest.

He glances up from his phone. "About time you woke up."

"I couldn't sleep last night," I mutter. Blowing out a breath, I step around the couch to get a glass of water from the kitchen.

"What's wrong?"

Where do I begin? A glass in my hand, I freeze. "For starters, Cam is missing."

His chest lifts as he palms the back of his neck.

"He's not missing if he doesn't want to be found," he says, and I shake my head.

"He's never been gone like this. Paige is worried—"

"Oh, Paige is worried? Because it seems you're more concerned than she is." My mouth parts at his insinuation.

"I do not like Cam. And I've made my feelings more than clear when it comes to him. That doesn't mean I want him hurt or gone. Paige needs her father, Heston."

His tongue snakes out, dampening his bottom lip. His ominous eyes hooded, he stares right through me.

"That's why she has me—that's why *you* have me. God put you in my path that day for a reason. Why don't you stop trying to fight it and be fucking happy?" he roars, his voice filling the room. I startle, and he pushes off the counter, grabbing his briefcase.

"Speaking of God, why don't you and Paige find a church for us to go to this weekend? A little Jesus would do ya'll some good." He raises a judgmental brow. Anger plumes in my chest, searing through my limbs. Who does he think he is?

I throw the glass in my hand at him, and he ducks, which sends it smashing into the wall behind him.

"Jesus Christ, Rain!" His eyes snap from the wall to me, the look on his face suggesting *I'm* insane. Me. Why am I even listening to this anymore?

"I have me! Why is it men feel like they have to swoop in and rescue the damsel in distress. She must be so weak and need me," I mock. "Get out of my house, Heston. And don't come back." Tears well in my eyes, but I'm not sad. I'm pissed off that I can't kill this asshole.

"Rain, look, you're obviously upset. Why don't we—"

"Do not tell me to calm down," I seethe, my nails nearly digging into the countertop. Glaring through my lashes, I whisper, "Get out, Heston. This isn't working anymore."

Huffing, he says, "I'll see you for dinner," before slamming the door behind him. Roaring in my ears, my heart rate spikes as I rush to the door and step outside before he has a chance to drive off. "You are not coming back. I said we're done!" I scream, hatred scathing every word.

He doesn't say anything, just climbs in his truck and starts it.

I toss my hair from my face and swipe at a falling tear. How did we get here? We were so happy, so stupidly in love. Now, we can't be in the same room without fighting, and I can't help but say I resent him more than half the time we're around each other. Legs shaking, I go back inside and into the kitchen. With one hand on the counter and the other in my hair, I force myself to stop crying. I knew we were moving too fast to actually know one another. It's all cute surprises and hot sex occupying your time together until the monsters want out of their cage for a turn. The first part of a relationship should be about getting to know each other. When the person you love is not only the heart-throbbing alpha they can be, but the asshole they really are.

Being alone really starts to set in. I don't have my mother

or someone to love and it's starting to feel like I never will. My chest starts to burn, causing me to breathe harder. I begin to pant and cry even harder. Heston was so sweet and said all the right things, only to become a completely different person. One I no longer want in my life.

Trying not to blubber, I don't want anything in this house that reminds me of him. Rushing back outside, I fall to my knees, the ground abrasive against my skin, and grasp and claw at the pink flowers, tearing them out of the ground. Elated that I'll never have to look at them and think about him again. I fall back on my ass and inhale a large breath, happy with the loose dirt, and torn roots all over my porch. Tears still trickle down my cheeks, and with my nails packed with soil, I sit there, staring at the stupid van.

"Rain?" Rhodes stands at the end of my driveway in a loose gray shirt with a Harley logo and ripped-up jeans with grease on them.

As soon as I open my mouth, I sob. Humiliated, I drop my head into my hands. His boots slap against the pavement before his spicy scent surrounds me. He kneels beside me, a heavy hand on my back.

"What happened? Are you okay? Did he hit—?"

"I told him to get out. It's over." My voice cracks. I finally look up, and he stares back, his lips lifting on one side.

"Well, hell, that's the best news I've heard since I moved here." He chuckles, and it takes me aback. He takes my chin in one hand and uses his other to wipe the tears from my face.

"It's just…my ex-husband and I didn't work. My mother died, and now Heston is gone. I'm alone. I'm always going to be alone."

Sitting down, he crosses his legs and rests his back on the cool stucco.

"I've been alone for about two years. My girlfriend and I

had a baby. My little girl turned one, and my ex decided she needed to get out there, see other people and live." He shakes his head. "I didn't take it well. I drank every night. Sat in bars and usually ended up with someone. Got arrested for a DUI, and lost my weekends with my girl. I know the feeling well."

"Is that why you moved here?"

He scratches at his beard, looking away. "Yeah. A family neighborhood, kids to play with, good school. I'd do anything for Nalini. Give her the best life I can," he continues.

"That's a really pretty name," I nearly-whisper. Silence falls between us, placing that awkward weight on my shoulders, so I say what I'm thinking, "I came looking for something better. The neighbors, the schools, the image of being a mother who carpools and bakes, but…I'm just not that person. I hate it."

"You don't want to be that person; those people are not as happy as they come off. Just be you, Rain."

Inhaling a breath, I lick my bottom lip. It's salty from my tears spilling onto them and drying from this damn heat.

Leaning my head back against the walkway, I mutter, "Yeah, maybe you're right."

"Mom?" Paige's voice has me snapping straight up and looking down the doorway. Her hair is down, not in her usual braids, and she's wearing a baggy shirt that I presume is her dad's because I've never seen it before, falling to her thighs.

"Right here, babe."

Her feet hit the patio, and she stops, her eyes wide, looking at the mess I made of our flowers.

"Whoa."

"Yeah...about that. I was thinking we should get black flowers. What do you think?" My voice wavers, and I have to catch myself.

"But Heston…he likes—"

"I don't care what Heston wants. This is my house and we want black."

She crosses her arms, a little smirk playing at the corner of her mouth. "I like it." She laughs.

"Plus, it'll take our minds off things."

"Let me go get my sandals." She looks to Rhodes one last time before going inside.

He stands and holds his hand out to help me up. I place mine into his much larger one, the pads of my fingers sliding over his calloused palms. A stark contrast to Heston's smaller, softer hands. He pulls me up in one tug, and I brush off my bottom and hands, trying to avoid eye contact. Now that I'm calmer, I can only imagine the medusa hysterics from moments ago. Embarrassing.

"Well, I'm going to let you ladies get to picking flowers. If you need anything, Rain, let me know." The sincerity in his deep voice has my breath hitching. I nod, my eyes snapping to his when the tips of his fingers graze the underside of my chin. His eyes, the color of moss after it rains, captivate me.

"I'm serious. If you need anything, no matter what it is, come get me." With affection in his voice and his stare holding, he leads me to believe he's being more than just a nice neighbor. Grasping his wrist, I pull his hand off my face and against my chest, causing my heart to quicken.

"I promise."

Dropping his hand by his side, he takes a step back, stares at me a second longer, then turns to head back to his place.

"Mom, I'm ready." I look to Paige, black slides now on her feet.

"Great. Let's go." I force a smile—something I've been doing a lot lately.

I've been trying to act like I have the perfect life, keeping secrets and telling everyone I'm okay when I'm really not.

30

On our way to Olive's Flower Shop, I text a locksmith to change the locks while I'm out. Heston is not coming back into my house. He and I burned from both ends of a candle stick, fast and hot, until our wick went cold. Jesus, he's starting to sound like a rebound but from who? Cam? My mother's death?

I pull onto the small gravel driveway in front of the shop. It looks the same as last time. A cute little brick shop with flowers of every kind.

"This is where you got the flowers?" Paige asks, skeptically. She's used to shopping in the city.

"Yeah. It's cute, isn't it?"

She gives me a forlorn look before opening her door and getting out. Meeting her around the side, we walk down a narrow path, rows of pots held up by railroad ties and cylinder bricks greeting us.

"Hey, you're back!" Olive says with a smile, a bottle of pink solution in her hand. Her hair is wispy and sweaty from working outside and she's wearing a garden apron with dirt rubbed all over the front, but what really stands out are those damn yellow boots.

"How are the Bougainvilleas doing?"

"Um," I hesitate, not wanting to tell her I ripped them out of the ground.

"She tore them up," Paige tattles. My head snaps in her direction, my eyes glaring at her. Her lips roll onto one another, as if she didn't mean to say what she did, but it's too late to take it back.

"Yeah, I can't say I'm surprised, dear."

My brows furrow, uncertain what she means.

"You don't seem like a pink flowers' kind of girl. I saw you eyeing the Queen of the Night tulip last time you were here. That's your flower." She points then walks past us. Paige and I give each other a look and follow her.

She stops in front of the deep purple flowers and leans in, inhaling their smell, a smile on her face.

"A flower can only bloom as much as its owner. You gave me the impression you're more complicated than a pink shrub. She glances at me from the corner of her eye, and I swallow, not sure what to say.

"Wow, those are really pretty. I want these. Can we get these?" Paige pushes past me and cups the blossom in her hand, staring at it longingly.

Olive steps back and looks at me.

"Um…yes. Let's get several."

Paige grabs a few pots, and I help her by grabbing two of them. Checking out, I set my hand on the counter and ask, "Is it a bad thing to be complicated? To not be a pink flower kind of girl?" I feel like most women want to be the bright, feminine color, capturing everyone's eye.

She looks closely at the tags as she jabs the register, putting in the price.

"Well, you aren't easy, but I don't think it's a bad thing. You're strong. It takes more to get your attention and thrive is all."

I think about what she says and look at the building behind her, wondering if she does psychic readings or something in there.

"I'm just an old lady who has seen many people come and go. What I say doesn't mean much, honey. It was just an observation," she says, handing me my receipt. I want to agree with her, tell her she has no idea what she's talking about, but…it does sound like me.

Back home, I follow the directions through a series of text messages the locksmith gave me to get inside the house, then Paige and I work on planting our new flowers. Without a shovel, I watch her scratch and dig at the rich soil. This feels right, but I can't help but think back to the day Heston and me planted our flowers. It was sexy, getting caught in the downpour, the sex on the stairs, but looking back, I felt more like a teenager climbing into someone's back seat, trying not to get caught, than finding the one to settle down with.

I clean my hands in the kitchen sink, dry them off, and open my phone to check notifications. Nothing. Sighing, I place it on the counter.

"Still nothing?" Paige asks, sitting at the kitchen table.

"No," I mutter, worry starting to turn into nausea. "Let's order pizza and watch trash TV, babe." Paige doesn't say anything, looking at her phone with a blank stare. I'm starting to feel defeated. I've done everything I can as a parent to lessen Paige's worry, but every hour that passes and nobody has called about her dad, I feel like we're going to have to accept something bad did happen.

My phone dings, and I snatch it up.

Tenly: *Don't forget the Block party is this weekend!*

I cuss under my breath, rubbing my forehead. I need to make a damn pie. Should we even attend with everything going on? My eyes sweep to Paige. She looks so lost…I wonder if going would help her get her mind off things. We can't just wait around. We have to keep living.

Me: *We'll be there.*

I just hope Heston isn't.

31

Lying in bed with the side-table lamp brushing a soft glow across the room, the bed feels larger than a king, lying in it by myself. Heston's texted twice asking to come home to talk about it, but I said no once and didn't say anything the second time. I don't want to be a bitch, but I'm just over him and over us.

Rolling onto my side, my tank riding up my stomach and my silk shorts giving me a wedgie, I wish my mother was here. She would help me through this. Losing her has been the biggest hurt of my whole life. She was my best-friend.

A loud knock causes me to startle and pull the blankets closer to my chest. I stay completely still, trying to figure out exactly what it was.

BANG! BANG!

"Rain, open up." Heston's voice carries down the hall. Holy shit, he's here. Sliding off the bed, I grab my robe from the back of the door and put it on. Walking out of my room, I stop at the end of the stairs, where Paige is standing and looking at the door with worried eyes.

"Are you letting him in?" she whispers.

Opening my mouth, I hesitate, unsure what to say and do. If I let him in, he'll think we're okay, and I won't be able to get him back out.

"Come on, Rain. I know you can hear me." The edge to his tone has me crossing my arms in front of my chest. He definitely doesn't sound like the Heston I thought I knew. Paige and I stand there, staring at the door, unsure how to proceed.

"OPEN THE FUCKING DOOR!" he shouts, kicking it and making me yelp. He steps away, the moonlight highlighting his shadow as he paces back and forth.

"Should we call the cops?" Paige asks, her face pale with worry. This is such a disaster.

"I'm sorry for whatever I did. I just really want to see you." His now soft voice is a complete switch from moments ago, his changing mood a complete mystery. But what does become clear is the fact that I don't have the slightest idea who Heston is.

"Just go away, Heston, we're done. I'll have a sheriff bring you your things," I finally answer back. He chuckles and goosebumps rise on my skin.

"YOU FUCKING BITCH!" he gnashes, jerking the door handle back and forth. He's not going to leave; I'm going to have to call the cops.

"Hey, I think it's a little late, don't you?" Rhodes' voice causes me to snap straight as a board. He's out there with Heston! Rushing to the living room window, I peek through the blinds and see Rhodes standing at the end of the porch with a gun in his hand. Holy shit.

My heartbeat quickens, and panic sets in. This is too much, someone is going to get hurt.

"You going to shoot me?" Heston asks, his arms stretched wide.

"Just doing a neighborhood watch tonight, Heston, and I think Rain is asleep, in fact, the whole block is asleep."

"You fucking her? Is that little slut coming over to your place at night? Is that what this is about? Because she's engaged, you know."

"Last I heard, you weren't engaged, so if you can kindly leave the property." Rhodes' arms suddenly look bigger than before, a black gun in his hand as he holds it in front of himself, so Heston can clearly see it.

"This is wrong. This is my house." Heston rubs the bottom of his chin, and Rhodes nods but doesn't say anything.

Stepping off the stoop, Heston turns around to face the house, his arms stretched out wide.

"I'll be back, Rain. I'm not giving up on us!" Letting the blinds fall closed, I take a step back, tears filling my eyes. He's so angry, hostile even. I don't want to know what would have happened if I let him in here when he asked me to open the door.

The sound of his truck roars like a lion in the night, and recklessly pulls out of the driveway, his headlights bouncing all over the walls of our house, before screeching off. With my hand on my forehead, I try and pull myself together.

"Rain, you okay?" Rhodes asks from the other side of the door. Hurrying over, I unlock it then open it. Standing taller than me, he looks down at me with a concerned look, placing his gun in the waistband of his jeans.

"Oh my God. I'm so sorry." Anxiety fills my voice, embarrassment flushing my cheeks. He pulls me in and wraps his arms around me. With my face against his hard chest, I can't help but feel safe for the first time in weeks, so much so that I close my eyes and bunch my hands in his shirt, pulling him closer.

"Shh, it's okay," he mutters into the top of my head. Blowing out a shaky breath, I wipe my tears and take a step back, noticing Paige on the bottom step staring, cheeks wet from crying.

"Thank you, I don't know what he was thinking—"

"You want me to stay over, in case he comes back?" He gestures toward the couch, and my mouth parts.

"Yes, stay!" Paige answers, stepping up beside me. Wrapping my arm around her, I look up at Rhodes.

"No, you don't have to do that."

"I know I don't have to, but I think I need to, in case he comes back."

"Mom, what are you going to do if he comes back and breaks in?" Paige asks, and the thought alone scares me. I don't know what Heston is capable of.

"Yeah, okay." I give in, the idea of Rhodes being here with a gun in his hand making me feel safer. His shoulders lift, his eyes meeting mine one more time before he turns to his house.

"Mom, what was wrong with Heston? He reminded me of when Dad used to drink."

Shaking my head I say, "I don't know, but he wasn't drunk. That was the real him, one hundred percent." His behavior like a Leopard. Gorgeous to look at, loveable and kind, but if he's not king of his territory, he'll kill and destroy whatever is in his path until he is. It scares me to think about what would have happened if I married him.

32

The sound of rain pelting the window wakes me from a light sleep; frustrated, I pull the blankets up under my chin and roll onto my side. I was too nervous to allow myself to fall into a deep slumber last night, the idea that Heston might come back and somehow sneak in haunting me, with every creak heard and shadow seen in the house. Thunder booms, making me startle, my heart beating so fast, you'd think I just got back from running. Slipping onto my back, my hands sliding down my face, I replay last night in my mind for the fiftieth time. I keep thinking I could have handled the situation better, or maybe I should have just called the cops. Sitting up, yawning, I grasp my phone from the nightstand. Owen messaged me.

Favorite Gay best friend, Owen: One, you'll have to give me the details on Heston becoming Ted Fucking Bundy on your doorstep, but first things first. I saw a brooding, handsome Rhodes enter your house and not come out!!!!!!! Spill the tea woman!

. . .

Pursing my lips, I back out of his message and look through my other texts and emails, finding nothing on Cam. Blowing out a deep breath, I toss the phone on my bed and change into some clothes. Normally, I'd grab my robe, but I know Rhodes is here. Keeping it comfortable, I put on some sweats and a camo t-shirt. Leaving my room in search of some food, I hear light laughter and deep guffaws. Stopping in the entryway to the living and kitchen area, I watch Rhodes and Paige sitting at the dinner table. Paige on her knees in her chair as she leans over half of it.

Unsure of what is happening here, I say, "What's going on?"

Paige's head snaps in my direction.

"Rhodes is teaching me how to play chess."

With my hand on the fridge door, I freeze and notice the gameboard between them.

"You can play chess?" My right brow lifts as I ask him.

"Yeah, I mean, somewhat. I know the basics." Leaning back in his chair, he places a hand on his thigh and shrugs. His dark hair is up in a hair tie, his deep nude colored lips pulled into a slight smirk as he watches Paige move a piece. He's really good looking, which makes me question why he's helping me out so much. Surely, he has a girlfriend to attend to. Maybe he's just a nice guy… but then I remember how we met and the asshole tendencies he possesses. Why are men so damn complicated to figure out. Seriously, they say we are complex creatures, but, I've come to realize, they're not any better.

Not seeing anything I want in the fridge, I shut it. Crossing my arms, I lean against it. "Thank you for staying over last night, it was…"

"Not a problem," he interrupts, his green eyes now on me, making me antsy. "What are you up to today?"

"Um, I have to make that pie for the block party thing." My brows instinctively furrow. The fact that I'm going through a bad break-up, have no idea where my ex-husband is, and now have this damn baking project to complete is just too much.

"You know how to bake?" he asks, moving his piece that looks like a horse on the boardgame .

Sighing, I reply, "No, but I'm sure I can figure it out with YouTube or something."

He chuckles, knocks the last white piece of their game off the board and stands. Paige's mouth drops open as she stares at the bored like he just completed some magic trick.

"Grr, I didn't even see that coming!" she shouts, causing Rhodes to smile bigger.

"My mom used to bake pies all the time for church. I learned a few tricks, if you want some help."

That antsy, I don't know what to say, but I'm thinking I know what I want to say, happens again, rendering me a mouth-gaping idiot.

"I don't know, I'm sure you have things you need to do today; I don't want to impose."

His shoulders rise, just as he slips his hands into his back pockets.

"I need to work on my bike and call my daughter, but after, I can come back over. Besides, I need to prepare some meat for the party, so we can just do it together."

His persistence makes me silently laugh. "What are you making?"

"Hell, probably just burgers and hot dogs." His 'I don't give a fuck' attitude is admirable. Taking his lead, I think about how I could use the company during this hell of a times, especially if Heston shows up again today.

"Yeah sure, let's meet up later then," I finally answer. His hand slaps the counter as he sucks a breath in through his teeth.

"Nice." The electric tension between us is definitely there and I can't help but wonder if he feels it. It's horrible to think he's sexy and strong, and that I feel safe around him when I am going through this break-up with Heston.

"I'ma run to the store and get what I need, do you want me to get anything for you?" I ask.

"Nah, I already have what I need," he replies, his hand rubbing his beard.

Getting dressed in a brown tank and black shorts, I slip into my brown slides. Grabbing my purse, I find Paige sitting on the last step of the stairs, waiting for me.

"Hey, I'm heading out. Want to come?"

She shakes her head, looking down at her hands that rest between her knees. I wasn't expecting her to say no. I can't leave her behind when Heston is out acting like a mad man.

"No, I'll stay back. Have you heard any news on Dad?"

Inhaling a deep breath, I reply on an exhale. "No baby, I haven't."

Without another word, she stands and stomps up the stairs. I should call the sheriff on my way into town.

Outside, the too hot sun smothers me with its intense heat, sweat instantly beading on my forehead.

Instinctively, I look over at Rhodes' house, but I don't see him. Inhaling, I think about the pros and cons of us spending time together weighs heavy on my mind.

One hand on the wheel, the other holding my phone, I dial Sheriff Reese to see where we're at with Cam's missing-person case.

"Hello, you've reached Sheriff Reese, I am currently unavailable, but if you leave a brief message, I'll try and return you call by tomorrow."

"By tomorrow?" I repeat angrily, just before the answering machine makes a loud beep.

"Uh," it takes me a second to get my head straight from her message, "yeah, this is Rain Adler. I'm calling to see if you have any leads or anything news about my ex-husband, Cam? Please call me back as soon as you can."

Hanging up, I slip my phone into the cup holder.

Finally reaching the market, its parking lot is full of cars, so I park in the shade, near the back, making sure to keep my windows an inch down to let it breathe. I hate getting into a car and feeling like you just slide into an airlocked crockpot.

Head down, purse hanging from my shoulder, I go inside. Cool air blows aggressively as if it's going to blast my body back to its normal temperature, and it feels good.

"Hey Rain!" Turning my head toward the friendly voice, I find Blair working register three. I've been in here a few times, and the fact she remembers my name like were friends feels great. It makes living here more personal and comfortable.

"Hey Blair." I wave and grab a small basket to carry the few items I need. Down the baking aisle, I stare at my phone for the ingredients for this damn pie.

I could get a graham-cracker crust, ready to-go pie crust, or make my own. Making my own is clearly what Tenly would want.

I'll meet her in the middle and get the ready to go pie crust, but get real apples for the filling. Reaching for a bag of Red Delicious apples, footsteps close behind me, causing me to look over my shoulder to see who is near, but there's nobody. I look the other way, nobody again. Goosebumps rise along my tanned arm, and I suddenly don't feel safe. Heston knows I come to this market, could he be here? Jesus I'm a paranoid loon.

Grabbing a random bag of apples, I shove them in the basket and get the last few items I need, without coming to a full stop. Zigzagging through people and cutting them off to get to Blair's lane, I dump my items on the belt, and she starts checking me out.

"You okay, Rain? You look sick."

Digging in my purse for my card, my eyes looking over my shoulder, I reply, "Um, yeah. Just in a hurry."

"Did Heston find you?' My head snaps up, and I almost drop my purse. "He came in looking for you a few minutes ago." I freeze, I knew someone was watching me.

"Did he say anything to you?" I frantically ask. Looking up from the scanner, she gazes at me, a confused look on her face from my sudden change in demeanor.

"You know what, here's forty, keep the change." Setting the two twenty-dollar bills on the belt, I grab my bags and rush to the exit. Outside, my feet make haste, my arms squeezing my bags against my chest. I hurry to my car, praying Heston doesn't find me. After the way he was last night, the idea of us being alone together is terrifying. Jerking my car door open and shoving the bags into the passenger seat, I turn the car on, make sure my doors are locked, and peel out of the lot.

Glancing in my rearview, I anxiously rub my neck. What am I going to do? Heston knows where I live, where I shop, and who I talk to. Maybe I should toughen up and sit down and talk to him. But his voice last night, and the words he chose to roar into the night, make me second-guess being anywhere near him. No, I should get a restraining order. That's stupid though, they don't work. Heston can show up to hurt me and I'll only have a piece of paper to protect me.

What I need is a taser or, better yet, a gun.

33

Pulling into the driveway, I shut off the vehicle and shove my door open, stepping out onto shaky legs. Even after the drive home, I'm still upset.

"Just in time." Looking up, Rhodes is heading my way with a couple of grocery bags of his own. Noticing my unease, his face falls serious, and he quickens his step.

"You alright? What happened?"

"Heston was there looking for me." Tears fill my eyes, and Rhodes pulls me into his arms and rubs my back. His jaw tenses, eyes going sharp as anger washes over him.

"It's alright, he ain't here. You're okay." He reassures me, and I exhale a trembling breath.

"I used to think he was a good guy, but lately, I'm scared of him, Rhodes."

His chest rises, a complex look causing his green eyes to turn the color of a burned-down forest.

"I have some buddies I ride with, I'll give them a call and see what we can do."

Biker buddies, like in a motorcycle club? "No, I don't want this to get any worse."

"You getting hurt, or Paige, is the worst that can happen, and I'm going to make sure it doesn't."

"Rhodes, this is our home not fucking *Sons of Anarchy*! We need to call the police…"

"Tell me, Rain, how many times have the cops helped you in the past?"

Ready to argue, I think back to Cam and me and the times I was able to slip from his grip and reach the phone to call for help. An officer would show up and Cam would give them some story and that was it. They asked me a few questions and told us to stay away from each other the rest of the night. That's it. That's the help I got.

"That's what I thought." His voice gets rougher, and I give in. My daughter is at risk because of a guy I brought into our lives, a wolf in sheep's clothing that couldn't handle a break-up.

"Okay," I accept his help, not that saying no would have stopped him. Rhodes is a man who has his own set of rules and he would have gotten into the middle of this situation either way. I still don't understand why though, since we're just neighbors, if that.

Inside the house, light noise comes from the living room. Paige is curled up in a corner of the couch, her elbow on the arm rest, her head using her hand as a pillow. She's expressionless; even as the people on the TV laugh, her eyes are sad.

"Hey baby, I'm back," I say, setting the food on the counter and masking my emotions so she doesn't sense something is wrong.

"Hey," she mutters, not lifting her eyes or head to look at me.

I should have taken her with me, got her out of the house for some sun and fresh air. Then again, I'm glad she didn't go because of Heston. Rubbing my forehead, I can't help but wonder how long it's going to be like this with him. When will he actually move on?

Rhodes sets his things beside me, his strong hands grabbing a chuck of meat wrapped in parchment paper and setting it out on a cutting board. He changed clothes, now wearing a camo-print shirt and tight Wranglers.

Pulling out another cutting board, I dump my apples on it and begin to slice them. After the second one, it becomes a mindless task, and I start to think about Heston. The way he sounded last night was unlike anything I've heard from him. Not the time he hit me or even when I gave the ring back. There is so much hurt wrapped around our relationship, like thorned vines pricking us every other way and yet, we kept going, hoping for a beautiful bloom in the end. But there's nothing pretty here, just ugly scabs that I keep picking at.

"Rhodes, have you ever hit a woman?" I ask, my eyes still on the task at hand.

"I like to smack a woman's ass, maybe a little throat grabbing in the bedroom, but I've never hit a female with ill intention, darling." A little southern twang presents itself in his reply, making me stare at him a little longer. This rough, wild man, wearing Wranglers with a southern accent, is attractive, a distraction, really, during a rough time in my life. Maybe God sent him to me to help the burden of my past. But the idea that Rhodes is an angel is laughable; he's a walking temptation ready to be licked and touched in every sinful way.

Jesus, what am I thinking!

"Are you and these motorcycle buddies the real thing?" I ask, because all I can imagine is Jax Teller rushing in with guns blazing.

He chuckles a little, sprinkling seasoning on the patties.

"Uh, I don't really know what qualifies as the real deal, but you don't want to cross any of them. That being said, they have loyalty and family chiseled into their bones—"

"Your bones?" I interrupt him, curious if he's anything like them.

He barely looks up, his hands still.

"I wouldn't be a part of it if I didn't."

Chewing the side of my cheek, I take that into account and grab my crust. Pulling it out of the package, I roll it out and knead it. Pulling the recipe open on my phone, I do what it says next, until I'm ready to put it in the oven. Now we wait for forty-five minutes, or at least I do.

Rhodes sits next to Paige on the couch, and I pull my phone out to see if the sheriff wrote me back about Cam, but there's nothing. When she calls, I need to mention Heston and see what my options are. My phone dings in my hand; it's a text from Owen.

Best gay best friend, Owen: Hey ho, I know you are occupied by lumberjack neighbor, but I want to know details!!!! Don't make me come over there!

Inhaling a breath, I close the screen and walk to the living room.

"Hey, Owen needs me for a second, will you watch her until I get back? I just don't want to leave her after—"

"After what?" Paige asks, her full attention on me now.

"Yeah, I got her." Rhodes gives a curt nod, before yawning.

"Thanks, be back in a minute."

"After what?" Paige yells, just as I walk out the door. I don't want to tell her about Heston looking for me; it will only upset her more, and I'm not sure how much more she can take right now.

Opening the front door, I look around for any sight of

Heston, my heart beginning to beat faster and harder as I start to think he's behind a bush, waiting for me to come out and shake me until I agree to take him back. Crossing my arms, I tap my toe anxiously, the feeling of being scared, washing over me and reminding me of when I was a kid getting up to use the restroom at night, and running and jumping to get back in bed because I was afraid something was under it, or behind me. Yeah, I can't walk across the street. Not happening.

Grabbing my phone, I text Owen.

Me: Come to my place

34

Looking at the black flowers Paige and I planted, Owen leans against the house with his legs crossed at the ankles.

"So, let me get this straight, you told Heston to get out, he came back angry as hell, frightening even, so Rhodes stayed the night to keep you and Paige safe, then the stalker was looking for you at the market and now biker man is getting his club involved and baking pies with you?" His index finger tips out just so, as he looks at me with a raised brow.

"Yeah, that's about it."

"Well to be honest, I never liked Heston. I think he was just a rebound."

My eyes snap to his, it's like he's in my head because I thought the same thing just yesterday. I really thought Heston and me had something great going, but somewhere down the line, things started changing between us, and I realized the only thing we had going was lust. I was sleeping next to a man in my bed every night, and I didn't even know who he was.

"And fuck you for not telling me about you two not

working out sooner." He sounds offended, and I shake my head, knowing I should have told him sooner.

"Cam was right, I should have done a background check on him," I mutter. I remember thinking how insane I thought Cam was for insinuating it. Figured it was just jealousy talking but now… I think Cam was on to something.

"Still no word of where he is?"

"He had a lot of debt with the wrong people before we split. I'm starting to think the way he lived caught up with him, and if they did…nobody is going to find him. I saw the people he made deals with when we were together, and they're not to be messed with."

"Damn," Owen whispers, so I just barely hear it.

"So, are you still going to the block party tomorrow? I mean, I know you're baking a pie, but what if Heston shows up?"

"I have to try and act normal for Paige. All I can do is pray he's not dumb enough to show up tomorrow or I'll kill him."

"You mean if Beefy Biker doesn't first?" Owen purses his lips, eyes serious.

"Yeah, I guess so." I sigh. "Why do you think Rhodes is doing all this, doesn't it seem strange to you?"

He scoffs. "No, he sees a single mother in distress, a hot single mother at that, and he's doing what he can to get your attention, babe."

"I don't want to be anybody's toy anymore, Owen." Relationships and I are incompatible, that much I've learned.

"Even if he's a big, broody biker, who comes to your side late at night?" Owen teases, forcing the corner of my mouth to pull into a smile. He might be a pain in the ass, but he always manages to make me laugh.

Rhodes slept over again that night.

Next morning

A loud knock on the door has me rising from the dead this morning and finding Rhodes in blue jeans and bare feet, a cup of coffee in his hand standing in my bedroom doorway.

"Tenly is here to see you." He jerks his thumb over his shoulder.

"Rain, up, up, up! Today is the day!" she hollers from the hallway, and I fall back onto my pillow with a loud groan.

"It's an evening party Tenly!" I grumble, wanting more sleep.

"Well, we have lots of setup to do, so let's get to it." Pulling the blanket from my face, Tenly is now standing over me.

"And while we're doing it, you can explain to me how you ended up with Rhodes answering your door this morning." Her voice lighter as if she doesn't want him to hear.

"Nothing to tell, he's my…bodyguard." I nearly laugh saying it out loud. Her brows furrow, eyes wider than before in that dumb, clueless way she has a tendency of making.

"From who?"

Sitting up, swinging my feet over the bed, I look over at Paige, finding her hiding under the covers, before I focus back on Tenly.

"Really? You have no idea?" She is always looking out her windows at what's going on. Blinking away the sleep from my eyes, I notice her tennis skirt and tight white shirt. I swear the woman's wardrobe is nothing but athletic gear. Does she even play tennis?

"Well, Asher came home the day before yesterday and

I've been busy." She purses her lips, pretending to pick something off her skirt.

"Wait, does that mean we will meet him tonight?" I ask.

Her mouth beams into a huge Colgate smile as she nods excitedly.

"Alright, let me change and get some coffee in me and I'll meet up with you and see what needs to be done."

Tucking a hair behind her ear, she spins on the heel of her white tennis shoe and leaves the room.

"Mom, we need more locks," Paige grumbles from under the blanket beside me, when did she slip in here to sleep?

"Well, it doesn't help if someone lets them in," I say, grabbing my robe from the door as I set out to find Rhodes. My feet pitter patter on the cold floor until finally hitting some carpet in the living room. Rhodes is sitting on the couch, his cup of coffee on the table in front of him, while the TV blares the news.

His head lifts up, and he rubs his chin.

"Sorry about that, I opened the door to see what she wanted and she threw a tantrum to see you, figured if I didn't just let her inside, she was going to wake ya'll anyhow."

"Yeah, if only I had an ounce of her energy," I mutter, walking to the kitchen for my morning fuel.

"So, I reached out to some brothers, a couple are going to ride out and stay at the party thing tonight, just to make sure everything goes smoothly."

"I bet Tenly will love that." I chuckle, imagining leather-cladded bikers standing like angry statues in the fucking suburbs.

"She'll get over it," he clips, sipping his coffee. His sharp tone has me looking up through my lashes at him, his wild anger quite attractive.

"Do you know what Tenly is wanting us to do?" I try to make small talk as I drink my coffee.

"I gotta move the grill and get that set up for the meat I'm cooking, but I said I'd get to it when I got to it."

"I swear if she's making me do some papier-mâché centerpiece shit, I'mma run," I mumble under my breath, looking up at the ceiling, thinking about the crazy shit she would do to one-up the other blocks. In fact, this all feels political in a way, and it's a competition Tenly is determined to win.

"I thought you liked art?" I freeze, my eyes pinned on him to explain how he knows I like art. "I saw your art room or whatever, you're good." He admits to snooping, but all I hear is him telling me I'm good at what I do.

"Thanks, I was going to go to a trade show, but everything happened at once, and I haven't been up there in what feels like forever."

He nods, but doesn't reply. Silence falling onto our shoulders things become awkward. I suddenly remember I haven't checked my phone this morning. Taking my coffee with me, I go back to my room and sit on the edge of my bed. Putting my cup on the nightstand, I unlock my phone, finding a text from Heston, and a text from Sheriff Reese.

Sheriff Reese: Tried calling. I have a lead. Cam got in a fight at a bar in Charlotte, so I'm going to check that out today and I'll let you know.

I sigh, feeling a tiny sliver of hope. I wonder if Cam has been crashing somewhere around the bar.

With every good thing that happens, something bad trails closely behind it, to test your strength and mind, because when I open Heston's text, it's him yelling at me in all caps.

Heston: THIS IS NOT OVER. YOU NEED ME. PAIGE NEEDS ME. You owe me!

I owe him?

The more this goes on, the more determined I am to stay away from him. I feel so stupid for falling in love with him, for moving so fast. Now that we're apart, I can admit I didn't want to be alone, that the thought of being in this new place without my mother or anyone but my daughter was terrifying, but I did care about Heston. We became friends, he made me smile, so much so I overlooked little red flags. But who I was sleeping next to was not who I thought he was.

Dressing in a red strapless top and my favorite pair of blue jeans, I head to the bathroom to look for a hair tie to pull my hair up. Looking in the mirror, I notice dark circles under my eyes from lack of sleep. Using my index finger, I swipe as close to my eyelid as I can, curious if what I'm seeing it just me or if it's really there. I can't tell and it's too hot to put concealer on. My eyes fall to my makeup bag, the end of a mascara sticking out. I grab it and apply it, my lashes doubling in thickness and making my eyes bolder. If I had any dark circles, you can't really tell now.

Somewhat satisfied, I drop the makeup back in the bag and go find Tenly to see what she needs me to do.

35

It's hot, the mid-summer sun shines down on everyone who's outside, helping Tenly in the middle of the afternoon. The smell of the BBQ grill makes my stomach growl, and I look to see if Rhodes is over there. He's messing with the grill, wearing no shirt, and those damn jeans that outline his ass so well. His dirty boots so different than the Hey Dudes, or Ralph Lauren's, men out here usually wear.

"Rain, I need you to put one of these on your house somewhere?" My attention's now on Tenly, as she heads my way with her hands full of American flags colored bunter banners.

She shoves one in my hands; she's out of breath and barely able to hang on to the unorganized mess in she's holding.

I watch her go to the next person, Owen, who begins to argue with her.

"Mom!" Paige's voice takes me away from the commotion, Paige walking my way with her arms crossed. She's wearing jean shorts, a blue top that is airy and flows down her shoulders, with a pair of flip-flops.

“Do you need any help?” she asks, and I hand her the decorations Tenly gave me.

“Here, put this up somewhere.”

Taking it, she looks it over, unsure of what it even is.

“Paige! Paige!” We both look up to see Layla waving in our direction. She’s wearing a black strappy shirt, with dark as night baggy jeans and chunky shiny boots. But what’s really catching is her parents are outside with her. I didn’t think they would participate, seeing as they don’t do anything with any of the neighbors.

Layla’s dad, Earl, is pale and balding, his belly robust and nearly popping through his striped button-up shirt. His wife, Melanie, is in a flowery blue tie-dye dress, her dark hair pulled into a tight ponytail. She’s pretty, her face clear of any blemishes, eyes wide and beautiful.

Paige turns on her heel and heads toward Layla. Not knowing when I’ll have another chance to meet Melanie, I head in that direction too.

“Hi, it’s so good to see you guys!” I say, with so much energy you’d think I was a kindergarten teacher. This place has really done a number on me, because if someone came up to me, the way I just did, I’d think you we’re trying to sell me something.

“We always try to make an appearance at these things,” she says, glancing over at her husband for backup.

“Yeah, but we like to stay to ourselves. Less drama that way,” he clips, and although he comes off as an asshole, I totally get what he’s saying.

The twins, dressed in red shirts and shorts, come laughing and running between us; they’re so cute but definitely look like trouble. I don’t know how Melanie does it with four kids; I can barely keep up with Paige.

"Sorry about that," Melanie mutters with irritation, "they are like little Wreck-It Ralphs."

"Little shits more like it." A tall boy that resembles Melanie grumbles from behind her. The oldest son I assume, he looks to be a little older than Paige and Layla, but he's not dressed in all-black like his sister. He's wearing a baggy shirt with an image of a rapper on it, baggy shorts with long socks and some Air Jordans.

"Excuse me?" Melanie whispers, turning her back on me and pointing her finger at her son while muttering at him.

"That's our son, Kingston," Earl says, placing his hands in his pockets, his fingers jumbling some change around while he looks out amongst everyone scrambling to get everything together for the party.

With a fake smile on my face, I nod. Feeling like it's time to walk away, I say, "Well, it was nice meeting you. I better get back and see what Tenly wants me to do next."

"Ugh, Tenly," Earl grumbles, his voice trailing off.

Turning around, I chew on my cheek, thinking over everything I just encountered. The mother seems normal, but that's about it.

I go to Owen and Flynn's table, and it's covered in a flowery cloth with two big jugs of lemonade and mason jars on each side with flowers inside them. Thirsty myself I grab a cup and begin to pour myself some.

"Hey, that's for the party, bitch!" Owen says, cutting up some fresh lemons.

"I can't help it. It's hot and your table looks so inviting!" I tease him about the decorations.

"It looks nice because we did it, not Tenly!" Owen sneers, as if I'm supposed to know what he's talking about.

"Tenly wanted us to put lemons all over the table, but it was a bit tacky and would attract flies, so we did what we wanted." Flynn explains with a shrug of his shoulder. Thank goodness my pie goes on a combined table of desserts, and I don't have to have my own table. I probably wouldn't have anything but my pie on it.

Hours pass by until the sun kisses the ground, leaving a hue of orange and pink in the sky. Neighbors from our block and others are here enjoying our festivities, the smell of cooked burgers and hotdogs hanging in the air and making everyone's stomach growl.

Paige is sitting in a chair next to Layla and her brother, talking and having fun. It's the first time I've seen her smile in days. It warms my heart to know she's okay, that she's going to be okay, no matter what happens in the coming days.

"Damn Straight" by Scotty McCreery comes on, and I can't help but sing the first few lyrics.

"Wanna dance?"

Startled, I turn around to find Rhodes standing there with a sexy smirk on his face.

"Is anyone dancing?" I look around, nervous everyone will look at us.

"Who cares." He shrugs and takes me by the hand. My cheeks flush, heart beating as everyone watches us. He stops in the middle of the road and pulls me close. His right hand clasps mine, while his other one wraps around my waist. I keep looking down to make sure I don't step on his boots as he sings along to the country music. His rough voice copies Scotty's soft tone. Trying not to laugh from the nerves bubbling in my stomach, I look to the left of us and see Paige looking at me with her mouth open, eyes smiling.

"Everyone's staring," I tell him, and I stop dancing.

"Let them stare, it's just a dance," he replies, ushering me to keep moving.

"I can't—" I try and pull my hand from his, but he stops me.

"Stop worrying, they're not staring at you, they're staring at me," he whispers, and I roll my eyes.

"They're staring at you? Why would they be doing that?"

His thin lips pull into a small smile, and I shake my head at his ego.

Inhaling a large breath, I close my eyes to ignore everyone and just focus on my steps while listening to the song. Getting close to Rhodes again his citrus scent and musk cologne become envelope me. I almost get lost in a place of zen, until the loud sound of exhaust has me freezing and looking up.

"Boys are here," Rhodes states, just as two motorcycles pull into the cul-de-sac. They're not wearing helmets, with angry scowls on their faces as they drive by everyone. The mean twisted alloy between their legs makes it look like their thighs are grabbing danger by the balls and I can't help stare at them. They park in Rhodes' driveway, the men even more intimidating as they stand straight with leather vests displaying a burning skull on the back. Glancing at Tenly, she's staring with her mouth ajar and wrinkles between her eyebrows. I can't help the slight laugh that escapes me. Rhodes is taking the suburbs and turning them into his own personal playground.

"I don't think we need them, Rhodes," I state, everything has been calm so far, and I'd hate for these guys, who have trouble etched into the lines of their face that the sun has marred them with from their daily rides, to start something with someone. I think Owen would piss himself if he got into a confrontation with one of them, but not before he tried to sass them.

"Then we don't. But they're already here, so let them enjoy some normal socializing instead of club…activities."

The way he says that last part makes me think they're criminals; they certainly look the part, doing things that outlaws do. It's as scary as it is exciting. Especially knowing they'd come here and pretend to enjoy country music with a bunch of yuppies, instead of being back at their clubhouse with half-naked girls and no sound mind of boundaries.

The song ends, and he winks at me before walking to his friends with broad shoulders and a heavy step. The way they stand there and wait for him, their hands in their pockets and expressionless faces makes me think he's in charge of them or at least of a higher rank.

"Rain, who is that and why are they here?" Tenly angry-whispers, coming up beside me.

Shaking my head I say, "Uh, some friends of Rhodes, it looks like."

"They have everyone staring," she hisses, crossing her arms, and she's right, everyone is staring. Bikers don't come here, and they definitely don't live here. But Rhodes, he does all these things because he doesn't give a fuck.

Turning on my heel, I paste a cheery smile on my face.

"Hey, where is your better half? I thought you were going to introduce him to me?" Her head snaps my way, her brows rising to her hairline.

"Yes! Yes, he is." Lifting her hand, her pointy little finger waves in the direction of Owen and Flynn's table. There he is. He's shorter than Tenly, his back muscled, and hair short brown. He's wearing a light blue polo and some khaki shorts, reminding me of someone who goes sailing rather than a famous plastic surgeon. I expected someone tall, dark, and handsome in highly stylish clothes because he has all the money in the world.

"Come on," Tenly says walking past me. Following her, she taps Asher on the shoulder and he turns, his face lighting up when he sees her.

"There she is!" he says with excitement, as if the few moments they were apart were torment for him.

"Hey, this is Rain!"

He looks to me, and I put on a smile. He raises his hand to shake, so I reciprocate. My eyes are stuck on how sharp his jaw is. There's no way he hasn't had surgery on it and his nose. It looks chiseled and defined and, in a way, it reminds me of a marble sculpture. Dark eyes, plump lips and not a mark on his face, including facial hair, I'd say there is nothing on him that hasn't had work done.

"Nice to finally meet you," he politely says, the manner in his grasp firm, but soft.

"Oh, has Tenly been talking about me?" I joke and follow it up with a little laugh.

"Only good things," he replies, taking his hand back and wrapping it around Tenly's waist.

"I love you, Rain!" Tenly says brightly, making me wonder if she's had more than a couple drinks. It seems like when you drink too much, you love everyone and the world is beautiful.

"Ya'll move it over, we have a visitor wanting some lemonade!" Owen throws his hands at us, his eyes straight forward. Looking over my shoulder, I find one of the bikers looking at the fresh citrus stand. This close, I can see tattoos up his neck and arms, and even on his hands. I try not to stare too long, but see glimpses of the devil, some skulls, and a woman's face. I try not to judge because he's here because of me. Speaking of, I casually look around the place to see if there is any sign of Heston, but as usual, there's nothing I can outright see. There's too much commotion and the setting sun licks the evening into darkness, making it harder to see everyone clearly.

"Rain...Rain?" My head snaps through the fog that hinders my surrounding, finding Tenly and Asher look at me with concern.

"I'm sorry, what were you saying?" I ask, trying to focus. Tenly looks to her husband before licking her lips and saying, "I've heard good things about your pie. I thought you said you couldn't cook?" Tenly asks.

I'm stunned, replaying what she just said, I hold my hand up.

"Are you sure it was mine? The apple?"

"You were the only one who brought apple, it had to be you." She laughs, her energy matching one of a parent proud of their child for acing a test.

"Nice!" is all I can manage to say; I wasn't expecting a compliment and I'm in disbelief that someone liked my baking, so the word nice is all I can muster at this exact moment.

Silence falls between us laying a thick awkward blanket onto our shoulders. I take a step back to convey I'm going to go do something else and Tenly says, "We're going to get the sparklers out, does Paige want one?"

Flicking my gaze to the porch, I find her and Layla sitting there talking.

"I'll ask her."

"Okay, just send her my way if she wants one." I nod in understanding and start weaving my way through the crowd. It's louder as the night goes on, people replacing their sodas with their choice of alcohol. Polite language now turns more colorful, to say the least.

Coming up to my house, Paige stops talking and looks up at me.

"Hey, Tenly has sparklers if you want to go check them out." She looks to Layla, who is staring up at me, her thick black colored lips pursed.

"You wanna go see?" Paige asks her.

"Hey, I'm sorry about your ex-husband, like, missing." My eyes widen, Layla's forwardness catching me off guard.

I offer her a smile, as both girls stand and head toward Tenly. Looks like Paige has been talking to Layla about her dad, hopefully, she can offer some positive feedback.

About a half-hour goes by and I try some of Rhodes' BBQ, talk to a few friendly faces and listen to music. Paige and her friend are laughing and smiling with sparklers, bringing me back to when she first held a sparker at three years old. If it weren't for her, I never would have believed in love. The way I see it, if you can love someone the instant they're put in your arms, the kind of affection where you would kill anyone who harmed them, where you would sacrifice your happiness for them… then it's proof that love has to be real between two people who pick one another to get to know.

The smell of spicy orange and musk causes the hairs on my arms to rise, my body knowing exactly who the scent belongs to.

Rhodes sits in the foldable chair next to me and hands me a Seagram's.

Taking it from him, I turn it around until the label is facing me. Strawberry.

"Thanks," I pop the top off and take a swig. Sweet tart fizz fills my mouth, and I nearly groan at how satisfying it is.

His lips pull into a slight smile, before taking a drink of whatever is in his red Solo cup. Leaning my head back, "Tomorrow" by Chris Young playing in the background, I watch Rhodes' jaw work as he swallows the liquid in his mouth. He's so angry but gentle at the same time. I bet his daughter never feels afraid when she's with her daddy.

"How is Nalini?" I ask.

I watch his chest inhale as if the name alone pains him.

"I tried to get her for the day, hell, I even asked her bitch of a mother to come if she wanted. I just wanted to spend some time with my daughter, but she wasn't having it."

My brows lift with sympathy. He's clearly trying, so why is his ex being such a monster?

"It's alright, here soon, we go back to court, and I have enough shit on her to send her to prison for a very long time. Nalini will be here…where she belongs, before Christmas." He gives a curt nod, his tone laced with promise.

"Good," I reply, then take another sip of my drink.

Both Rain and Layla come running up to me, their shoes smacking against the pavement.

"Hey Mom, can I stay over at Layla's?" she asks, and the first thing that pops to mind is no, but Paige could use this distraction from everything that is going on with Heston and her dad missing.

"Are we going to behave?" I lift a brow and stare at both of them with a hard look.

"I promise we won't do anything we're not supposed to," Layla quickly answers, and Paige nods in agreement.

"I guess," I mutter, and they start cheering. I can't help but laugh at their reaction and watch as they run toward Layla's house. Her parents' Melanie and Earl went inside right before dark; they simply made their rounds and were done. I don't reckon we'll see them until next year's block party.

Finishing off my drink, I set the bottle in the chair's cupholder.

"Want another?" Rhodes asks, and I smile at his attentiveness.

"It's getting late," I say. Several families have left, causing the party to die down. Silence brings upon the end of the summer and the sweet smell of honeydew on the ground as the temperature drops.

Standing, I stretch my arms above my head, watching what Rhodes does next.

"Come on, I'll walk ya home." There's no question in his voice, he might as well have said, move, I'm walking you home. Grabbing my pie dish off the table, I wave to Tenly, who is in a heated argument with Owen, again. We pass the flowers Paige and me planted, and their beauty makes me happy to be home. I stop right in front of door and turn toward Rhodes.

"Thanks," I say.

"Wasn't a problem."

Rolling my lips together, I brush the stray hairs from my face and look down at his boots.

"Do you want to come in?" As soon as the words leave my mouth, a warmth fills my chest and I feel like I can't breathe. Nervous at what he'll say next, I don't dare look him in the eye.

"Yes," he finally replies, and I smile. Opening the door, I step backward into the dark foyer, baiting him inside with the flirtatious grin on my face. I don't know what I'm doing; I shouldn't want to have sex with Rhodes, not with all this shit going on with Heston, but I need to sow my oats or eat them.

However the saying goes. But the way this man looks and makes me feel can't be tamed any longer. Wrapping my hands around his neck, he kicks the door shut, just as our mouths meet. His lips are hard but fit perfectly against mine, his tongue flicks against mine, filling my mouth with the taste of Jack and Coke. Moaning, I reach up his shirt and feel his hard chest, the same one I've seen strutting around my house for days now. His hand greedily kneads my tits, my leg wrapping around him as I gyrate my hips against his hard bulge.

WHACK

Rhodes headbutts me, and all I see is white light searing behind my eyelids. I hear the noise again and the shadow of Rhodes falls to the ground. Blinking a few times, unsure what is going on I yell "Rhodes? Are you okay?"

Agonizing pressure thunders against the back of my skull, causing fire to strike like a match in that exact spot. Dropping to my knees, I wince in pain. I want to puke, cry…but all I can do is black out.

The pain in my head feels like I just had a railroad spike thrusted into the back of my skull. It's wet, cold, and hurts so bad, I can't help but sob. Trying to open my eyes, at first, all I can see is blurriness. I have no clue what is going on and it takes me a second to remember this was no accident. Lifting my hand to feel my head, I can't because my arms won't move. I try to wiggle my fingers, and they move enough for me to figure out I'm restrained. It feels like there's tape wrapped around my wrists like a vise, my fingertips puffy and pulsing from lack of blood.

Male mumbling has my eyes snap wide open. That's Rhodes' voice. I open my mouth to reply, only to feel my lips stuck together, they're taped shut. I suddenly feel like I can't breathe, I panic and look down at my body, finding that I've been duct-taped to a chair. I jump and jerk, trying to get out. But the adhesive won't budge; if anything, it only gets tighter.

My eyes fill with tears as I look around the room. Everything is painted in a soft glow. There are candles all over the house; it would be incredibly romantic, if you weren't for being held hostage. How long was I out for? My eyes land on Rhodes, who's strapped to a chair at the other end of the dining table, blood matting his face and tape across his mouth. My eyes search the rest of the room for who is responsible for this. The curtains have been drawn, an unexplained amount of burning candles lit, but no sign of anyone else.

The urge to puke becomes overwhelming, and I gag. Closing my eyes, I try to breathe through it, focusing on inhaling and exhaling.

"Surprise!" My eyes whip open and land on the one and only psychopath, Heston. His brows lift with excitement and his smile is bigger than I've ever seen. He looks disheveled, his shirt untucked and wrinkled, and his blue jeans dirty. In fact, I think it's the same clothes he was wearing the day I kicked him out.

My nostrils flare with fear, my eyes wide and watching.

"Did you miss me, wifey?" He puts on a pouty face, his bottom lip sticking out. I can't reply because of the tape, but I'm sure whatever I'd say would only bring Rhodes and me pain.

"Of course you did," he states, standing straight. "Sorry I'm not wearing my Sunday best but I've been living out of my truck because of you." He walks to Rhodes first, putting his hand on the table, and scowls. The emotion locks his features into place like he was born with that look, every smile, joke, and laughter I've known from him merely a façade.

"You know this one's a whore, right?"

What the hell does he mean? I never cheated on him. I loved him!

Pissed at his accusation, I mumble behind my tape, catching his attention. "Don't worry, princess, I have something for you." His promise laced in poison, I still.

"You know, Rhodes, I blamed you for everything. Crazy right?" He starts toward the kitchen, both Rhodes and I left with nothing to do but watch.

"I thought she wanted you instead of me, that you had something I didn't," he continues to explain. "But then I realized!" He turns on his heel, a crooked grin gracing his face despite the disgusting words he's saying. "She's a whore… like her mother."

Wait what? My mother? Instinctively, I turn to look at the urn, my mother was a lot of things, but not a whore, so I don't know what he's getting at with that insult.

"Oh, don't worry, Rain, Mommy gets to be here with us while I…well, kill you." His head turns to the side, the darkness from the room shadowing his jawline ominously. Taking a plain white candle from the counter and leaving behind probably twenty more, he brings it up to his face and looks into the dancing flame. He's mesmerized by it, as if the devil has reunited with his everlasting love.

"You know, when I was a kid, there was this bad winter, one unlike any other in Carolina. My mother and I were freezing. I even got sick. My skin was chilled to the bone, and I couldn't tell if the blue hue on my toes were just veins or frostbite. My father went to the market and stood in line for three hours, making sure he'd be the first to get inside for a kerosene heater. Later that night, when we were snuggled in our bed, I woke to the fire alarms going off and the lick of a flame burning my leg. I remember kicking the blanket, crying from the feeling of my skin melting off. My mother rushed in and saved me, carrying me out of the house. I screamed for my father, who was left inside, demanding someone go back in…only to find out that he wasn't home." Heston's glossy eyes slowly look to me. "He was out with another woman. He cheated on my mother and me and because of his indiscretions, I almost died." I don't understand what he's saying, and my head throbs trying to figure it out.

"So, as you can see, I have a disdain about cheaters." He slowly puts the candle back down and scratches the back of his head, walking back to the table Rhodes and me are at. Leaning down, his face inches from mine, he whispers, "Your mother killed my father."

I don't understand. Piercing irises stab into me. "Your whore of a mother killed my father!" he repeats. "The day I almost died, and the day he did die, he was with the same woman. Your mother!"

Suddenly everything comes together. The man my mother was dating, the guy she was with when she had her wreck and died was Heston's cheating father.

"DING DING DING!" he yells, pointing at me. "I think she finally gets it, Rhodes."

"My mother didn't do anything wrong. She did everything for him, and it still wasn't enough. I wasn't enough!" He slaps his chest. "If you can take my father, my lifeline to a family…then I can take yours," he yell-whispers. Heston scouted me out and hit on me on purpose that day. He played with me like a toy baiting me into his sick vengeance. "I was going to kill you right away, but then I met Paige, and I wanted you both for myself. I longed to have you as my new family, but you had to pull away from me. You just had to."

Shaking my head, tears falling down my wet cheeks, I look at Rhodes, who is staring right back at me. He doesn't have to speak a word for me to know he's telling me not to feed into Heston's bullshit, but the psycho has been in my head playing mind games with me since the day we met.

"Oh, and your ex-husband had to get in the way of us, too. I couldn't have him exposing me before I was ready…so I killed him."

Sadness and anger spark in my chest. I was a fool. I put me and my daughter in danger and now Rhodes, but right now isn't the time for me to cry about it, I need to fucking do something, anything to save us.

Using my nail, I saw and tear at the duct tape, my wrist pulling against the adhesive to loosen it.

Heston walks into the living room, the filtered light from the candles illuminating his way, so much so that it casts a dark shadow over him, reminding me of the Devil in Stephen King's *Stand*. Reaching down, he takes a candle and sets it under the curtains. It blackens before finally igniting and zipping up the cloth material. My heart beats faster, my stomach feeling like I'm on a roller coaster, as I watch him start a fire.

He kicks another candle over and topples a few others. The temperature rises, heat blossoming off the carpet and couch. Smoke bellows into my lungs, making me cough and wheeze. I'm going to die here.

"Looks like you took another man to your place, got romantic and put one too many candles out." He looks at me. "You should have blown these out, you know. They might catch fire." His condescending tone makes me scream. I start kicking my legs, shifting my body with my movements until I tip over and fall to the ground. I freeze since the fire is only five feet away from my head. Closing my eyes, I try and tell myself I'm not going to die! Heston steps over me, and the sound of skin smacking skin can be heard and then crackling and popping. He's beating Rhodes, punching him in the face over and over again. Using the floor, I brush my face up and down, my cheek burning from the rug's abrasive touch, but I manage to get my gag loose.

"STOP! STOP IT!" I scream, my foot kicking the left of the table. The commotion stops; Heston's stained-up shoe all I can see from this angle.

"Aww, baby. Don't worry now. Shhhh." He straddles my body and grabs my cheeks with both of his thumbs, his touch rough and my skin feeling like it might split at any second. He lifts my head, dragging me a foot closer to the fire, and I scream. Panic makes me want to pass out, but I fight it and slam my head into his, headbutting him.

He stills, his hand touching his forehead to check for blood.

"You little bitch!" He raises his hand and slaps me across the face, but the pain is nothing compared to the back of my head. Jerking me upward, he jostles me forward another foot, the smell of burnt hair telling me how close I am to the flame. Closing my eyes, remembering Paige, I try to think about the good times. The times we laughed, the nights my mother and I would stay up and talk, being able to watch Paige grow up. If I'm going to die, I'll go thinking about all the good things in my life.

Something falls on top of me, thrusting the air from my lungs. My eyes open and Heston is lying on top of me with a dazed look in his eyes, something happened to him. I look around his body to see if Rhodes is up, but he's still lying on the ground, blood smeared all over him so I know he wasn't the one that knocked him out.

"You asshole!" Paige screams, kicking Heston's limp body off me, a wine bottle in her hand covered in blood. She grabs the chair I'm stuck to by the legs and pulls me away from the fire and closer to the dining table, before fussing with the tape.

"Tear along the seam where it's the thinnest," I tell her, and she does, releasing my hands. I tear at the tape on my lap, and free my legs. I grab onto Paige and kiss her forehead, hugging her to my chest. I didn't think I would ever have another chance to do this with her. A small explosion in the living room throws dirt and debris at us, our time growing short. We need to get out of this house.

Grabbing onto Paige's shoulders, I make her look me in the eye. "Go out front, and do not come back. Do you understand?" I tell her, and she nods. Pulling away from her, I go to Rhodes. His face is bloody, his lip split and his eye bulging. He doesn't look good.

"Rhodes? Rhodes?" I shake him to see if he'll respond, but nothing. I slap him, but he doesn't budge. Shit, I can't carry him. Glancing down at the bottom of the chair, the legs come into view. I can do what Paige did and slide him along the kitchen floor and outside. Kneeling down, I grab the wooden legs, digging my nails in and jerking Rhodes and the chair. We slide about a foot and I have to stop for a breath, my head painfully pounding with every move. Taking one more breath, I tug with all my might, and we move more than before. I pull him, take a break, and then tug some more. Almost to the door, the sound of sirens makes me nearly fall to my knees in relief. We're going to be saved; someone is coming to help. The next five minutes, everything happens in slow motion. Men in yellow rush the house, I'm pulled away from Rhodes, and he's instantly circled by four firemen. I'm taken outside to one of the trucks, as men spray water at my house, trying to put out the fire, and someone asks me my name. In a daze, I stare at the house that is stamped with death, flames rushing from the windows. The roof looks like something straight out of hell. The place where lies are masked by love.

I'm placed on a stretcher and shoved into the back of an ambulance, the light so bright I have to close my eyes. My body is jostled, causing me to reopen my eyes, and Rhodes is slid in next to me, someone squeezing a pump that's attached to his face to help him breathe.

The top of our hands touch, the skin warm and layered with soot. The sirens blare as we careen around corners, and the stretchers shake back and forth. Suddenly, my hand is grasped by someone. Peeking one eye open, I find Rhodes holding it. He's worried about me as I am him. Squeezing it back, I can't help but wonder if the connection we feel bred from where love lies. Two hurt individuals who were molded into different people because of the deceit they were fooled into loving. Coming together as two broken souls, I can't help but think we might have a shot at being together.

THE END

EPILOGUE

TWO MONTHS LATER

Sitting on the stained wooden porch of Rhodes' house, I chew on my nail and stare at the house I lived in just two months ago. It's now a charred disaster; everything eaten from the fire, nothing to be saved. Except my mother's ashes, the urn withstood the heat. After we lost the place and had nowhere to go but a hotel, Rhodes told us to come stay at his place until we found somewhere else to live. I want to stay around here, so I'm waiting for another place to open up close by.

"There you are, I thought you were outback messing with the flowers," Rhodes says, walking out the front door, shirtless in only low-slung jeans. Sitting next to me, he hands me a cup of iced tea and stares at the place where he almost died. His wounds are still healing and are a constant reminder what could have happened that night.

"I wish they would clear the lot already," I mumble, tired of looking at it and remembering.

"They had to investigate, which took longer after they found Cam's body in the crawl space," he reminds me and I cringe. I can still hear the Fire Chief hollering they found another body. The shock and trauma constantly ringing in my ears. The firefighters couldn't pull Heston from the fire, he was basically melted to the living room floor, so when the structure was finally declared safe, they let the investigators in to take his body. He never had a place in Charlotte, he lived with his mother. He never had a real estate career, he went to see his mother on days he supposedly worked. It was all one big lie. Looking at my old place I can't help but think of the movie *Carrie*, where if I walk across the rubble, Heston's hand will drive through the ground and grab me. Forcing myself to look away from it, I glance at Owen and Flynn's house. They've been gone this week, visiting with a little girl looking to be adopted. I hope they get to bring her home; it'd be nice to have a little one running around. Owen claims he knew all along that Heston was pretending to be someone else. I love him.

After Cam's funeral, Paige went into a deep depression, where I had no choice but to put her in therapy. She's better now and I haven't had any more incidents with her and Layla. I hope it stays that way.

"I'm going to go inside," I mutter, standing up. Walking into the house, the smell of wood and leather fill the house. Rhodes' large brown leather sectional in the living room, and his wooden farm door dinner table the first thing to see when you walk in.

"I'm going to take a shower before Paige gets home from school," I tell him, and he nods. That tension that has been pulled so tight between us is ready to snap at any moment. We haven't had sex, but it's gotten close. I think he's waiting for me to be ready, and I just want to make sure I'm fully in before fully giving myself to another man. Using the hall bathroom, I turn the shower on and set my bath caddy on the sink. Biting my nail, I look at the pink and white box still in the package. I haven't had a period in two months. Undressing, I sit on the toilet, the lid cold against my skin and pee on the stick. I instantly look at it and only see one line faintly coming in. Looks negative. Thank God. I don't know how I'd feel about having Heston's child. The seed of a demon kicking me from the inside is too much to think about. There was something definitely wrong with him and the idea that his DNA would be in something I created is scary.

Stepping into the shower, the hot water caresses my skin, wetting my hair. Closing my eyes, I lift my hands and scratch at my scalp, making sure not to touch where my cut was. I was able to take the stitches out, but it's still so tender there.

Steam rises, fogging the glass of the shower. With the sound of the door opening, I freeze.

"Paige?"

The shower door is pulled open and Rhodes stares directly as me.

"I'll only get in if you want me to," he says, his body only in a towel. My body pulses, need growing in my core.

Biting my bottom lip, I take a step forward and pull him inside with me. Hot water splashes on us, our mouths connecting as our hands explore one another. He's hard where it counts and soft where I need it. My fingers slip up and down his tattoos, my skin contrasting amongst his golden.

Grabbing me by the hips, he lifts me and presses me up against the wall, the tip of his cock fat and thick, I hold my breath as he presses into me. Closing my eyes, I focus on it stretching and filling me, and it feels so damn good. With his face in the crook of my neck and my legs wrapped around his waist, he thrusts in and out of me. This is something that has been building between us for quite some time, the temptation making it that much sweeter. Resting my chin on his head, I feel his hand grab my breast, his mouth enveloping my nipple, sending a burst of pleasure through me. I moan, rocking my hips faster. Needing to hold onto something before we both slip and fall, he slaps his hand against the wall and continues to drive into me. He grunts, the low growl a turn-on.

"I'm coming," I tell him, and he takes advantage. He thrusts harder, grabbing my ass cheeks hard. Stars burst behind my eyes as ecstasy takes over my entire body.

His body tenses, and he comes seconds after me. Standing in the shower, both of us trying to catch our breath, we stand under the waterhead that is slowly turning cold.

Grabbing my face, he leans his forehead against mine.

"That was better than I could have imagined," he mutters, rivulets of water dripping from his lips. I kiss him, feeling so much closer to him now.

Turning the water off, I open the door and grab my towel and dry off. Stepping out, he takes the towel he was wearing and starts drying his body off. Walking around him, my eyes fall to the test where there are two bright pink lines. I freeze, heart pounding, not from what I just did in the shower with Rhodes, but rather out of fear of what this test is telling me.

Noticing me staring, he looks down at the sink and stills.

I open my mouth to say something, but I'm speechless.

"Shit," he whispers, picking it up to look at it better.

"No, no!" I yell, thinking about a little Heston living inside me.

Moss-colored eyes look at me, his hand setting down the test. "This is okay," he states, but all I can do is shake my head.

He glances at the test in thought and then back up to me.

"Hey," he grabs me by the hips and pulls me closer, "Heston was fucked up because of his up bringing. You're a great mother, just look at Paige. Her father was shit but she turned out great. This child is yours and will be just as amazing."

Blinking rapidly, hypnotized by the pink lines, I'm frozen in place. The doctor said I couldn't have any more children. How is this possible?

Two large palms grip my face, forcing me to stare at Rhodes.

"Let me be a part of your life, Rain. Help me get my daughter back and do things a mother should teach a young girl and let me be the father your kids deserve. Have this baby. Here, with me."

"You don't know what you're asking, Rhodes." There are late nights, breastmilk, shitty diapers.

"I'm asking God for a second chance to be a dad," he says seriously, and my eyes widen. His sincerity takes over my fear, and I think about our girls playing, and him and his biker buddies attending a softball game, or orientation at preschool.

"I don't know, I like how things are slow and sweet between us, this would be throwing us into something—"

"I'm in no rush, Rain. I like us just hanging out and being together." He chuckles, as if the idea of being stuck together isn't an option. I like that, no urge to marry and tie us down.

"We're going to need a bigger house," I mutter, and he laughs pulling me into him.

NOTE FROM THE AUTHOR

First off, let me say that if this book becomes what I hope it will because then there'll be more to come of Fairview Suburbs.

I don't know what got into me to write this book. It's different than my fast pace biker books, for sure. It took me a year to build my characters, the story, and every chapter has things weaved into the words and scenes to make up the big twist in the end. That being said, I really loved putting this world together. I can see myself doing this again!

I wanted Heston to come off very pushy and over the top nice at the start. The romance to brew quickly, and for things to move so fast Rain didn't even have to think Heston was crazy.

Heston lost his family due Rain's mother and wanted to kill Rain for it that day on the highway. Only his plan didn't plan out the way he'd hoped. He saw her face, and her daughter and instantly wanted them both for his new family. Only when she wouldn't play perfect house wife he started to slip and let his true colors bleed into their relationship.

Rhodes tipped his psych0 scale into know return.

Aww. Rhodes. What a fucking hero! Big, strong, and gentle. He sees Rain and fucks with her because he likes to see her react. They both discover they're damaged from past lovers and start to connect on that level. They want to keep things casual because they're both scared of what happens when they make things "official".

Their story ends with them together, an unborn child from a psycho that will determine their future is what really fucks with your head.

It's up to you to wonder if Rain can nurture this child to be just like Paige or if it's DNA is more dominant and Rain will soon have another Heston in her life. Only she can't escape from this bad seed.

I hope you enjoyed this read, and this layout helps if you were confused on anything in the story! Thanks for reading and I would be OVER THE MOON for a review!

KEEP IN TOUCH

Amazon

- Twitter
- Instagram
- Newsletter
- Reader Group
- BookBub
- TikTok
- www.mnforgy.com

36

ACKNOWLEDGMENTS

I want to thank everyone who helped make this book possible. If there as a bump in the road, I hit it. I couldn't have overcome the journey without so many bloggers, editors, proofreaders, readers, and more!

Thank you Rebecca from Fairest Reviews for stepping up and offering your services when I needed them the most.

Shout out to Michelle Edrington-Areaux. Very quick proofreader!

Hugs to the bloggers who signed up to spread the word about Where Love Lies. The reading community wouldn't be possible without you.

My readers - You are seriously the best. You have been so understanding and are always there no matter if it takes me a month to write a book or a year. I'm very grateful to you.

To my husband who had to juggle all three kids, dinner, carpooling, and chores while I was deep in the cave. There are no words for me to describer how much you mean to me. My career/dream wouldn't be possible without you.

ALSO BY M.N. FORGY

Devil's Dust MC Series (All in Kindle Unlimited)

What Doesn't Destroy Us

The Scares That Define Us

The Fear That Divides Us

The Lies Between Us

What Might Kill Us

Devil's Dust Boxed Set All 5 Books

Devil's Dust MC Legacy

The Blood That Drives Us

The Long Road To Us

The Prospect Who Saved Us

Sin City Outlaws MC Series (All in Kindle Unlimited)

Reign

Mercy

Retaliate

Illicit

Bloodlines

Sin City Outlaws MC Boxed Set

Fallen Gods MC Series

Coming Soon

Omertà Law (mafia trilogy) (Both In Kindle Unlimited)

Beautiful Criminal

Beautiful Thief

Standalone

Relinquish (Escort romance)

Love Tap (MMA Romance)

Love Me Crazy (Modern Day Bonnie & Clyde)

Made in the USA
Columbia, SC
07 January 2025

51342125R00143